All The Reasons I Love You

January Kelly

Wandering Reads Press, LLC

Cover design: Black Widow Designs.

Published by: Wandering Reads Press, LLC

ISBN Paperback: 979-8-9916267-0-5
ISBN E-Book: 979-8-9916267-1-2

Trigger Warning

While this book is a work of fiction, it contains situations of domestic violence [alluded to, not depicted] and sexual assault [alluded to, not depicted] that some readers may find triggering. Please put your mental health first.

Contents

Also By

Paranormal Romantic SuspenseThe Hidden Series:

The Night They Knew- a short story from The Hidden

Hidden Intent

Smoke and Shadow

Relative Deceit

Standalone:

The Last Lament of the Late Shawn Reilly

Contemporary Fiction

All These Days

Romantic Suspense

Dangerous Flame

Wandering Reads
PRESS

www.januarykelly.com

Follow on Facebook:

https://www.facebook.com/profile.php?id=100067850730415

Instagram:

https://www.instagram.com/januarykelly.author/?next=%2F

For the good guy [or gal]. The hero. The one that makes you feel human. You know who you are, and this is for you.

Acknowledgements

I want to express my gratitude and thanks to all the beta readers out there. Creative endeavors are difficult enough, but without you, a lot of authors wouldn't know if the words and feelings they put on the pages accurately encompassed the vision. You are invaluable.

Authorship is hard. Book writing is hard.

To anyone who reads and enjoys the art of books: Thank you for all your time, money, and energy you've spent falling in love with the characters that have taken over our minds and hearts for months [and sometimes] years. Please, find a place to review those books; especially if the author is new or independent. Even if you just leave a score, it means the world to that writer and pushes their creativity further. We love to create as much as you love to consume our art. We are symbiotic. We love you.

The night is darkest just before the dawn. —Thomas Fuller

Chapter One

Natalie

"It's a full moon, you know?"

I shook my head. The cobwebs of exhaustion and boredom were thick within the walls of my mind, "What?"

"It's bound to get a little crazy this weekend is all I'm saying," a thin woman behind the rounded desk added before noticing my deer-in-the-headlights expression. "Girl, are you even paying attention?"

"Yeah, sorry," I yawned. "Just didn't get much sleep...I'm sick of pulling double shifts twice a week."

"I know that's right," Cece, the woman at the desk, and my very best girlfriend murmured as the radio behind her crackled to life.

"Bus twenty-three one niner en route. Sixty-three-year-old male, code ten with pain. ETA to Southwest Haven, three minutes."

Cece's eyes rolled, "Christ, that's the fourth MI in two days."

I threw my gray stethoscope around my neck, "I'll prep room one."

My tennis shoes made a soft squeak on the highly polished tile as I turned away. As I reached the midway point between the station and the exam room, I rotated, mid-stride and pointed at my friend, "Next time, shut your mouth about the moon."

Cece, rolled with hearty laughter from the desk, calling back, "I didn't think you were listening."

"I wasn't. But the universe was!" I walked into the exam room, the ring of my friend's laughter still hanging in the stark and dull hallway. I cleared the large suite in a matter of a few minutes, making sure all supplies were ready. It really had been a quiet night, and I was grateful for it. I prepared to turn and leave when the large glass door to my back swished open, allowing the ensuing chaos to pour in.

"What the hell?"

"Grab the crash cart!" Cece yelled from behind the gurney, pushed by an older paramedic with salt and pepper hair. His partner, a younger and fit man with piercing blue eyes straddled the patient's hips, driving the heel of his palm into his chest with rhythmic motion.

"Rafferty, out of there," the older man barked as his partner leaped off the gurney.

"What happened? I thought he was stable?" My eyes bounced to the older man as I grabbed supplies while Cece evaluated his airway. The patient stopped breathing.

"Tube!" Cece commanded. As if second nature, I already had the intubation kit ready as I handed off the flexible plastic tubing to her. The three of us watched as Cece skillfully opened his jaw and slid the tube inside.

The older paramedic let out a short breath that secretly told everyone he was holding it in, "We opened the bus doors and he just crashed."

I worked to hook the man to monitors just as Dr. Stoffel, the attending physician in the emergency room swept in the door. Sudden and skilled movements swirled into action as we worked in tandem like the internal gears of a clock.

"Looks like VT...anyone shock him yet?" Dr Stoffel removed the stethoscope from his ears, staring at the monitor reading his heart rate.

"Pads are in place," I step back. "Everyone clear?"

The small group confirmed and I pressed the button. A high-pitched beep rings out as we watch the monitor.

"Again," the doctor ordered and I complied. The monitor began to make beeping sounds at regular intervals. "Alright...let's get some blood work and turn up his o-two. Let cardiology know and send him upstairs."

Just like that, the whirlwind of action was done. Turning, Stoffel left the room as Cece looked up at me, "Can you grab the report from the medics? I've got this."

I found the two paramedics finishing their paperwork at the edge of the nurse's station. The younger of the two, the one referred to as Rafferty, turned to me, and I was taken back by the way his sapphire eyes sparkled. Shaking off the weirdly intimate feeling, I nodded in the older man's direction.

"Hey, Marc...long night?" I smiled at the pair.

"Ah," he grunted, "Gotta feeling we're just getting started." He closed his metal clipboard and handed me two documents; one white and one pink, from a triplicate form.

Rafferty, with the brilliant blue eyes, closed his laptop, "He's just grouchy because he left his dinner on the table."

"The most beautiful steak you've ever seen," Marc's eyes glazed over and shone like he was in love.

I laughed, "Well, Marc, there's your problem. You thought you needed to eat during a full moon."

"Oh, hell, Nat...is CeCe going on about that again?" he chortled. I giggled along as I watched Cece approach the older man from behind.

"Now, you get yourself out of here with all that non-believer bull," CeCe waved her hand at him before raising her chin in Rafferty's direction. "You got yourself a new partner, old man?"

"Hey! You watch that old man stuff," Marc grinned wide. "This is Finn Rafferty. He ain't green...been around a bit up in Sonoma."

I smile, "Sonoma County? Huh."

I knew the place well. Picturesque with rolling hills and horse farms, that section of the state oozed money and presumed status. It was a far cry from the endless noise and dirt of any city.

"You know the area?" Finn narrowed his eyes on me with sincere interest. The look sent a little spark through my core.

"I should...it's where I grew up," I chuckled as the radio's cracking sputtered once more. I watched a smile spread across the new medic's face. It was warm and friendly like connections were ready to be made and it continued up to his eyes.

"Really? It's beautiful there...made it hard to leave," he said.

Cece put her signature on a clipboard and handed it back to Marc, "Well, we're glad you're here. I'm just sorry you got paired with this old coot."

"You keep talking like that, and I'll have to ask you to marry me, " he laughed.

Cece's eyes lolled before her face formed into a devious grin, "Baby, you only wish you could afford me."

Snickers and laughter enveloped our group as the pair continued with their flirtatious banter. Finn's smile brightened but his eyes never left mine.

Chapter Two

Finn

"We should probably grab something before we head back...I know Huang ate my steak," Marc said with a little discontent. "Little shit. I don't know where he puts it."

I huffed out a laugh, "Is that all you can think about?"

"It was a beautiful piece of meat," he shrugged.

I wound our way through the sparse parking lot of Southwest Haven and out to the busy road. I'd only lived in Hanford for a couple of weeks but was happy with how easy it was to navigate the city.

"So, what's the story with that girl?" I asked, thinking about the beautiful brunette with the golden-flecked eyes.

Marc smiled, "Ah...I like to flirt with her. She's hella fun...and she doesn't take me seriously. Besides, I'm married...happily for twenty years and even if I weren't I think Cece would be too much for me anyway."

His round frame joggled as he laughed. But I shook my head, she wasn't the brunette I was asking about.

"No," I corrected. "Not her, the one with the scar in her eyebrow...Natalie."

My partner eyed me with mock suspicion, "Already looking to move in on someone, Rafferty?"

I started to protest but I felt my phone vibrating in my pocket. I dug it out and saw the name on the screen. My eyes involuntarily rolled and I looked for somewhere to pull the bus over.

"How about a burger?" I suggested.

"Yep, sounds good," he replied as I found a spot in the Carl's Jr. parking lot. Marc hopped out and waited for me to follow but I waved him inside.

"You go ahead," I held up my phone. "I need to take this."

I knew she would call back if I didn't pick up. She was relentless. She had called no less than a dozen times in the past two weeks. Most of the time, I let it go to voicemail, but when I did, the frequency of her calls always increased.

As if on cue, my phone vibrated again.

"What?" I answered.

"Hey...whatcha doing?" she tried to sound cute. I had to take a deep breath and center myself.

"What do you think, Lori? I'm working. What do you want?" my words were clipped and harsh.

She paused, "I wanted to hear your voice. I miss hearing your voice."

I met Lori during our sophomore year of high school at Sacramento High. I played football and ran track, she was a budding artist with a more than spicy attitude, but we had an instant connection. By the summer, we spent every waking moment together, and by our graduation two years later, we were completely inseparable. Lori Marcum was a five-foot zero-bottle blonde-explosive-pain-in-the-ass nightmare. She was also my ex-wife.

"Lori, I don't have time for this—"

"Finn, hear me out. We both made mistakes back then...we need each other. You are the only man for me...I love you, Finn," she cooed through the receiver. "Maybe we can get together this weekend. We can...you know...stoke those old flames."

"Lori, I want you to listen to me very carefully," I spoke slowly and deliberately. I wanted her to understand every word that was about to come out of my mouth. This was far from the first time I had said this exact thing, but I hoped it would be my last.

I knew it wouldn't.

"Are you listening?" I asked.

"Of course."

I took a deep breath, "Lori...I want nothing to do with you. Ever. We've been divorced for over six years and our marriage was over long before that because of your cheating ass. Mistakes were made, but not by me. Get this through that burned-out brain of yours. I will never...*never*...stoke anything with you again."

"You know, Finn—" she began, but I was quick to cut her off.

"No, Lori. I don't care. Stop calling me. And stop going through Danny's phone to get my number...don't use him like that," I demanded.

She was dangerously quiet and I knew the storm was building.

"You're a fucking asshole, Finn! I'm trying to spill my heart out to you and you just don't care, do you?" she screamed so loud I had to hold the phone away from my ear.

"I think you're finally getting it!" I laughed. "Now, go do what you do best...go snort something and knock one out with some random guy."

I disconnected the call as she screamed profanities in my ear. I honestly didn't like being a dickhead, because it's not who I am. But Lori's life choices have cost me more than my savings account over the years. I tried civility and taking the high road. I've given her money for rent, car payments, and bail but it's never enough. And all of that I can let go of, allow it to slide off my back, because, it's just money and I never did any of it for her; I did it for her brother, Danny.

I saw Marc making his way to the glass door with a large bag and two cups. I slid back into the driver's seat and pulled the bus to the sidewalk to let him inside.

"What the hell happened? I thought you were coming in," he put the two cups in the center holders and clipped on his seatbelt. The smell of greasy hamburgers and salty fries filled the cab of the rig.

I shrugged, "Sorry...had to take that."

"Well, I hope you like everything on your burger," he tossed a thick wrapper at me.

I shrugged again, unwrapped my sandwich, and took a large bite. I had to get Lori out of my head or my night would be ruined. That's when I saw the hazel eyes flecked with golden sparks in my head and I smiled to myself.

"So, tell me about Natalie."

Chapter Three

Natalie

Coffee cups and dishes clattered from every direction as Cece and I sat with two other nurses in the Pig and Fly, a diner within walking distance of the hospital. The crowded room smelled of eggs and bacon and was exponentially more appealing than the cafeteria at the hospital. It was our group's regular spot and general meeting place after nearly every shift.

"Did you see the ass on that new medic? What was his name?" Cece whooped with pleasure.

"New medic? How did I miss that?" Becca, a round-faced woman with platinum hair, replied hastily.

Rolling her eyes, Cece sipped from her cup, "Girl...he ain't your type."

"What do you mean?" Her giant blue eyes batted in coy misunderstanding. "You did say *he*, right?"

"She said *paramedic*, not doctor," the brunette on her right replied with an evil grin.

Becca feigned hurt, "I don't just date doctors, Carrie."

Our table erupted with laughter before I finally added, "Finn. His name is Finn Rafferty."

"Uh-huh. Someone was paying attention," Cece teased.

I shrugged. Was he cute? Hell yes. Do I have the time to date? Not a chance.

At least, that's what I tell myself.

"Only because we're going to have to train him like we do all the newbies," I sat my cup down with a clink.

Becca's nose wrinkled, "Oh god...remember that one that transferred from the county? Glen, I think it was?"

"Stinking ass, nasty man," Cece spat. "I don't think he knew what a bar of soap was."

"I heard he got fired for playing grab ass with a nurse over at Southshore," Carrie added, her eyebrows raised in conspiratory fashion. She leaned in, "Apparently, they got caught while a woman was coding in the next room."

Gasps of disbelief and shock circled our table.

"Now, how do you know that?" Cece demanded.

Carrie shrugged, "I've got a friend that works in the HR department over there. They had to keep it all under wraps in case the family sued."

"Well, all that aside...I wouldn't mind playing grab ass with that skinny white boy, Rafferty," Cece chuckled heartily, filling the space around us. "He's cute...and you know with that butt, he's got a body to go along with it."

I smiled but disagreed with my BFF's definition of skinny. Finn was broad in all the right places and his eyes were like sapphire flame. But I listened and joined my friend's laughter and it was like soup to my soul. Our kinship soothes me in ways I have a difficult time consciously processing or expressing. Being an only child and with both of my parents gone, I had no family to speak of; these women were my tribe.

A few years ago, I lived day by day and one breath at a time and I had my reasons. Now, only six years out of nursing school, and with no one at home other than my cat, I have goals and plans and some trash to work through. I saw my life as though it was laid out on a map; the road taking me from the next town then to the next in orderly succession. I was motivated, but sometimes that internal drive to keep moving forward was exhausting. My friends were the rest stop along the way.

"I think Nat's thinking about it too," Becca's eyes sparkled in a giggle.

"What?" I blinked.

Rolling her eyes, Cece waved her hand dismissively at the group, "Ignore her." She turns to me, "She's running on caffeine and no sleep. Nat. Go home. Enjoy your days off...I know I'm gonna enjoy mine."

She waived the server over for the check before retrieving her card. "On me today, ladies. Let's get out of here."

Chapter Four

Natalie

Southwest Haven Medical Center was a sprawling edifice of concrete and granite covering several acres of beautifully landscaped lawn at the southern corner of Hanford, California. With one thousand sixty beds, it was the largest hospital in Kings County. After our short absence from the maelstrom that was the emergency room and trauma center located within its walls, Cece and I found ourselves back, just days later.

The outgoing day shift gave their daily report; one motor vehicle accident still waiting on x-rays. Three children under the age of four with some toy or craft supplies lodged in some hole where they didn't belong; a new record for one day. One elderly woman with a possible stroke. One assault victim, a dozen or more triaged patients, and a full waiting room. We settled in with the rest of the team for another night of coffee-fueled caretaking. I hoped that the customers of our particular store would trickle in and not become the dinner rush at Pig and Fly.

That dream was short-lived.

"Twenty-three one niner in route...possible code four, bravo one...juvenile female is unconscious. ETA to Southwest Haven, two minutes..." the radio chirped around eight that night.

I noticed Cece's face fall simultaneously with mine. If I had to give a definitive opinion of what I dreaded hearing on any given day, it would be this call. Any sexual assault is horrific, more so when the victim is a child.

"I hate this job sometimes," I sighed. Cece shook her head.

We only had to wait by the door for a moment before unit twenty-three-one-nine backed into the bay. We held our breath and watched as Marc opened the door and his partner jumped out of the back. Together, they gently took the gurney onto the ground before releasing the mechanism that pulled the wheeled bed to chest height. Finn grabbed a blanket from a storage compartment and held it in front of him to block any view from lurking eyes.

I hit the large red button on the wall, releasing the door. Marc pushed the cart gently as Finn walked beside him shielding the tiny girl on the bed.

"Room six," Cece whispered.

Finn stood just inside the closed glass doors of the private room, the blanket still raised until I could pull the curtain. My throat tightened at the devastation in front of me and my eyes darted to Finn's and I thought I saw them fighting tears.

"Do we have a history?" Cece asked softly, placing the tiny pulse oximeter on the child's thin finger.

Marc turned, grabbing the clipboard off the gurney, "Mother came home from work...found her in the child's bedroom like this. She said she thought she was sleeping at first. She should be here shortly."

My heart sank as Finn snarled, "The boyfriend was babysitting. Police are en route here...chain of custody for any DNA you get out of her."

I pulled back the blanket covering the girl when Finn rushed to touch my hand, "Don't. We'll come back for it."

I frowned at him, watching the muscles in his jaw clench, his eyes spoke volumes. Hate, anger, and pain all in one look. He had already been a witness to her violation and it was something he didn't want to do again. Finn closed his eyes as I peeked to see what was being concealed. The sight was heinous and the lump in my already dry throat morphed to become a pit in my stomach.

It was in moments like these that I questioned human existence and it was the part of my job that I hated the most. The city could send me every stabbing, every shooting, and every car accident and it wouldn't come close to being as horrific as any crime against a child.

I caught my partner's eye, "We'll need to set up the assault kit. And get plenty of towels."

I turned back to Finn and his eyes instantly opened on me into a glower.

"We've got her now," I whispered. "She's in good hands...I promise."

Finn turned sharply, pushing the glass door hard enough that it slammed shut again. Cece and I give each other a look of recognition. We knew that feeling all too well.

***

Luckily, the night dragged on without much more incident. Marc and Finn returned one more time with an elderly man who fell off a step stool in his home trying to get his cat off a kitchen shelf. At the end of our night, the late spring sun was just peeking through the glass doors as the first of the day crew filtered back in with fresh faces and clean scrubs. After finishing our report for the next shift, Cece and I walk outside weaving through the parking lot.

"Up for breakfast?" I asked.

"Not today, I'm wiped. God, I'll be glad to be back on day rotation next week," Cece's dark ponytail bobbed with a shake of her head. "But, if you see Becca, tell her Dr. Peters asked about her.

I laughed and waved my hand, "Will do."

The Pig and Fly was packed by the time I squeezed in the front door, dodging the exiting patrons. Briefly looking around for my friends, the rail-thin waitress with a stack of bright red hair, a woman by the name of Bea, touched my arm.

"Hey sugar, girls didn't show up today. If you still want breakfast, I can get you something to go or you can sit at the counter," her smile was as bright as her pink lipstick.

"Thanks, Bea." I smiled back but, deciding that I would rather get the night washed off, I turned out the door and bumped into a man's thick chest. I backed away with my head hung and gave a polite "So sorry," in his direction.

A familiar and jovial voice boomed, "Hey, Nat! Nope, that's my fault."

"Hey! Sorry...I'll get out of your way," I maneuvered around a small group working to get inside.

"You having breakfast or just leaving," Marc checked his watch.

It was then I noticed Finn standing behind him. He looked weathered and defeated. I knew exactly what he must be going through because I felt it as well. It was a look of disappointment in the world. His eyes met mine and he gave me a small smile that told me he was trying not to see all of humanity in gray.

"I'm actually headed home. You guys working tonight?" I adjusted the bag on my shoulder. Marc shook his head and held the door for another couple walking out.

"Nope, we're on a seventy-two after this," he referred to the rotating schedule that was common for emergency personnel in the area. "Then back to dayshift for the next three weeks."

My eyes stayed on Finn. It was as though I could feel his thoughts. He seemed to be sensitive to this undesirable muck the world held and an unlucky few of us see. I wondered how he did it until I turned the thought internal and contemplated for a second how any of us did it. I forced a small laugh, "I know you're in love with Cece, Marc, did you have to have her schedule too?"

The man's eyes rolled in amusement, "I can't do this job without her. We'll see you in a few days kiddo."

As Marc stepped inside, I moved to the edge and teetered off the sidewalk, missing my footing. Stumbling sideways I felt Finn grab my arm and pull me upright. It was then I knew Finn definitely wasn't the skinny boy Cece alluded to; he was thick and muscular. When I regained my balance, I realized our faces were no more than an inch apart. I was so close I could see the fine stubble on his jaw and smelled his light cologne.

"I got it, thanks," I grinned, a little embarrassed. Finn nodded but stood frozen in place. His eyes locked with mine before I took my arm gently from his fingers.

Taking a step back, he put his hands up in apology, "Sorry."

I nodded, but my words came weakly because I was drawn into those eyes, "No problem. Enjoy your seventy-two."

Chapter Five

Natalie

F our days wasn't quite enough.

I threw my beat-up duffel over my shoulder as I glided out of the automated doors. The final day of another never-ending week has been longer than most and excitement filled me at the prospect of taking a long, well-deserved shower when I got home. I preferred the dayshift, but after today, what I wouldn't give for a slow night with just an overreactive parent or two instead of a unit full of patients who have overinflated expectations of the care they should receive.

And Bob.

It was mid-afternoon when Becca came down the hall in a hurry and I could already tell from her face that she was frustrated. When she finally rounded the half-moon-shaped desk, she shoved the wheeled chair out of her way, stomping into the small supply closet located within our work area. Cece eyed me and I shrugged. If she wanted to know, she could ask her but I knew better than to get into Becca's way when she's having a day.

"Something wrong?" Cece smirked at me and I wondered if she already had an idea.

The petite blond returned a few seconds later with a bedpan and an enema kit, "I'm just swell. Why is it that I always seem to draw the short straw?"

Cece and I looked at the items she carried and choked back snorts of laughter. For as much love as I had for my friend, Becca was the person who only attended college to get her MRS degree. But when that didn't pan out by the time graduation came, she realized she had to work. She was genuinely a hard worker, but, most of the time when was her turn to be on a night rotation, she usually got someone to trade with her or she was placed on standby. She always had the best luck in that regard.

"I'm serious you guys!" she whined. "I've got a non-pooper in seventeen."

Cece leaned over her computer and tapped on the keys before bellowing in laughter.

"What?" I asked, trying to see her monitor. "Who is it?"

"Bob Johnston."

I, too, erupted in laughter and Becca looked at us in sheer bewilderment. Bob was not unknown to Cece, myself, or anyone who worked the night shift. In his early eighties, Mr. Bob, as he had come to be known, usually wandered in a couple of times a week looking for assistance in a particular kind of relief. He never complained if he had to wait and had the brightest smile; eventually.

"Put that stuff away," Cece told her as I picked up the phone and called our pharmacy. "Run to the cafeteria and grab one of those cartons of prune juice."

Becca only stared.

"Girl, just do it. I promise it's better than your plan."

Twenty minutes later, the medications I ordered arrived and Becca returned with the juice. I poured the juice into a cup and microwaved it for twenty seconds. Cece took it from my hands and mixed the two laxatives in the cup with the warmed liquid.

"Oh my God. You're gonna have him drink that?" Becca curled her nose.

Cece handed her the cup, "No. You are. Tell him Cece and Nat said it's cocktail time. And don't leave him. It works fast.

I couldn't help but snicker. We watched Becca's blonde head bounce as she walked Mr. Bob's drink down the hall and disappeared into his room. We gave each other a look of relief because we knew what awaited on the other side. We busied ourselves with other patients and paperwork and had all but forgotten about Becca and Mr. Bob when everyone at the desk heard a scream of frustration. Before we could make a single movement in the direction of the noise, Becca was running up the hall toward the desk followed by a very recognizable odor.

When she was within just a few feet of the desk, she slowed her pace to a casual walk. She didn't speak as she slid a chair to a computer out, sat, and put in her password. We stared at her as she logged her notes and calmly exited the program. She turned down an adjoining hallway in the direction of the cafeteria and said as she passed, "If anyone needs me...don't. After that horror show, I need a drink."

Cece and I fell away into laughter.

So by seven, I was glad to be clocked out and well on my way to a long weekend. Luckily, I put a small pot of chili in the slow cooker that morning and Delilah, my rescued Maine Coon awaited my arrival. Looking down at my feet, I realized I was still wearing foot covers. Huffing a long sigh and dropping the bag with a heavy thud, I reached to flick off the paper slippers from my shoes.

"Hey!" a man's voice called to me from the sidewalk. I looked up in time to see Finn Rafferty jogging toward me.

I stopped, "Hi...Finn, right?"

I knew his name but it was a stupid attempt at flirting.

He smiled, seemingly amused by my fake recognition, "Yeah, that's right. You're Natalie."

"Or Nat. That's what they call me inside," I noticed his dimples. Suddenly remembering the warmth of his hands on my arm a week earlier, the combination of memories made me blush. "Either work."

A short pause dropped between us, "How's the training going?"

I stepped onto the concrete walkway, allowing an ambulance to pull safely into the half-moon drive as Finn laughed. It was the kind of sound that was genuine and joyful. He flashed a brilliant smile of perfectly white teeth in my direction and my heart thumped in my chest.

"Well, I'll be honest...I think I'm teaching the old man more than he is me."

I shrugged my bag on my shoulder again, chuckling, "I bet. Well, it was nice seeing you Finn."

"Uhm...can I ask you something?" Pausing, he took a breath, "Before you leave?"

His eyes were even more gloriously blue when draped in the shadows of the parking lot and looked like orbs of beautifully clear gemstone. My heart beat faster staring into them. I needed to get it together.

'What the hell is wrong with me?' The thought roared.

What I really wanted was to stand there for as long as he would talk to me, but my tired mind and muscles were fighting against me. I smiled sweetly, "Absolutely."

Finn danced in place for a moment. Entertained by his sudden nervousness, I raised my eyebrows a bit.

"I was wondering if you would have dinner with me? Sometime?" he let out a long, slow breath as the words fell from his mouth.

Even with the noise of traffic in the near distance, and the rumbling of the parked bus, his words were overwhelmingly loud in my ears. Time seemed to slow as I immediately thought about the last time I was asked out on a date. Had it been a year? Two, maybe.

A look of concern fell over Finn's face at my long pause, "You okay? I wasn't too forward—"

I shook my head, "No, of course not. Dinner sounds great. How does Friday work?"

Friday seemed far from today, an unrelenting Tuesday, and it was plenty of time for me to back out if I got cold feet.

"Friday is perfect!" Finn's entire body relaxed. Handing me a slip of paper he continued, "This is my number. I'm kinda old fashioned so, I'd like to pick you up, if that's okay. Text me your address?"

"Sure...we can work out a time before then," I replied.

"Great! I'll let you jet...have a good night!" Finn turned, walking away leaving me still and stunned for a moment.

What had I just done? A date?

Hefting my bag again over my shoulder, I contemplated the idea. I couldn't say that I didn't find him attractive, because I certainly did. He seemed like a nice guy and everyone at work thought the same. I made my way closer to the car, my mind still wandering and preoccupied with a soft internal monologue that questioned my sanity. It took my brain a moment to register the movement from the corner of my eyes. A silhouette lurking nearby sent the hair on the back of my neck straight up. Keys already woven in my fingers and sticking out like jagged brass knuckles, my pace quickened.

The shadow moved between vehicles on a line to intercept me at my destination. I took up a smooth jog but he was already within arms reach and stood between me and my car. I stopped suddenly, standing off with the figure in shadow.

"Hey, Nat," it spoke.

The bile churned and I immediately wanted to vomit, "Drew. What are you doing here? You're not supposed to be within five hundred yards—"

"Don't get your panties in a wad...my girlfriend is in the ER. I'm going to see her. I just recognized you and wanted to say hi."

I could almost see the oily grin on his face and my stomach turned again. I wanted to run from our standoff, but my feet felt cemented to the ground. I had to remind myself, for whatever comfort it warranted, that there were cameras everywhere.

"Get out of here Drew. I've got a panic alarm that will call security in a matter of seconds," I lied, gripping my handful of keys tighter. I was fully prepared to gouge one or both of his eyes.

Drew put his hands up, "There's no need...I'm going. It's...*really* good to see you, gorgeous."

The tenor of his voice shot revulsion down my spine and he walked so close to my frozen form that I smelled his cheap cologne.

"Hey Nat! Wait up!" Cece's distant voice was like a lifeline in the spotted darkness.

"See you around," Drew whispered close to my head as he brushed against my shoulder. "By the way, I'm not a fan of the new perfume. You should go back to your old one. I liked that one."

He walked toward the sliding doors.

My eyes were squeezed tight when I felt Cece's presence next to me. I let out a long cleansing sigh. It was a close call, and I knew it.

"Girl, who was that?" Cece chortled with a distinct sound of attraction before noticing my face. "What's wrong?"

I shook my head, "No one. Really...I think he just startled me is all."

Cece, not buying my story, leveled a cautious eye, and took a second glance behind us, "Uh huh...Wait a damn second. That better not be—"

My eyes flashed an answer only she would understand.

She nodded cautiously, "Did Finn find you?"

"Oh, yeah," I replied, but knew my answer was distant.

I saw worry sweep Cece's face but she kept her thoughts to herself as she looked back over her shoulder at the door, "Girl, go home. Get some rest...I'll see you on Sunday."

Chapter Six

Natalie

"Ok...what do you think about this?" Cece laid out another outfit on my already over-filled bed. Piles of clothes and shoes scattered on every surface and looked more like a thrift store than a bedroom.

I laughed, "Do you really think a hot pink lace crop and palazzo pants are the way to go?"

My friend shrugged, "You're probably right...this is more of a club ensemble. Where did you say he was taking you?"

"No idea," I mindlessly flicked a scattering of lime-colored sequins.

When Cece said she wanted to help me get ready for the date with Finn, I had no idea she would be trucking her entire closet to my house with her. I didn't mind, honestly. She had impeccable taste and was a connoisseur of trends and fashion. Unfortunately, where Cece was slender and rail-like, I had hips; not everything looked the same on me.

Cece's head whipped in my direction, "What do you mean, no idea? He didn't give you a hint?"

I shook my head.

A scoff clicked in Cece's throat and her expressive eyes rolled, "Girl, you need information. Dressing for a movie night isn't the same as..."

She pondered for a moment, "...horseback riding."

"Horseback riding?!" I roared with laughter. "Where did you come up with that?"

"I don't know," she shrugged, returning to the closet. "I'm just saying, you need to have some idea so you know what to expect."

I couldn't disagree with the logic but something about Cece's tone felt off. Like it was hiding a story that didn't *want* to be hidden.

"Ce?"

She glanced over her shoulder, "Yeah?"

"Spill it," I lifted a suspicious eyebrow in her direction.

Her eyes rolled and the expression brought me such delight. She was my very best friend and while she liked to know all of my business, she was sometimes a little shady about her own.

"Alright," she relented. "I went out with that radiologist last night."

"Oh?" I was immediately and completely invested.

She threw a yellow sundress in my direction, "Yeah, so, get this. I am looking sharp. Girl, the hair is done to perfection, the makeup...ooo ..chef's kiss."

She kissed her fingertips in the air as I rolled off the bed stripping down to my underwear before sliding on the dress she tossed at me, "Of course."

"Of course," she repeated. "This man rolls up in jeans, a cowboy shirt, and dirty boots."

I tossed a look of disgust at her over my shoulder. I wasn't judging the radiologist, but I knew Cece and her type. Dirty boots wasn't it.

"So?" I zipped the dress and shifted from side to side looking at myself in the mirror and decided this one would go on the shortlist.

"Well, I went out with him anyway and where does this man take me? To one of those places where you do trail rides." She flipped through the shirts in my closet at breakneck speed, "Oh hell no...here

I am with my Jimmy Choo's and smelling like an expensive tropical vacation thanks to some Simone Andreoli and he thinks I'm getting on that animal. Nope."

I was quiet. Not because I was in shock, but because I was trying not to bite a hole in my lip as I fought the impending outburst. But it didn't work. Suddenly I was doubled over in raucous roils of laughter.

She whipped around on me, "It's not that funny."

I could hardly breathe. It was indeed that funny.

Her eyes narrowed, "You better stop with that nonsense. I'm telling you, it was a disaster."

Taking a deep breath, I tried not to smile as I choked out, "Please, continue."

My best friend in this entire world had expensive taste. It didn't matter what it was, food, makeup, shoes; Cece always sought one hundred percent quality and was willing to pay for it. Many people would say she was high maintenance, but that couldn't be further from the truth. She just knew what she wanted and wasn't afraid to work hard to get it. Sometimes, it put her in some pretty sticky, and often hilarious situations just like this one.

"Try these shoes with that dress," she tossed a strappy pair of tan sandals my way. "Well, I politely declined...then, he suggested we just go ahead and have dinner. So, we drive over to Visalia to that cute little French place, Le Cafe Parisien."

She pronounced the restaurant name in perfect French.

"Oh! Well, that's nice." I felt her eyes drill into me before I even looked up, "What?"

"You would think so, wouldn't you?" her voice playfully acidic. "But, you know the one thing you need, on any night, even a Wednesday, to have a meal at Le Cafe Parisien?"

I shook my head, my teeth still clamped onto my inner cheeks.

"A reservation!" Cece blurted and I again doubled over in torrents of laughter.

"He didn't think to get a reservation? In one of the most popular restaurants?" My giggles were almost too consuming.

Cece rolled her eyes, "He wanted to impress me."

"Yeah, well, bang-up job. Dirty boots, live animals, and no real meal plan? What did you end up doing?" I turned back to the mirror to admire my friends' outfit selection. Yeah, this was definitely in the running.

"Cheesecake Factory. Which, is fine...you know I do like the Key Lime," she shrugged.

I paused.

"Wait a second. That's in Fresno. You guys went from here to Visalia to Fresno and back?" I chuckled again. "You got dressed up for a road trip and cheesecake."

"Which brings me back to my point," she tucked in the tags on the dress I tried on. "Girl, you got to know the plan. Don't be me...I'm a cautionary tale."

The seriousness on her face forced me to erupt in full-body laughter, "Dramatic much?"

A grin spread across Cece's lips as she finally broke, "I know, right? But seriously, that was the worst date ever. For your sake, I hope the tight-assed paramedic wears clean shoes, at the very least."

Chapter Seven

Finn

I knocked gently on the door as my mind raced with nervousness. I didn't know about her, but it had been a long time since I had been on a date. Cupping my hand around my mouth, I huffed a couple of times and sniffed. Breath was good; check. I glanced down to validate my appearance. My khaki-colored pants were neatly ironed and the blue oxford shirt was untucked. I was going for sophisticated casual but worried that I may be too laid-back. We probably should have discussed where we were going, but our recent text conversations always seemed too short and veered into another territory.

Within a few seconds, I heard a slide lock, a deadbolt, and a chain release on the door before Natalie appeared behind it. My breath caught in my chest for a moment as it suddenly occurred to me that this was the first time I'd seen her out of her normal Ceylon blue scrubs and ponytail. She was dressed in a simple yellow sundress and sandals, her brunette hair hung in long waves around her face. I was so taken aback that I almost forgot to speak.

"Right on time!" she chirped.

I blinked, "Uh...yeah. I'm usually pretty punctual. Are you ready to go?"

Natalie's rosy lips spread into a grin, "Absolutely!"

She threw her purse strap over her shoulder and then pulled the door closed before we walked the short sidewalk to where my pristine 1980 Bronco sat parked. She watched me pull a fob from my pocket and unlock the doors. One of my little upgrades on this passion project.

"This is your car?" Natalie mused as I held the door open.

She had to wait for me to jog to the driver's side for an answer.

I slid in, "Yeah. Just so you know, if you say you hate it, it will break my heart."

Her eyebrows rose, "Why is that?"

"Because," a teasing smirk formed at the corners of my mouth as I turned the engine over. "It would be the end of our date. I'd hate to walk you home now without a kiss goodnight."

Natalie's neck and cheeks flushed crimson, "Well...then I guess you'd miss out on all my stories of family road trips in my dad's."

"Oh yeah? Can't wait to hear about it," I smiled and eased away from the curb.

As I drove, I saw her eyes discreetly watching me with quick, side glances. She took in every movement and motion I made as my hands slid over the glossy walnut wheel. I wasn't certain if it was because she was a nurse, but she seemed to pay special attention to my hands. I was nail-biter but what I had left on my beds was clean and neatly groomed. Her studious eyes made me a little self-conscious, but they didn't linger in any one place for long before she pretended she was looking out of the window.

"So, do you like pizza?" I cleared my throat, breaking the silence growing in the space.

Natalie's skin flushed again like she'd been caught with her hand in the cookie jar, "Uhh, yeah, pizza is good."

"There's this great little place in Visalia that makes the best Pizza Napoletana. Nonna's...you heard of it?" My quick glance in her direction caught her eye.

"No...but it sounds great," I heard a smile in her voice.

The doom of silence fell between us again. It was the awkward absence of sound made by two people who probably had so much in common but didn't know where to start and neither dared to be the first. I was afraid of making her as nervous as I felt, so I continued to glance in her direction in hopes that a truly thought-provoking question would come to me. I knew she had to feel my eyes on her and I made a mental note to apologize for it later.

"So, look...I'm not really good at this small talk thing..." I said after what felt like an eternity.

Natalie huffed out a chuckle, "Good. Because I was thinking it was just me."

A full smile spread across my face, "We work together. None of this should be weird, right?"

She nodded her agreement.

"Okay. Let's not make it that way. I'll tell you what...let's do this like an intake," I suggested.

A wrinkle formed between Natalie's eyes, "How do you mean?"

I shrugged, "We can ask questions...the other person answers until we have a good history. I think we can skip the name section though."

Natalie giggled. What I suggested is a more lighthearted game of Twenty Questions. But, she considered my request for a short moment and eventually decided it would be an effective icebreaker.

"Ok, I'm in," she paused. "Where did you grow up?"

"Oh, getting right to the depths, huh?" I laughed, but I was quietly pleased I didn't go first. "I'm from Medford, Oregon...but my mom moved down to Sacramento when I was eight."

Natalie concentrated on a follow-up, but I beat her to the punch, "You?"

"I'm from Cloverdale...born and raised," her words cut short. I knew the area was just as pleasant and picturesque as it sounded as it sat in the north of Sonoma County.

"Cloverdale? That's a nice place," I mused.

Natalie was quick with her next question, "Have any hobbies?"

"Yeah," I nodded, "Anything outside."

I cut my concern at her and was grateful she didn't notice. The abruptness of her question startled me for a moment, but, not wanting our night to be awkward, I ignored it and continued with my answer, "My favorite is the water...anything that gets me in, I'm down for."

Relief of common ground swept over her face, "Oh! Me too!"

The tension of just moments before dissolved between us. We chatted about rivers and lakes and our mutual stories of white water rafting and skiing filled the cab of the truck until I pulled into the parking lot of the restaurant. Our conversation finally made natural turns into comfortable areas and brought genuine smiles and laughter. After sharing the most delicious pizza either of us ever tasted, I took her for ice cream and we ate in a park to watch the sunset over the distant Sierra Nevada mountains. Our fervent exchange still lingered through the drive back home and to Natalie's doorstep.

It felt like we'd known each other for years.

I watched from behind as she climbed the three steps onto her porch before I followed her. She turned to meet my gaze and time stood silent and unmoving around us. The world just seemed to slip away. Suddenly, my mouth felt like a desert and I didn't think I could get words to form. Taking a deep breath, I held it in my mouth while I memorized her hazel eyes.

"So..." I dropped my breath slowly, "I had a great time tonight."

Natalie's smile seemed to brighten every inch of the dimly lit stoop, "Me too!"

I flipped a thumb behind me, "I'd better go...I'm on my forty-eight at seven."

I watched her face droop ever so slightly and a thin veil of disappointment glided over her eyes. The sight made my heart ache; I really liked this girl, and the thought of ending such a great night bummed me out too. I knew most guys would go in for the kiss at this point but, I respected her too much and didn't want to cheapen the great time we had. I knew I'd have to do something and act fast before any thoughts of rejection crossed her mind. I stepped forward, picking up her hand.

"I would...uh..." My mouth was dry again. "I'd like to do this again...maybe Thursday?"

Natalie's voice was as soft as her fingers, "Yeah, I'd like that."

"Great!" I knew my face wouldn't hide my excitement. Before she could respond, I lifted Natalie's delicate hand to my lips and kissed it gently. "I'll call you tomorrow."

Chapter Eight

Natalie

I never thought Thursday would get here.

It was so weird. I hadn't felt this giddy in, well... years. I had to temper my enthusiasm though because I didn't want Finn to get the wrong idea. But, he was just so...cute. And kind. And funny. He called me, like he said he would, the next night. We talked until around midnight when a call came in for a possible heart attack, and he and Marc had to run the scene. But we saw each other the next morning when I walked into Southwest Haven for my shift. His brilliant baby blues sucked me into another world and left me suspended in their cosmos. I allowed it. I acquiesced to the pull and harmonious sound of his voice until Cece had to draw me inside to reality.

"Girl, get your head out of those eyes," she laughed.

I blinked quickly but felt the flush rushing through my cheeks. Turning toward my computer screen, I hid from what I knew was going to be an onslaught of teasing. But before she could light into me, a well-dressed woman who looked to be in her sixties approached the desk.

"Excuse me, may my mother have a drink of water? Someone was supposed to bring her something thirty minutes ago," she asked timidly.

I jumped at the chance to get away from whatever torment my best friend had in store for me, "Of course, what room?"

"Twenty-one," she replied.

I nodded and retrieved a styrofoam cup with a lid from the supply closet before filling it with water at the fountain. I walked the request to the room as the daughter met me at the door.

"Thank you so much," she smiled.

"No problem at all, if you or your mother need anything else—"

"Ma'am! Ma'am!"

I turned to find a second woman, this one clothed in a standard-issue hospital gown and grip socks shuffling in my direction. She was waving her thin arms in frantic motion and worked hard to get my attention.

"Ma'am!" she yelled again.

I faced the woman with the cup of water, "I'm sorry...one moment."

I turned back to the shuffler who nearly reached me as she continually yelled "Ma'am!" at the top of her lungs and flailed her arms. As she skated past the nurse's station, Cece made a double-take at her. Her eyes rolled and she held in laughter as she hurried around the desk. I realized from the look on her face that the back of the gown was splayed open.

The shuffler reached me, "Ma'am I said!"

"Yes!" I replied sternly. "What can I do for you?"

My voice was low in hopes that she would follow suit but she did not.

"I am trying to tell you something!" the shuffler bellowed.

My smile was tight and I reached for her arm, "What can I do for you?"

"I've lost it! I need your help! You need to find it!" the shuffler's face was distressed. What in the world could she have lost? Did she come in with a small child? Or maybe it's her personal belongings she's concerned over.

Cece finally caught up and I asked, "Okay, we can help you. What are you looking for?"

"My clitoris! It just fell out!"

The daughter behind me gasped with a pearl-clutching sound and I watched my best friend and colleague melt with stifled laughter as she turned on her heel back to the desk, shuttering with repressed giggles and shaking her head. I immediately bit my lip and steadied my reaction, which took every last bit of my resolve.

I ground my teeth, keeping my laughter at bay, and took the shuffler by the arm, "Well, I'm sure we'll find it here somewhere. Let's go check your room."

***

After my extraordinarily long day, and reporting to the night shift that the aforementioned female anatomy was still missing, I raced home to give myself enough time to shower before Finn picked me up around eight. We planned on a low-key late dinner and a movie so I dressed quickly in comfortable jeans and a tee shirt, before adding a sweater for the cool theater. Walking into my living room, I watched Finn jog onto my front porch and I opened the door before he could knock.

"Hey...you," his face filled with that smile that made my internal butterflies wake. I asked about his day and listened as he delved into the details of the most interesting calls of the week.

"It was a week for sure," the growl of exhaustion emanating from deep inside. "Some are like that...I'm sure you know."

I nodded and described my flailing woman and he exploded in laughter. As he drove, I watched the street lights flicker on as the early summer sun finally set and we passed out of my neighborhood and onto the busier areas of the city center. It didn't take us long to reach our destination and slide into a spot near the door. The scent of spice and fresh tortillas from my favorite restaurant perfumed the air as Finn held the heavy wooden door for me at Casa Azul.

After we were seated and our drink orders were taken, a smile crept over my lips as I tried to avoid his stare. I was an introvert, by nature, but I could usually handle one-on-one interactions perfectly fine. But, there was something about Finn Rafferty that set me off balance. He was handsome and charming in an all-American sort of way. He looked like he should be riding waves in SoCal instead of saving lives here in the central corridor.

"Why are you avoiding me?" he asked and his devilish grin set me on fire.

My lips purse and I shook my head coyly, "I'm not."

Finn bent his head to force eye contact, "Oh yeah, I can tell."

He paused.

"You really are shy, aren't you? Face to face."

"I'm sorry," I looked up sheepishly, but I was begging for forgiveness in my head. This guy probably thought I was an insecure nutjob. I wasn't but I sure felt like it. I didn't think I'd dated anyone so nice and free with acts of kindness.

"Why?" his brow furrowed. "It's who you are...why apologize for that?"

I smiled at him but it wasn't out of agreement, it was because I didn't know how to respond. He seemed fine with my bashfulness, even if I wasn't. I didn't want him to see any of my weaknesses and there are so many of them. Part of me worried about how long I could keep them hidden. Forever was my hope. I needed to redirect the focus of the conversation if only to get out of my own head.

"You know, this is one of my favorite restaurants. Did you talk to Cece?"

"No..." was his answer but the slight shift in his chair told me otherwise. I raised a suspicious eyebrow at him.

"Okay, yeah...maybe," he finally admitted.

I giggled, "I knew it!"

I had to give him points for being resourceful.

"Do you have a Cece in your life?" I propped my chin on a hand.

Finn smiled wide, "I do. Cop buddy of mine in San Jose, Elias. We worked a lot of scenes together when we both first started out. He's good people...helped me through my divorce. Pushed me to move when I couldn't get a moment's peace being in the same city as the ex."

"Is that when you moved to Sonoma?" I sipped my wine.

"Yeah," Finn nodded. "It's beautiful there...but, I missed being in a larger city. I kinda like the rush."

Other than a few text messages when we chatted at night, this was the first time Finn had mentioned his ex-wife or their divorce. I wanted to know more, but I didn't want our date to turn into a gossip circle comparing exes; I certainly wasn't ready for all that. Our vibe had finally relaxed so we enjoyed our tacos and each other's company. Before long, Finn paid our check and we were on our way to the movie.

"What are we seeing again?" I asked.

"Delmar is having a re-release of the original Twister. I thought it might be fun," Finn glanced in my direction as he rounded the corner.

"I'm not sure how people can live in someplace that has tornados. Terrifying." I laughed.

His eyes glinted in the city lights, "We live in a place that has earthquakes, fires, and mudslides. At least they get a warning when Mother Nature is pissed off."

I considered his answer, "We have warnings with slides and fires. You can't outrun a tornado."

"Two words: Earth. Quakes," he smirked.

My laughter filled the truck, "I've got two words for you: Flying. Cows."

Our hot debate on the worst natural catastrophe continued as we parked and walked toward the theater's doors. Our discussion elicited stifled chortles between us as we waited in line for popcorn and snacks. When Finn was making a last-ditch, desperate retort for the absurdity of flying farm animals my eyes wandered to take in the surroundings and landed on a familiar face staring back at me from the self-service soda machine.

The second his darkness locked on me a rock formed in my throat and my hands went numb. I felt the cold beads of sweat forming on the back of my neck and at my temples as my heart beat from my chest. I felt his oily leer lean on me like a falling house and I couldn't make my eyes peel away from his.

"Natalie?" I heard a voice in the distance. It was like a beacon on a stormy sea.

A warm hand gently held onto my wrist and the signal called out to me again but this time it was softer but closer.

"Natalie...can you hear me?"

The world came more into focus and I heard my own whisper, "Popcorn. Poster... Finn."

"Yeah, I'm right here. Are you okay?" his eyes met mine.

I tried to swallow but my throat was like sandpaper. I looked back at the drink station, but Drew was gone. Glancing around I noticed we were removed from the line and tucked in the junction of two video games, Finn's fingers still holding onto my wrist at my pulse point.

I knew my voice would be unsteady but I did my best to hide my fear from him. I rubbed my finger over the scar on my brow, "Yeah...you know, I'm not feeling well. Would you mind if we called it a night?"

Chapter Nine

Finn

I knew this much was one hundred percent true: I had just witnessed Natalie having a panic attack not ten minutes ago. I didn't know why or what caused it, but I'd seen it before. But somehow, this time, it was so much worse than anything I'd witnessed at work. Probably because it happened off the clock, unexpectedly, and to the woman I'm dating. We rode with silence layered between us but there were so many things I wanted to say to her. I couldn't. I didn't want her to feel bad about cutting our night short and I didn't want to ask questions whose answers were none of my business. It did made me wonder, however; What did she see, smell, or hear that would push her to a survival response?

'It's none of my business,' I whispered in my head, but it killed me to think it.

I gently rolled up to the sidewalk in front of her small craftsman and jumped out of the truck before she had a chance to argue. I pulled the door open and her hazel eyes met mine briefly. In that instant, they were tired and embarrassed with just a slight edge of fear that was fortunately fading by the second. I knew I was looking at her for far too long when she broke the lock with me and hung her head.

"Thank you for driving me home," her voice was soft yet, apologetic.

I bent my head and tried to get another look at her face, but it was as if she didn't want me to see her. She tried her best to move her eyes anywhere but mine. "I'm sorry you're not..."

Her terrified face flashed to me for a split second. I felt a crack in my chest as I saw the beginning of tears glistening in the streetlamp. It wasn't my place, but I wanted to pull her to me and tell her everything was okay; that whatever happened was over and she didn't need to feel ashamed or afraid.

"...Feeling well," I finished as our swollen pause gained its foothold again. "Do you need anything? I'm a great listener if you want to tal—"

"No!" she snapped and her face fell again. She took a shaky breath before she dared to look up, "No, I'm fine. Raincheck on the movie?"

I knew the second the words fell from her mouth that she was lying. I could tell she was trying her damnedest to lighten the heavy weight that was pressing down on her and me, but I didn't want her to. I wanted to feel every crushing ounce of it because if I could bear it myself, maybe she'd let me carry it for her someday. Her stare cut through my veins and sank in my gut. I fought the urge to grab onto her and shield her from whatever was going on in her head.

Instead, I said, "Absolutely. Maybe next week?"

The surprise on her face was another ripple of pain in my chest. In whatever way this woman was treated before, I knew immediately it wasn't the right way. It was like she never expected me to make another date with her. Not wanting her to feel any sort of apprehension, I continued quickly.

"If you're not busy, maybe lunch tomorrow? I've got some errands, so I could swing by around eleven if that works?" my gaze held hers as I waited for an answer.

Her head nodded slowly and a soft smile almost pulled at the edges of her mouth, "Eleven is perfect."

I wanted to reach out and touch her hand and kiss her flushed cheek, but I didn't. I wouldn't invade the space that she so desperately needed at that moment. She seemed so fragile, but I knew she wasn't; she couldn't be. Anyone who was fighting as hard as she was to hide her pain and fear couldn't be a broken-winged bird. Natalie Shire was all iron and steel. I knew it because I felt it.

"Goodnight, Finn," her voice soft as she walked the short sidewalk and porch steps to her door.

I waited by my Bronco until I saw the living room light and what I can only imagine was the light of her bedroom flip on and spill onto the yard below. I sat inside the truck and watched her house for just a few more seconds before I turned the engine over and drove away.

Chapter Ten

Natalie

As promised, I saw Finn's truck pull along the sidewalk at eleven o'clock. It wasn't as if I didn't know he was on his way because he texted me before he left his apartment with vague instructions.

I opened the door with my shoes dangling from their leather straps over my fingers, "You may have an iron stomach, but I don't. A sweater and sunscreen seem like something that will give me heartburn."

Finn's smile was magnetic, drawing me in, "Don't most doctors say everything in moderation?"

A laugh bubbled from my throat and his eyes sparkled in the shade of my porch. I wanted to say so much right now. I thought I owed him, not an explanation because I didn't think I could give him that, but at the very least an apology for last night. It was like he could read my mind because his next words eased the pressure I felt inside.

"I'm glad you're feeling better," his voice was soft as he spoke. "I wasn't sure you'd feel like doing anything today."

I didn't want him to know that I saw him from inside my house last night and knew he didn't immediately leave. If that small gesture didn't make me a little more confident that he wasn't going to run for the hills after the way I behaved, then the text message when he arrived home to tell me he had a great time, despite my becoming "ill" certainly did.

I gave him a pleasant smile, "I am. Although, it would be great if you'd give me a little more of a hint than two items I'm sure aren't necessary for a meal."

This elicited a devilish smirk, "You sure about that, are you?"

He waved his hand in a gesture that asked me to walk with him to the vehicle, "After you, ma'am."

I giggled, grabbed my purse and keys, and followed him to the truck. As I stepped into the cab, I looked into the back seat to find a large cooler, blankets, and something that looked like fabric rolled inside a long plastic bag. On the front floorboard was a smaller cooler, just big enough for a six-pack. I eyed him as he shut the door. He took a look at the items behind us and then back at me before he lifted his shoulder in a dismissive shrug. I pursed my lips in suspicion, but this only threw him into a fit of belly laughter.

"You're really not going to tell me, are you?" I pressed.

Finn shook his head. "I know I haven't earned it yet, but can I ask that you trust me?"

My body was screaming no, but my mind immediately quieted all the anxiety. A small voice whispered, *'Yes'*.

I nodded but didn't let go of my playful suspicion, "Okay..."

Finn laughed again, but his eyes were relieved. He looked as though I gave him the answer to a long-awaited question that had been squirming its way around the dark recesses of his mind. I wondered what else happened in that brain of his; the things he didn't say out loud. I was lost in my thoughts when I realized we had left the city and were driving west. As if I'd just woken from a nap, I scrutinized the passing scenery.

"I thought we were going to lunch?" I asked.

Finn's lips parted in a grin, "We are. But, it's going to be a couple of hours before we can eat. If you're hungry, I packed snacks."

He gestured to the smaller container on the floor in front of us.

"A couple of hours?!" my voice pitched high and incredulous.

"Yeah," he shrugged again, chuckling.

"Finn!" I protested but hoped he would take it as playfully as I intended. "There are a lot of places to eat between Hanford and two hours."

He only laughed again and it rang like bells in the truck, "It's a surprise! I don't know about you, but I hate it when they're ruined."

I knew that whatever offer of dissent I gave would be rejected in short order, by his child-like excitement. We made our way closer to our secret destination and I watched Finn's enthusiasm grow with each passing mile. He occasionally glanced at me during our time-passing conversations and smiled with his wickedly charming grin.

We were just five minutes past our two-hour timeline when we cruised by a city limit sign and I shifted in my seat to turn toward him. His smirk told me everything I needed to know.

Welcome to Morrow Bay, California, Population: 10, 757

"Really?" I was in disbelief.

Easing into a parking spot on the dirt-colored and nearly empty lot, Finn put the vehicle in park. Even through the vents of the Bronco's cooling system, the ocean air permeated my nostrils. I rolled down the window and pulled in a lung full of the sweet, briny breeze as the roar of the water filled my ears and I felt all the tension leave every cell of my body. Water, particularly for me, the Pacific, was nothing short of magic in how she tugged at my soul and commanded me to release any distress into her.

My eyes fluttered open and Finn was already out of the truck loading everything into a fat-wheeled wagon made for beach terrain. Meeting me at the door as I stepped down, the once devilish smile was softer and content.

"You hungry?" he asked. "I think our table is about ready."

I smiled at him, really trying not to look completely like a kid in a candy store, but I knew I couldn't help it. I offered to help with the load, but Finn only shook his head as we headed out onto the sand. We found an area of beach where we wouldn't be disturbed by the family units with children frolicking in the cool water and set up our large blanket. Once seated, I pulled on the sweater that was requested while my date unloaded a variety of delicious-looking offerings.

"I have fruit, cheese, crackers," he dug into the cooler. "Oh! And Curried Egg salad from—"

"Rothery's!" I interjected, recognizing the familiar label. "It's so good."

"Right? There's nothing like it."

"How did you get this? I thought this was a special order item," I asked.

The corner of his mouth fought from curling into a smirk but it failed miserably. I rolled my eyes, "Your morning errands?"

Finn shrugged, "The Chief is a friend of the Rothery family. They always keep a few containers back for us."

My eyes rolled again in faux exasperation and it made him laugh.

"I tried to recreate it once," he chuckled, passing me a compostable bamboo plate.

"Oh yeah? How did it turn out?" I handed a set of silverware in his direction.

His lips curled in disgust, "Let's just say there's definitely a reason to get it from Rothery's."

I waited until he was finished laying out the spread before I served myself. I felt his eyes on my skin as I picked strawberries from the deli container and scooped the golden wonder that is Rothery's Curried Egg salad onto my plate. His gaze watched every twist of my hands and twitch of my face. Under normal circumstances, I would be wholly creeped out by this kind of behavior, even though, it seemed like we've known each other forever, but Finn was different. He had an aura of gentleness about him and sometimes it seemed to exude from him. I glanced up and locked on his sparkling blues. I could feel my cheeks redden, so I quickly looked away and we ate in the crash of the waves for a moment.

Finn cleared his throat and shoved an olive in his mouth, "I hope this isn't too cheesy."

"What?" My brow furrowed with unasked questions.

"A picnic on the beach," a short laugh huffed over his lips.

I sat my near-empty plate on the blanket next to me and wiped my hands, "Absolutely not. It's actually..."

My words faded. I didn't know how to finish the sentence. I couldn't tell this God-like man in front of me that this was, without a doubt, the sweetest thing anyone had ever done. And he did it on his own; I had no hand in the planning or execution, save for the sweater and sunscreen. I wanted to say all of that and more, but... *I. Can't.* I realized he was staring at me and I hurried to finish my sentence.

"...very nice."

I watched his face fall just a bit but before I could decipher what kind of disappointment he just allowed to slip, Finn jumped to his feet and pulled the rolled fabric from its plastic sheath. I watched as the material splayed out to show a large colorful bird, a crane, as he fitted small rods into channels of fabric at its edges. Once the cross bars were set, he attached the reel of thick twine before turning to me with a beaming grin.

"It's a kite!" I giggled and immediately my insides churned with guilt. It's as if the synapses in my brain finally put the pieces together to communicate that Finn's look before may have been hurt and not disappointment like I thought. Before he could stand and raise the ornate bird in the air, I laid my hand over his, "This is pretty awesome, Finn."

Pausing to give me a short look of confusion, he asks, "What?"

I took a deep breath of the ensorcelled air, "All of it."

Chapter Eleven

Finn

Natalie's gleeful giggles were like music over the thrumming of the ocean as I handed her control of the enormous kite. The giant bird had drawn a small clutch of nearby onlookers as it set against the wind and drove higher into the air. As the kite's tip began to dive, Natalie gasped with frustration.

"No, no, no!" she ordered through short laughs.

"Here," I moved behind her, reaching around either side and guiding her hands into keeping the bird flying. I felt the heat of her skin through my henley as the breeze blew her sweet scent into me. She smelled like honeysuckle and something soft. I closed my eyes for just a moment to burn it into my memory like a brand.

"Oh no! Finn!" Natalie's squeal turned into rolling laughter as the kite landed in the wet sand like a jart.

I chuckled, "Well, let's be glad no one was standing there."

I realized she was still in my arms as she turned to look up at me. I fought the urge to pull her warmth closer and envelop her body with mine. Her hazel eyes glowed in the sunlight and her hand brushed against my forearm as she reached to sweep strands of her dark hair from her face. Fire grew in the depths of my gut as my eyes moved over her.

"I...uhh...I better get the bird," I said but I didn't move away and just continued to stare. She had to feel this too, right? The electricity that sparked when we were within a mile of each other? I watched her throat swallow hard as she took in my face. I wondered if her pulse was beating as hard as mine.

"Right. Get the bird," she cleared her throat.

I blinked out of my hypnosis and jogged out to where the crane's beak was buried halfway into the packed sand. After prying it free, I held it aloft as Natalie cranked the reel and spooled in the slack of the line. I secured the framed fabric to the ground and plopped back onto the blanket. Natalie sat next to me and we stared off into the water, listening to the rumble of the waves onto the shore.

"Did you always want to be a paramedic?" she asked over the thunderous crashing, her words breaking our meditation.

I shrugged, "I always wanted to help people, I think. I knew someone a long time ago that helped me and I wanted to pay it forward."

Her eyes asked the question.

"I had cancer as a kid," I began. "I got really sick after one of my rounds of chemo...I threw up for two days. Became dehydrated...almost died. My mom called nine-one-one and had a bus pick me up. The guy who worked on me, Jason Harris was his name, made jokes to take my mind off how terrible I felt. Told me to imagine the IV he started was ice cream and how much better I would feel by having my dessert before dinner and not telling on him to my mom. I guess I wanted to be Jason for someone else."

A wrinkle formed between her brows, "What kind of cancer?"

"Leukemia."

"Well, if you're going to have one as a child, statically..." her voice trailed off. "I'm sorry...I'm not telling you anything you don't already know, clearly. Sometimes it's hard to turn the nurse off."

I watched a blush rise on her cheeks. The snicker that left my throat sounded more bitter than I intended, "Stats aren't always a comfort."

There was meaning in my words. I knew as soon as they left my mouth that I'd said too much and I was desperate to rewind our conversation. I wanted to tell her everything because she needed to know. I didn't want her to feel like I misled her or burdened her with images of a future that would never happen. My mouth was dry and the words were lost.

Her round eyes widened, "I'm sorry. I'm sure it was a really scary time for you and your parents."

"Mom," I shook my head. "Just my mom...and my little sister, although she was too young to understand."

"What about your Dad?" she pulled her knees to her chest, resting her chin there. I scooped a handful of sand and watched it fall through my fingers before I answered.

"He took off when Sadie, my sister, was a year old," I stated as a matter of fact. While his absence was old hat now, I still remembered my mother's tears as she waited for him at our kitchen table.

"I'm so sorry," her hand was warm on mine as she reached out to me.

"Nah," I dismissed, "Memories of him used to infuriate me, now, I just pity him. He's the one that missed out, not us."

"What does your sister do?"

I realized Natalie had a way of switching topics like a pro and always stayed in the shallows of the emotional pool. I knew what I hid in my depths. The thoughts of broken dreams and experiences permeated my darkness like the shadow of a predator. It made me wonder about hers. But talking about my sister brought me joy and I couldn't help but offer an uncontrollable smile.

"She's a third-year law student at Stanford. She just went back after she and her wife had their first child...with any luck, she'll graduate next year," I knew Natalie could hear the pride in my words.

"You're an uncle? That's awesome! Boy? Girl?" she asked with genuine excitement.

"A girl! Harbor Grace...and that little girl has all of this uncle's heart," I beamed. "Seriously...she is going to get anything she wants. Candy...clothes...ponies."

Natalie giggled, "Do you see your sister and the baby often?"

She ran her slender fingers through unwieldy tendrils fighting for her face.

I sighed, "Not as much as I'd like which would be every day. I plan to drive up tomorrow for a few hours." I paused to watch the wind blow through Natalie's long hair. She was indescribably beautiful against the backdrop of the roar, the waves, and Morrow Rock. "What about you? Any nieces or nephews?"

She shook her head, "No, it's just me."

"No siblings? What about your parents?" I asked.

I wasn't sure if it was a more private setting or if it was the backdrop of the sea, but Natalie seemed more open to personal matters today. I didn't want to pry into her life, but the more time we spent together, the more I liked this woman. I was drawn to her in ways I'd never been to anyone else and I wanted to know her. In our hours of conversation over the phone or a meal, she'd never given me the chance to do that.

"My parents died a few years ago. First my dad...heart attack. Then my mom...a stroke." She took a deep breath and looked at the dwindling sun, "It's just me. I've never had a lot of family anyway...I think

I've got a cousin and aunt in San Diego still...obviously, we're not close."

Her chuckle was tight but there was also an edge to it. I couldn't be sure, but it sounded like that of someone who has been through the hits that life could throw but fought them alone. Those were the bits I wanted to see. I wanted the stinging, acerbic edges that destroyed her while also keeping others at arm's reach. I needed to know what eruptions happened in her core that created the walls of razor-sharp stone that surrounded her now.

"Well, in my experience, a lot of family is overrated anyway," I shrugged. "It's the tribe you create that becomes your family."

She smiled and her lips trembled. It was then I noticed her whole body shiver. I pulled my jacket from the wagon and scooted closer to wrap it around her shoulders. Her eyes thanked me and we were so close. The setting sun glittered in her almost-green eyes and I again caught her perfume in my nose. I became acutely aware that my hands hadn't moved from her shoulders and she hadn't pulled away.

The wind blew a lock of hair onto her face and before she could move it, I drew my fingers across her cheek, tucking the piece behind her ear. Her skin was like velvet under my hand and even in this dull light, I saw the rosy hue appear. God, I wanted to kiss this woman. The pull between us was otherworldly but I couldn't bring myself to reach out and take her beautifully full lips on mine.

She leaned closer and I wrapped my arm around her, pulling her to my side. Our bodies were warm together as we watched the last few seconds of the twilight fall beneath the horizon. She reclined into my chest and I drew her tighter in my arms. My heart raced with a need to stay like this all night, but I hoped she couldn't hear the thumping drum inside me over the rumble of waves.

I buried my face in her hair and nuzzled her ear. I felt her let loose a contented sigh and she leaned her head on my bicep.

"What do you want most in life, Finn?" she turned her head to look at my face.

I couldn't tell her what I knew my heart wanted; it was way too soon for that. I also couldn't leave the question unanswered either.

"I don't know," my eyes focused on the profile of her face. "To live a meaningful life and share it with someone. To have a purpose."

I let out a chuckle, "That sounds cliche, huh?"

I felt her body shake with a laugh, "Maybe a little. But, I believe you mean it."

"What I mean, I guess, is that I've already been close to losing my life. I don't take anything for granted...unless you've been to the edge of that cliff, you just can't understand how to really live," I explained.

Natalie was quiet for a long time and the waves crashed and receded a dozen times before she said, "A couple of years ago, I was in a situation where I thought I was going to die. I didn't think about who would miss me if I was gone...because I don't have anyone *to* miss me. Except for Cece, of course... but the thought that crossed my mind was that I would never see the ocean again. When I didn't die, I promised to live for me...but it's not as easy as it sounds."

She ran a finger over the white scar in her eyebrow.

"It sounds like you and I should do something about that," I smiled. "What is something you've always wanted to do, but haven't yet?"

She grinned at me softly as a breathy laugh fell hesitantly, "Take a road trip on the back of a Harley down the coast."

"Okay," I guffawed. "What else?"

Her head cupped on my shoulder, "I don't know."

"C'mon!" I urged, "You better come up with something more or our summer is going to be pretty boring."

"*Our* summer?" I felt her eyes searching my face for any sign of retraction.

I leaned away from her so I could get a clear look at her face. Reaching out with my hand, I swept more strands of hair from her forehead and cheek, "Well, yeah. If that's okay with you."

Natalie smiled and lit my heart on fire once more. That smile. It's all I wanted to see when I looked at her and I'd do anything to see it again.

"I love the water...maybe we could go SCUBA diving?" she offered.

I raised my eyebrows before pulling her back into me, "Alright, SCUBA diving, now we're getting somewhere."

Chapter Twelve

Natalie

The sounds of ceramic cups clashing against countertops and plates mixed with the chime over the door and tables in conversation in the small diner. I sipped my tea carefully as my amusement at Cece's gaped mouth permeated my heart. Becca and Carrie's eyes bounced between my nonchalant expression and my best friend's disbelief.

Cece finally closed her lips and her dark eyes narrowed, "You mean to tell me, that you spent your entire weekend with the medic?"

"Not the *entire* weekend," I clarified. It's not often that I was able to shock her, and to her credit, I was a creature of habit. And while I'd never been able to confess to her why that is, she understands that routine is what keeps me grounded. Also, I wasn't great with dating, so for me to have more than two dates with anyone would come as a surprise to everyone at the table. "He did visit his sister and her baby in Stanford on Saturday. I stayed home and Delilah and I did laundry."

"Oh my God...she's killing me," Carrie flopped against the leather booth.

Becca pointed a perfectly manicured nail at my nose, "Get to the good stuff, sis."

"There is no good stuff," I choked a laugh, "At least not in the way *you* mean."

Her eyes looked from me to Carrie, "What does she mean by that."

Carrie jabbed an elbow in her ribs, "Probably that you're a slut."

Laughter erupted from our group, except for Cece; her eyes were still fixed on me.

"What?" I demanded through softening chortles.

"Huh-uh," she shook her head. "I'm not letting this go. I want details. What do you know about this guy that you would let him take you out to Morrow?"

An awkwardness descended on our table and Cece carried the weight of it. She was relentless and protective like a dog with a bone. Gnawing and rabid and willing to bite at any threat. It was one of the countless things I loved about her.

I sat my cup down, raising my fingers in capitulation, "He's a really, really nice guy, Ce. And honestly, the water is exactly what I needed. I got to spend the day hanging out with a great-looking guy with ocean air in my hair. We just got to talking and before we knew it, the sun was setting and—"

Before I could finish my thought, Becca interjected, "And?!"

I stared at her, rolling my eyes at her eagerness for a dirty detail, "And nothing, Bec. We held hands and that's it."

She groaned in disappointment.

"You know, it's actually kind of nice to spend time with a man who doesn't have sex on his mind every second he's with me," I snapped. It was bitchy, and I knew it.

Cece sat back in her seat, her body a little less tight, "All you did was talk?"

"Yeah. It was actually kinda...awesome," I smiled.

Carrie leaned into my story, "What about a kiss goodnight? Any-thing?"

"He walked me to my door, hugged me, and kissed my hand," I lifted a shoulder before I reached again for my cup.

"Christ, he's not a virgin is he?" Becca's nose puckered in disgust.

It was instances like this where I had to remind myself that I loved her, but I didn't like her all the time.

"Yes, Bec. He's a virgin. That's why he and his ex divorced," the sarcasm dripped from my mouth like venom.

"Whoa! Ex? He has an ex-wife?" Cece's muscles coiled again. "How much ex are we talking about?"

I shrugged, "Five, six years."

"And?" she pressed. "What do we know about her?"

"Her name is Lori, she lives in San Jose. They were together in high school, and got married almost the second after graduation," I sipped from my cup.

Cece's fingers tapped her lips, "No kids?"

"Nope," I shook my head.

"I wonder why they divorced," Carrie mused.

Cece's eyes rolled, "Girl...how many people do you know that got married as teenagers are still together?"

"Yeah, I guess you're right."

I watched for the second time the loaded spring that was Cece unwind. I would admit, if the tables were turned, I might be just as reactive as she. I had secrets that she knew I carried, albeit, not how many or how deep the darkness could become. It was like she could sense it though. She could see into me and catch the images of shadows that were there, but not clear.

Our group sat in discussion for another hour before I threw my part of the bill on the table and announced that it was my bedtime. I faked a yawn before I excused myself from the table and walked out into the warm night air. I hustled to my vehicle and only after I'd locked the doors did I pull out my cell and read the messages that vibrated on my leg for the past ten minutes.

> Finn: Hey! Just wanted to know how your day went.

> Finn: My lunch is in an hour. If you're not busy, it would be great to hear your voice.

> Finn: :-)

My heart was weirdly light when I tapped back a response. His reply was immediate as my car came to life and I pulled from the parking lot.

"Hey," his greeting was weak when he answered. I could feel the weariness even over our call and I already knew what kind of day he had.

I didn't offer a preamble, "What happened?"

I heard his voice break and the air catch in his chest. The sounds broke my heart, but I understood them. It was something we all dealt with: the emotions. Some were better at closing them off than others, but we all had our limits. I didn't push or urge him to speak, because I knew he would when he could. I listened and waited for the wave of raw emotion to break so Finn could find his voice.

He coughed, "Car accident out on forty-three. Marc and I were first on the scene after the CHP."

He referred to the California Highway Patrol officer and I nodded as if he could see me.

"It was a mess. A father, two kids," his voice cracked again. "Marc and I took one of the kids. They uhh...he..."

I heard him cough again, this time louder and harder than the last. His breath was heavy and he tried to reign in the sadness and prevent any tears from forming or falling.

"It's not my first car accident with kids involved. It's not even my first where the driver is so high he wouldn't be able to fight his way out of a paper bag...but it's the worst yet. That kid didn't have a chance! A fifty-pound six-year-old has no chance when pitted against the back end of a semi-truck and a piece of shit dad who is so out of his mind that he can't be bothered to put a damn seat belt on him!" The pained growl that emanated from him came from somewhere deep inside. I allowed his angry, grief-filled panting to subside before I spoke.

"I am so sorry, Finn," my words were soft but full of depth. "I know nothing I can do or say will change what happened...but if you need to let anything out, I'm here."

His sigh hit my ears and I heard a faint smile return to his voice, "Thanks, Natalie. You know you can do the same. Any time."

The sincerity in his voice lingered and I hoped he could hear the appreciation in my tone when I told him goodnight and disconnected the phone.

Chapter Thirteen

Finn

I stared at the sliding doors of the emergency room and waited for that angel with the high brunette ponytail to make her way outside. As luck would have it this week, our shifts had aligned and we were getting three whole days off together. I walked out of the station an hour prior, deciding to surprise her with a nice bottle of the Reisling she likes and a bouquet of hydrangeas; pink and purple.

I parked in the visitor area so I would see her as soon as she existed. I looked at my watch and knew it wouldn't be long now. As I waited, I watched people mill around the lot before they walked with a determined purpose into the building. I knew some had been here most of the day; it's just the way this area of the hospital worked sometimes. The guy in the Atlanta Braves hat was one of them. I'd watched him pace a trail between his Charger and the low bushes just to the left of the doors, four times in ten minutes.

The glass slid open again and I saw Natalie's familiar and gorgeous smile flash to Cece who walked next to her. I gathered the wine and flowers as my keys slid out of my hand and to the floor. I looked down for a second to slip their ring back on my finger when I heard nearby voices rising in anger. My head snapped in Natalie's direction and I watched ferocity flash in Cece's eyes with Atlanta's finger in her face.

I tossed the gifts aside and jogged to where the trio stood. I entered the space they filled to find Atlanta with his hand gripped tight on Natalie's wrist. Her face was already blotched red with tears which immediately set my blood on fire, but the fear in her eyes sent me over the edge. I grabbed Atlanta's collar and spun him out and into the bushes.

"I don't think the lady likes your hands on her," I bellowed over Cece's verbal assaults. "And frankly, neither do I."

Atlanta, who was around my height, but not as toned, took a step toward me and we were inches from each other. "I don't fucking care what you like. Mind your business."

He turned, stepping in Natalie's direction, but I blocked his path, "Natalie, who is this guy?"

Natalie was silent but Cece interceded, "His name is Drew and he's not supposed to be within five hundred yards of this place or her."

"Shut up, Bitch!" Atlanta's finger pointed over my shoulder.

"Boy, you're fixing to lose that finger if you point it at me one more time," Cece challenged angrily.

"It's time for you to go," I ordered and used my body to back Atlanta away from the women. "Cece, take Natalie back inside and get security."

Atlanta laughed, "That's okay, Nat. I'll catch you later at home."

My eyes narrowed as every muscle in my body tightened. I wanted nothing more than to make a patient out of this guy. He was still laughing when I heard the doors slide shut.

He glowered at me, "I don't know who the fuck you think you are, *hero*, but next time, you'd be smart to stay out of my business."

Atlanta shoved me with his palm on my shoulder. It was at this moment the world turned red before my eyes; like someone dropped a sheer fabric over my face and held it there. The next few sequences happened in a matter of seconds.

I heard the doors slide open again when my fist pulled back and I hit Atlanta square in the mouth with a right uppercut. I watched his head loll back as he lost his balance and fell to the sidewalk on his ass. It took him a moment to recover, but when he did the knot on his face was already swelling and he scrambled to his feet, charging my direction.

Bill, the night security guard, who also happened to be an off-duty Hanford Police officer, stepped between us with his hand extended, "Whoa! What's going on here? You got business here, son?"

Atlanta looked from Bill to me, "You saw what he did! I want to press charges!"

Bill pulled a dry sucking sound through his teeth, "You sure about that? You aren't supposed to be here, Andrew Bonetti. I'm pretty sure that restraining order says five hundred yards." He looked over his shoulder at me, "And to be honest, my eyesight is pretty bad these days."

Atlanta's head bobbed as he understood the full scope of what was happening. He spat a mouthful of blood and saliva on the ground at our feet before he smirked, walking back to his car. Bill and I watched until we saw his taillights turn a corner in the distance. Bill finally turned to me, looking at my hand.

"You okay?" he asked.

"Yeah," I said absently because my mind was elsewhere. I wondered where I'd find Natalie and I hoped she was okay. As I moved to enter the building, I turned back to Bill, "Hey, how long has that guy been on the no-fly list?"

"A couple of years," he answered.

When we looked up again, Cece and Natalie were walking toward us and my guts wretched as I saw the fear still lingering in her eyes. Whatever this is between Atlanta and Natalie, it set every nerve ending in my body ablaze. How dare he put his hands on her like that; I almost wanted him to come back so I could finish what I started before Bill walked out.

"Shithead gone?" Cece asked, her glower still prominent.

Bill nodded, "Yeah, we watched him to Bayberry." He turned to Natalie, his voice softened, "You okay, kiddo?"

She smiled, but there was pain in it, "Yeah, I'm good. Thanks, Bill."

Our eyes locked for a minute, but she pulled them away from me. I didn't want her to. I needed her to keep them on me so she knew I was a safe place. She didn't need to be afraid or anxious when I was around and I knew at that moment, I would die before Atlanta hurt her again. Cece adjusted her backpack over her shoulder and gave a concerned glance at me before her eyes darted to Natalie.

"We good here?" she asked.

I nodded.

She flashed a tense smile, "Alright then...I'll call you tomorrow girl."

"Okay," Natalie stated, her tone a little stronger than a moment before. Bill offered to get Cece an escort, but refusing, she walked to her car alone and he returned to his post inside the ER doors. Once alone, I watched Natalie's nervous shuffle as I was sure she was trying to decide what to do next.

I cleared my throat and forced a smile, "I-"

"I don't want to talk about it," she sliced my words before I could say another syllable.

"Yeah, okay," I nodded emphatically. "I have something for you in my truck."

Her ponytail bobbed and we walked a few feet to where I was parked. Reaching inside I pulled the wine out first then the flowers. I watched all the tension in her body release and tears well in her eyes.

I panicked, "Oh, hey...I'm sorry. I screwed something up—"

"No! No...not at all. This is very, very much the opposite of screwed up," she buried her nose in the petals and took a deep breath before wiping an escaped tear from her cheek.

I took her free hand in mine, "You don't have to talk about anything that makes you uncomfortable, but, hear me out, okay?"

She nodded and I let out a sigh.

"Whatever that was, it's dangerous. And I will never assume you need my protection. But, Atlanta there is a threat and from the sounds of it, he knows where you live. So, I have a proposition for you," I paused and waited for her response.

She nodded again for me to continue, but I worried how she would respond. We had only been dating a little over a month and my idea may seem a little forward; hell, I hadn't even kissed this girl yet. Not that I haven't wanted to, I just didn't want to rush her and I didn't have a schedule.

I took another deep breath, "I want you to come stay at my place for a few days...stay out of Atlanta's line of sight. We've made plans for our time off together anyway... this just means that we won't be on the phone the whole time I'm driving home. I mean, unless you want me to text you from the living room, I can do that too."

My last comment finally elicited a soft giggle, "I appreciate the offer, Finn, but I can't ask you to do that."

"You're not asking! I'd feel better knowing that you are out of his way for a few days. And, before you think this is somehow an inconvenience, I have a spare room," seeing the blush creep into her cheeks, I took her hand. "This isn't a *move* if that's something that worries you."

Her flush deepened, but she shook her head, "No...I wasn't."

"So, is that a yes?" I raised my brows.

She rolled her eyes playfully and nodded one more time.

In the next hour, I followed her sedan through the tree-lined streets of her small neighborhood and watched from my truck as she parked in her garage. I waited for the lights to come on and for her to open the door before I made my way onto the covered porch and into her house. A bounding, ball of white fur and energy met me as I walked inside.

"Who is this?" I knelt and scratched the cat under its chin.

Natalie laughed, "That's Delilah. She thinks she's the boss...I don't tell her anything different. She gets moody."

Delilah purred fiercely as I rubbed her belly and watched Natalie add kibble and water to the auto feeder. She gathered what personal items she needed for the next few days into a small suitcase before setting her alarm. It wasn't long before we were back on the road to my apartment.

After parking in my covered spot, I pulled Natalie's suitcase from the backseat along with my gear as she slid out with the wine and flowers. I unlocked the door and stepped to the side for her to enter.

"Mi casa, es su casa," I offered, reaching in and flipping on the light.

She smiled, "Nice place...and huge."

"Oh, yeah, you also have your own bathroom," I sat her suitcase next to my bag. She turned, giving me a quizzical look and I shrugged. "I was supposed to have a roommate...my buddy flaked."

"I'm sorry," she laid a hand on my arm. It was warm and sent a gentle current through my skin.

"No big deal," I smiled, "I can more than cover the rent and my neighbors are great. I have no complaints."

I led her through the spacious kitchen, a room I rarely used, down a short hallway to a set of four doors, two on either side of the corridor. I pointed to the left, "Bathroom and bedroom."

I paused as a thought came to me, "If you'd rather have more privacy, you can take the master suite. The bedding is clean..."

I stared into her forested eyes and lost myself for a moment.

"I uh...changed the sheets before my rotation. It has a more private bathroom," I found again, like so many times, there was no moisture left in my throat.

Natalie shook her head, "That's not necessary, I won't kick you out of your own room. The guest bathroom is fine."

Her smile was determined but appreciative. She had no idea that I would sleep outside if it made her more comfortable. I nodded and turned back down the hall, allowing her to get settled. While she was busy in her room, I called for Chinese delivery and changed into my basketball shorts and a tee shirt. When dinner arrived we scooped Lo-mein and Szechuan chicken onto plates and settled on opposite ends of my overstuffed sofa to catch the end of the local evening news.

We finished and I gathered the plates, placed them in the sink, and watched her stare out of the window, lost in thought. I opened the bottle of Reisling, poured her a glass, and dropped two fingers of whiskey in a glass for myself. I padded around the island and she didn't notice me until I said her name.

"Natalie?"

She startled.

"I'm sorry...I thought you could use this."

"Thanks," she took the wine from my hand. Our fingers grazed slightly and I felt her trembling. I choked down my rage and sipped on my amber liquid slowly, letting the burn in my chest dissipate my anger. I tried my damnest not to think about Atlanta's grasp on her wrist, but it's all I saw.

"Drew is the reason I thought I was going to die," her soft voice snapped me back to reality.

I didn't move and I hardly took a breath. I just let her continue.

"We dated when I was in nursing school. We broke up for a while and I moved here to Hanford."

She took a sip of wine and turned on the sofa to face me. I was still holding my breath, afraid she'd lose her nerve and tell me her story was none of my business. And she would be right; it wasn't, the only caveat was that I wanted her safe. She locked my eyes and gave me a look that screamed for strength. I slowly sank into the spot next to her.

"We eventually ran into each other again and decided to give it another shot." She sipped again, whispering, "Huge mistake. We really just casually dated before, this time was different...we were a *couple*. Right after we moved in together, I saw a whole different side of Drew."

My heart raced in my chest and a fire that wasn't from the whiskey burned in my stomach. I didn't know how much she would share but I knew none of it would be good.

"The first time he hit me I was in shock. We were out with friends and he thought I was talking too much to his sister's boyfriend. He shoved me into the back door of our house and punched me right in the sternum. I should have packed my shit right then and left. I let him apologize and make excuses until the next time. It just didn't stop," her eyes were distant, her voice somber.

I nodded and Natalie sucked in a deep breath before she continued, "One night...we got into a fight that turned out like it always did: Drew using his fists to get his point across. This time though, I had enough of being his punching bag, so I fought back. My second huge mistake."

Tears welled in her eyes, but as quickly as they appeared, I watched them disappear as she fought against her closely held emotional turmoil. I wanted to take her in my arms and hold her there, but I was unsure if I should. What other things did this asshole do to her? I didn't do or say anything then because I didn't want to be the reason a panic attack was triggered. I wanted this place to be somewhere she could come to whenever she felt uncertain or scared or she just needed to hide for a few days. But I had so many questions. Why wasn't he in jail? Why was he still allowed to walk free and torture her? Why had someone not given him a taste of his own medicine?

I felt a new life goal being set.

"I grabbed the wood block that we kept our knives in and smacked him in the head. He went down for a minute...just enough time for me to barricade myself in my bathroom with my phone. He was furious when he came around. When the police broke down our door, he was using a meat cleaver to cut down the door of the bathroom," it was then that the tears she fought so hard against moments before ran down her cheeks.

I took the wine glass from her hand and sat it and mine on the floor next to us. Slowly, I laid my hand on her cheek and brushed the stream away with my thumb. I could not imagine how painful these memories were for her, but for me, I felt my soul being ripped to shreds seeing her like this. She laid her face into my cupped hand and closed her eyes. We remained this way for several moments before I slid my arm around her shoulders, pulling her into my chest.

"I am so sorry you had to go through that...I'm so sorry Natalie. You're safe here...you're safe with me," I said gently, but the fury was stoked in my stomach. "I promise...he'll never touch you again."

Her wide eyes looked up into mine, "You can't be sure of that."

"Yes, I can," I declared and moved to the floor so I could look her in the eyes. "Look at me."

She did and I grasped both of her hands, "If I have to sleep on your porch every night for the next five years, I will. Natalie, he will *never* hurt you again. I swear, he won't get a chance."

We stared at each other for a long moment when I saw Natalie swallow hard, "Why would you do that?"

I felt like I'd been punched in the gut and my mouth was inexplicably dry again. This woman stole my heart from the moment I laid eyes on her. It baffled me that she didn't see how crazy I was about her because I wasn't hiding it. Or maybe she did and it's not something she thought she deserved. Atlanta turned this woman inside out and she had no idea how fantastic and utterly perfect she was. I ran my fingers over her cheek and smiled at her. Slowly, my face moved toward hers and I half expected her to pull away, because it was such bad timing.

But she didn't.

I was close enough to smell her shampoo and the wine on her breath. With one final caress of her face, I laid my lips on hers, and my universe exploded.

Chapter Fourteen

Natalie

I knew he thought I was an absolute wreck, but I couldn't help that he sent chills down my spine with a simple stroke of his fingers on my face. Finn's hands were gentle and nimble and I knew this because I'd seen them in action. At that moment though, I reveled in the way they drew out the gooseflesh on the back of my neck as he weaved his fingers in my hair. Our lips were dancing in a gentle waltz that I felt like I'd waited a lifetime for him to ask. He took his time and so did I, trading between his push and my pull.

God, what terrible timing.

He pulled me to the edge of the sofa and I put my legs on either side of him; even on his knees and me seated, he was a head taller than me. His broad chest was like a shield when he cupped my face in his hands and lifted me toward him. More gooseflesh raced down my neck and arms as my body pressed into his and his tongue finally skimmed along my teeth. I wrapped my arms around his nape and lost my fingers in his short hair while our kiss deepened.

Finn pulled back and groaned softly, "This was not why I asked you over."

"I know," I whispered then waited for a beat. "Can I ask you a question?"

He rocked back on his heels, but his hands never left my waist, "Of course."

"What took you so long?" I asked as a grin pulled at the corner of my mouth. It's a question that had confounded me for weeks and one for which I was already prepared to demand an answer.

His eyes narrowed as he searched my face, for what, I don't know. It took him a while but he finally replied, "I was holding off for the right moment...this wasn't it, but I couldn't wait anymore."

"In the future, you run a serious risk of giving a girl a complex," I scoffed sarcastically. "I was beginning to think you didn't like me."

For a split second, Finn's face contorted into something resembling grief, it's as if my words were a knife and I just stabbed him in the heart. His recovery was quick and he squared himself in front of me again. His thick chest blocked me from seeing anything but him.

"Not like you?" his voice incredulous. "How can you not see that I'm crazy about you? I don't have a good excuse for not kissing you...but just know I think about it all the time...every second we're together and every second we're not. I dream about you, Natalie...but, I'm not someone who's out for a thrill. Everything....all of this means something to me."

My breath caught in my chest and my heart was racing to keep up. It seemed all my recent memories were raw and bloody and stained. I did a great job forgetting Drew and putting it behind me or so I thought. I'd turned into an expert at just keeping the anxiety at bay and hiding the darkness that lingered in the recesses. But I couldn't hide from Finn. He was here and all my attempts to keep him just out of reach had failed and for the first time failure felt good. He was so perfect in every way and so different from Drew.

The crystalline blue of his delicious eyes made my stomach flutter as they searched my face. I wondered if I sounded as awkward when I spoke to him as I felt in my head. Was I being ridiculous? Probably. But the more time I spent with him the more off-balance I felt. He didn't make me *afraid*, but I did feel like I was back in high school and the football team captain just asked me out. It was a giddy kind of nervousness; one that made me feel sixteen. Maybe I was afraid, but the good kind. The kind that gently pushes into only good.

"I hope I didn't freak you out," he said.

I shook my head, "No... it's just not something I'm used to hearing."

I looked away from him because my embarrassment was at a level ten. Even at his best, if it could have been called that, Drew would never say anything so beautiful. Finn moved closer to me, lifting my chin again.

"Are you okay...really?"

"Yes," I bobbed my head. "Honestly. I'm okay."

Seeming satisfied with my answer, Finn drew back and kissed my temple. We sat on the sofa, entwined in each other's arms in silence until our eyes were heavy but neither wanted to let the other go. At around one am, Finn finally decided for the both of us.

"You know, we have a pretty cool day planned tomorrow...think we should get some rest?" he yawned.

I groaned with feigned irritation, "You're a party pooper."

"Some party," he laughed and pulled me gently from the couch. "Thank God we didn't invite anyone else."

He held my hand and led me down the hallway to my room. Tiny remnants of clumsy insecurity hung around as we both fumbled how to say goodnight. Finn finally pulled me against him and I could feel every muscle in him tighten as my body touched his. I saw his pulse racing in his carotid artery and his breath came in shallow huffs.

He finally let go of a deep sigh, "Goodnight. If you need anything, I'm just a door away."

He smiled and kissed me softly on my lips.

I returned his affection and added before shutting my door, "Sweet dreams."

The handle clicked shut but I thought I heard him say, "Only of you."

Chapter Fifteen

Finn

"Are you sure about this?" I asked with a small twitch of a grin pulling at my jaw. Natalie's eyes were gleaming with excitement.

"You're kidding, right? This is what we've been training all day for," she laughed and turned her back to me. "Zip me please?"

For the third time today, I helped close the neoprene she slid over her swimsuit, a little black one-piece with keyhole cutouts around her navel. We arrived at Turano Dive School in Pismo at ten to meet with a former firefighter-turned-diving instructor friend, Jake Turano, for a full day of private lessons. When I surprised Natalie with the plans a week ago, she looked at me with such disbelief.

"Are you serious?" her eyes wide with shock. "I can't accept this...you're too much."

"Jake and I go way back. We worked together in San Jose...not too long after I moved to Sonoma County, he was hurt on the job. Decided he'd had enough so he moved to the beach and never looked back. Trust me...we're gonna have a great time!" I told her.

Natalie was reluctant to take the gift, but after a few minutes of reminding her that this was her idea and if we didn't the summer would be exceptionally boring and who wants that, she agreed through laughter-induced tears.

The small vessel rocked gently on the water as we clipped our gear into place and adjusted our masks. Jake stood nearby watching and making sure we didn't miss any of the steps. Once we checked all our equipment, he prepared and readied himself. After a thumbs up, we rocked back, falling into the deep blue. We followed Jake further into the depths as we ran through everything we'd learned that day.

Natalie glided through the water like it was her second home. It was mesmerizing to watch her skim over and around rock formations and I thought if it weren't impossible, I would have believed she was a mermaid in a past life. Time seemed to speed up and stand still all at the same time. Before long, Jake soon gave us the sign that it was time to surface.

We bobbed along the boat as first Jake, then me, and finally Natalie exited the water. I watched her face as she climbed the ladder and stripped out of her gear. She turned back to gaze at the lapping ocean and I would have sworn her eyes looked homesick. She wasn't kidding when she said she loved the sea.

By the time we arrived back at the dock, returned the equipment, and got quick showers, the sun was starting to set. We met with Jake as he was shutting off the lights and ready to lock up for the night.

"You guys did great today! I'd call you officially certified for open water," his tan face beamed.

Natalie smiled serenely, "Thank you, so much. I had an amazing time."

Jake looked from her to me, "Don't let this guy let you be a stranger. I expect to see you both on your next days off."

"Thanks again, man. Say hello to Selene for me," I shook his hand.

"Absolutely. You guys come back, the four of us will do dinner," he turned the key in the lock. "Be careful on the drive back!"

We waved goodbyes and I held the door on the Bronco for Natalie. After a cruise through a drive-through for burgers and shakes, we hit the road back to Hanford. The first several miles were spent devouring our meal.

Natalie pulled her thumb over her mouth to wipe the remnants of her dinner, "I think that is the best cheeseburger I've ever had."

"I think we're on the brink of starvation," I laughed. The two-hour trip home flew by, much like the city lights outside the truck's windows as we recounted our day's adventures.

"Thank you for today...I've always wanted to learn to dive," she remarked as our headlights grazed the Hanford city limit sign.

I looked her way and gave her a quick smile, "Of course! Jake's been hounding me for a year to come out. You gave me a great reason not to put him off any longer."

"He seems like a really great guy," she laid her head back on the seat. "You said he was hurt on the job?"

I nodded, "Yeah...he and another guy from his station got trapped in a four-alarm. Jake was pulled out...some minor burns and smoke inhalation. His partner didn't make it."

"My God, that's terrible."

"I think he was just done with it...Pretty sure his wife Selene is the only reason he's even still here," I shook my head against the memories. I forced the rest of our ride to turn more lighthearted as I cranked on the radio and we sang together until we pulled into my driveway. I carried our gear into the house as Natalie went to her room to change. I was sitting on the sofa watching an old movie when she returned.

She pointed to the television, "Is that Twister?"

I looked up at her and back to the screen with a chuckle, "Yeah...I guess we could have saved money on those tickets."

Natalie didn't laugh with me. When I turned to see why, a light came on in my head. Her panic attack. Even though she still hadn't admitted to it, we both knew what happened. It was the reason we never actually watched the movie that night. I rose to her and took her by the shoulders, "Hey, are you okay?"

She nodded and put a smile on her face, but knew she was lying. If she was trying to spare me from seeing her fall apart, we were way past that. I was also pretty tired of seeing her try to be strong for everyone around her as if that's what they expected from her. I wanted her to let go, at least with me.

"Natalie, it's bad enough that you put on a mask and pretend everything is fine for everyone around you. But what's worse is that you're lying to yourself," I observed.

Boldy.

She glowered, "No, I'm not."

"Stop it. Just stop," I ordered gently. "Let's talk about this elephant. You had a panic attack the other night at the movies...you know it, I know it...no matter what we called it later. Was he there? Was Atlanta there that night?"

My words came out hard but there was no stopping them now. I was going to get it all out in the open. "Well?"

Her eyes were huge. But they weren't hurt or sad; they were determined. Under my hands, I felt her back straighten and the roll of her shoulders. She squared her eyes to mine and let out a long, low breath.

"Yes."

I lifted my brows, "Yes? To what, exactly."

She sighed, "Yes, he was there. And yes, my anxiety got the better of me and I couldn't control it. In my defense, it was the second time I'd run into him in as many weeks."

She moved to the sofa and sat facing me. I could hardly move with my mind racing so fast. Her revelation only created more questions for me, but now, I thought she could handle them and I wasn't afraid to ask.

"Wait. The second time?" I crouched next to her. "Where else?"

"In the parking lot of the hospital...he was there with his girlfriend."

I stared in disbelief, "How do you know that?"

"He told me," she shrugged. "Of course, this was after he scared the shit out of me and I threatened to call security."

A familiar surge of rage boiled in my gut. A gnawing feeling relentlessly poked my brain and told me it was no coincidence, that nothing this man did was. I worked entirely too many DV incidents for this not to make the hair on the back of my head stand straight. "Can I ask you a question?"

She nodded, "Sure."

"You have a restraining order on him, right?"

She nodded again.

"So, this is going through the court system?" I asked.

A third nod.

"Why isn't he already in jail? Natalie, he's stalking you," I explained.

"You don't understand—"

I was exasperated, "Then help me too! You said this guy has already tried to kill you...now he just happens to be at your work and a date you're on? I think that's more than convenient."

Desperate fear and denial clouded her eyes. She either didn't want to believe that her abusive ex had become a stalker, or she was afraid to think about it. I wouldn't blame her for the latter.

"Natalie, I know you're scared," I lowered my voice to a calm level. "I'm just trying to put the pieces together. It doesn't make logical sense that he isn't locked away somewhere."

I saw she was trying to gather the courage to say what needed to be said. Her struggle killed me. I had never been one to go looking for a fight, but Atlanta might just be the one to change my mind.

"His dad is a big-shot lawyer in Sacramento. We went to court...but he claimed I was trying to hurt myself and that's the reason he was busting down the bathroom door. The judge didn't buy it...well, not all of it. He got six months in the county jail and an order to stay five hundred yards away from me. Which I get to renew every three years because god forbid I get a permanent restraining order."

The complete lack of punitive enforcement was astonishing and infuriating. It was shocking that in this day and age, people abused by their partners were still forced to face their abusers year after year and dredge up old pain just so they could continue their lives under the guise of peace. I didn't know what to say. I knew some women talked about how frustrating it was to have their partners want to fix every problem and I didn't want to be that guy, but it still didn't make me not want to try.

I was still balancing on the balls of my feet when I leaned forward, sitting on my knees to her. I thought about what I wanted to say and my eyes narrowed on her. I took her shoulders in both of my hands because I wanted her to know I was serious about every word getting ready to come out of my mouth.

"I want you to be careful. If you ever feel unsafe, no matter where you are, I want you to call me. If I can't come immediately, I will make sure someone does. Think of a word." I told her.

"What?" her eyes puckered at the corners.

I released my hold on her and leaned away, "Think of a safe word. Something you can call and say to me that tells me you're in trouble."

Her lips tightened and I saw her thinking about what our word should be and I knew she'd choose something meaningful. Until we could find a more permanent solution, I resigned myself to this plan. I knew I couldn't be everywhere, but I wanted to help her protect herself from him all the same.

"I've got one," she nodded sharply.

"Okay. That word will be our code. You call and use it, I'll know he's nearby. If someone gives it to you, you will know they're safe," I explained but she still looked unsure. "Natalie, I will do everything in my power to make sure he never gets close to you again."

Chapter Sixteen

Natalie

Beams of the early morning sun streamed through the blinds of Finn's guest bedroom. I stretched the stiffness out of my muscles when I smelled it and it was glorious and heavenly: coffee and bacon. I picked up my phone to check the time when I realized I had slept in a bit. We stayed up way past midnight talking about Finn's plan to keep Drew away. I wasn't very confident it would work, but I was willing to try anything if it meant I wasn't looking over my shoulder at the grocery store and I had some dependable backup if needed.

I slid out of the warm blankets and pulled on a hoodie over my white tank and matching shorts. After a quick divert to the bathroom, I padded to the kitchen to find Finn standing shirtless over a small waffle iron, its small wisps of steam floating and disappearing in tiny waves around him. My heart fluttered and I stared for longer than I should have because I finally noticed him staring at me staring at him.

"Good morning," he smiled wide. "Coffee?"

I nodded.

"Black, right?"

I felt the warmth of embarrassment leaving my cheeks and I nodded again. He poured a cup out of a glass French press and handed it to me, "How did you sleep?"

"Good...really good," I blew over the dark liquid before I took a sip. He watched me take a few more pulls before he spoke again.

"Hungry?"

I smiled, "I could eat."

I was starving. The growling in my stomach said the temptation of salty pork and warm waffles soaked in syrup was almost too much to handle. He built plates of food for the pair of us and sat them on the island before pulling out barstools. We devoured our meals quickly and after some debate about his willingness to let me help clean up, we sat back in the living room with our warm cups in hand twenty minutes later.

"So, you feel like a walk today?" he asked, that familiar grin pulling at his cheeks.

I pursed my lips in mock suspicion, "Why is it when you suggest something as simple as a walk, I get a weird feeling that you're lying?"

"I'm offended by the notion, Shire," his laughter filled the room. Reaching out with his foot, he linked one of his bare toes with mine.

My spine tingled.

"Really? Offended, Rafferty?" I pushed his foot away playfully.

"And a little hurt."

The belly laughs were mine, "Oh my God, you poor thing. Must be terrible to have your misdirections exposed. Are you mad because I've caught onto your game?"

Without realizing it, Finn had finished his coffee, sat his mug on the table, and was inching his hand toward my foot. With the swift movement of someone who had studied martial arts, my ankle was in his grasp in seconds, his fingers waggling dangerously near the bottom of my foot. I squealed and pushed back with my free leg, but it wasn't free for long as Finn slid closer and locked it in the crook of his knee.

"Let's discuss my hurt feelings," he winked, moving his fingers closer to my very ticklish foot.

"Oh my God, Finn...don't!" I laughed out in short puffs. "Please."

A wicked grin spread along his lips as he stroked his index finger along my arch. I bucked and scream-laughed.

"No! Stop!"

Releasing my trapped leg, Finn threw my held ankle behind him as he lunged for me, and worked his fingers along either side of my rib cage, "Oh! So it's not just the feet."

I squirmed and giggled until I lost my breath. Our play slowed and the heat from his body fell over me like waves off blacktop. My lips found him and we fell into long, deliberate kisses that curled my toes and set my nerve endings on fire. I draped my arms around his neck and pulled him into me, scooping handfuls of his dirty blonde hair through my fingers.

I waited for him to make the next move. I wanted him to slip his fingers under my sweatshirt and feel my skin; to find me braless and excited. The need for him to strip me down and feel all of his warmth on me made the butterflies quake. I would settle for one hand on my bare hip or a firm grip on my ass cheek.

But he didn't. Instead, he released my mouth and pulled back.

"You..uhh," he stammered, a little embarrassed. "You ready to yield?"

I smiled back, "You ready to define that walk?"

Chapter Seventeen

Finn

I woke up this morning and felt a cloud already descending on my day. I knew that at some point today, I would have to drive Natalie back to her house and we would be forced to return to reality. It was certainly not something I wanted, but I had no choice. If it wouldn't scare her away or make me look like a lunatic, I'd ask her to move in with me. When I said that I was crazy about her, I knew I meant more than what I could admit out loud.

The past couple of days hadn't been exactly perfect, but they were incredible. I'd learned so much about how strong this woman was and we'd been able to get to know each other in ways that I never imagined. Our conversations were endless. Natalie worked her way through college, saving every penny she could, and within her first year as a nurse, she paid off what school debt was left. As a child, she loved animals and always wanted a cat, but because her mother was allergic, she was never able to own one. After her mother died two years ago, Natalie came across a feline rescue and Delilah's picture; it was kismet.

I watched her mannerisms and how she moved in her environment. She called herself awkward and shy, in a self-deprecating humor sort of way, but I saw her as a perfect balance of a quiet extrovert. I knew she felt compelled to take time in her day to read on her phone, losing herself in other worlds besides her own and I knew that she rubbed the scar over her eye when her anxiety was high.

She liked order but wasn't controlled by it. She would let a glass sit on a table for the day but made sure all the dishes were cleaned before bed; no matter how many times I told her it was okay to leave them for the next morning. It was funny how quickly accustomed I'd become to having her around. I didn't know that I'd ever want the intimacy that a relationship provided especially after my ex, Lori, and I split.

She and I were disastrous. We were too young, too inexperienced, and too opinionated for each other. As it turned out, Lori was also too dramatic, too devious, and too much of a cheater for my liking as well. Even this far out from our divorce, and up until six weeks ago, I was perfectly happy with bachelorhood and thought if I got to the point that I needed companionship, I'd adopt a dog.

The world worked in mysterious ways.

I enjoyed sitting on the sofa every morning with Natalie drinking coffee and talking. I loved watching her get excited over the enormity of the trees yesterday and the peacefulness wash over her every single time she put on dive gear and rolled into the water like the ocean was a part of her soul and she was returning home. The way she carefully filled each hole of her waffle with syrup before she took even the smallest bite brought an immediate smile to my face. But, what I would remember and miss the most of this weekend was the soft sound of her feet as they came toward me in the morning.

After two days of adventures that included our walk in the Sequoia National Park, Natalie decided last night that we needed a day inside. One day to just spend in the quiet confines of my apartment and ignore the world. There will be nothing but us, some movies and board games, and the sofa. I promised pizza delivery from Deltano's and homemade strawberry milkshakes; her favorite. I promised this place would be a refuge for her in whatever form or fashion she needed. A haven of comfort and laughter.

I would make the world safe and right again.

Chapter Eighteen

Natalie

"Girl, you better start talking," Cece ordered as we walked toward our only real solace in our part of the hospital—the vending machine hallway.

I giggled, "You know where I was...you texted no less than forty times."

"I want details! This is the first time we've had a second to breathe today," she slid her card into the reader, then pushed the buttons for a pack of peanut butter crackers. "We're gonna walk back real slow so you can tell me everything."

I laughed and grabbed my bag of chips and her crackers out of the machine's tray. "We went diving in Pismo, hiked in Sequoia, then had a quiet day...that's it!"

I was being purposely vague because I knew how to push her buttons. She would want every single detail including what we ate, who drove, and especially what I wore. But, I was going to make her work for it.

She thumped me on the arm, "Damn it. I know what you're doing...and you stop with your games. Spill it."

I recounted every event, in excruciating detail, beginning from right after the incident with Drew up to Finn walking me to the door of my house last night.

Well, almost every detail.

"So, you slept in his guest room?" she took a small bite from her snack. "Nothing happened?"

I smirked.

"Oh, you liar!" she bellowed. "You shady little liar—"

"No...not exactly. I did stay in his guest room the whole weekend. But,"

"But, what!?"

"I can tell you for certain how good of a kisser he is," I laughed but it was directed more at the look of shock on my friend's face.

Suddenly, Cece threw her hands in the air and did what I would call a small jig, "Hallelujah!! There is a God!"

I laughed harder. Her dancing stopped as quickly as it started and a look of suspicion fell over her.

"Just kissing? Or is there more? God, please tell me there's more."

"No, just kissing," I smiled at the slight disappointment on her face.

She linked her arm with mine and we moved down the hallway toward the nurse's station, "Oh, well...that's fine for now."

She paused, cutting her eyes at me, "Are those lips as strong as that perfect ass of his?"

I knew a flush rushed through my cheeks as I thought about his mouth on mine but I shrugged nonchalantly, "Stronger."

Chapter Nineteen

Finn

I glowered at my partner, daring him to say it. My last night on shift, one good day of sleep, then I could spend time with the woman who never left my mind. This asshole was going to blow it and my *calm* night was toast.

"I'm just thinking that this night seems..." Marc faked trying to search for the right words.

"I swear to God, if you say the Q word, I'm going to beat the shit out of you, old man," Darren Sanchez, another firefighter on duty, warned.

He feigned his offense, "That is no way to speak to your elders, boy."

"Jesus, how long until you retire?" Another of our teammates, Nate Yung, laughed.

"Four weeks, two days, and..." Marc rocked back in his seat, checking his watch, "Fourteen hours."

"Too damn long to wait," Sanchez shook his head, laughing.

My partner wasn't wrong, it had been really quiet that night. But, it allowed us to deep clean the house and the trucks and get caught up on paperwork. I was getting ready to prop my feet on the table and settle in with a book when my phone pinged in a text.

"The girlfriend must be on break," Marc teased. "Tell that gorgeous woman I said hi."

I shook my head in confusion. It was three am and I knew Natalie was on the day shift for the next month. Pulling my phone out of my pocket, I read the lone message and my blood turned cold.

Pacific

Before I typed out a message or grabbed Marc for a quick drive over, the overhead buzzer went off and my partner and I were ordered to a call.

"Goddamn it!" I growled.

"Hey, I didn't say it...looks like a Code ten. Let's go partner," Marc referred to the call for chest pain as he jogged towards our bus and a small crew climbed onto a nearby truck.

"Sanchez!" I called out and Darren came toward me before I got inside.

"What's up?" he asked over the squawk and clicks of radios.

I gave Darren a quick rundown, "Natalie's in trouble...I need someone to go check on her and stay until I can get there."

He frowned but I saw he was ready for action, "What kind of trouble?"

"Long story...he's the kind that doesn't take no for an answer," I ground my jaw as I slid into my seat and rolled down the window. "When you get there, say the word *Pacific*. Thanks man...I'll be there as soon as I can."

He thumped the door with his fist, "I'm on it...I won't let him near her."

The doors of the garage rolled up and we lurched forward as my partner gave the rig a foot full of gas. I tried to concentrate on the task at hand, but Natalie was all I could think about. What if she was hurt? What if he was there? Did she call the police?

I was a little too quiet as we loaded our patient, who was not having a heart attack but instead got choked on a mouthful of hotdog he was having as a midnight snack. Evidently, lying to one's wife when you were supposed to be on a diet results in a ride to the ER. My silence did not go unnoticed by my partner.

"How's he doing?" he called back.

I grunted, "Fine."

I heard Marc radio our location but I didn't pay much attention. I just wanted to offload our would-be cardiac patient and get to Natalie. I checked my phone for any update from her or Darren, but my phone was silent. I remembered how grateful I was to work in this field; we weren't just a team, but a family. I knew I could count on anyone in that house for anything and I owed my friend a beer.

"Rafferty? Where's your head?" I heard Marc bark from the cab as he turned into the entrance for South. As soon as he was parked, I was out of the doors and collecting the chart.

I didn't say anything as we got our guy into the building and rolled him into a triage bed. Marc stood at the nurse's station and chatted up Becca as I signed off on the forms and dropped them on the desk. Grabbing the end of the gurney, I started to roll back to the bay doors. I made it about twenty feet when my pulling hit resistance.

Turning around, Marc's large hand was grasped onto one of the railings, "What's your hurry?"

I was pretty sure he saw the anger and anxiety on my face.

"Rafferty, what's going on?"

I pulled back on the gurney, "We gotta go, *now*."

He followed me back to the bus and as we finished loading, I turned back to my partner, "We need to make a stop before we go back to the station."

"Son, you wanna tell me what's got you jumping like a frog in the desert?" Marc narrowed his dark eyes on me making his lids appear closed.

My partner was nearing sixty years old and still had the energy and sense of humor of a twelve-year-old boy. But there were times he gave off an air of fatherly compassion and this was one of those times. I waited until he climbed back into the driver's seat before I told him where we were headed and why.

"Jesus Christ," he said under his breath, giving the truck more gas as we turned off the parkway and into Natalie's neighborhood. "That poor kid. And this asshole? Drew? You said you met him?"

I nodded, pointing to his next turn, "Yeah, two weeks ago. Caught him outside South harassing her and Cece. I took Natalie home with me for the weekend because I didn't think she needed to be alone."

"Good call."

"It's this one," I pointed to her house and we rolled up behind a red F-350 with Hanford Fire emblazoned in gold and black lettering on the doors and tailgate. Before Marc could put the bus in park again, I was out on the sidewalk in a near run to the front door. I knocked twice on the fully lit home and saw a tall silhouette move to the window. Darren opened the door.

"Where is she?" I whispered hoarsely, walking past him.

"In the bathroom."

I shook his hand, "*How* is she?"

Darren's eyes widened, "Scared as shit man. But, better than when I got here. The asshole sent one of his friends over to apologize for scaring her the other night at the hospital."

"In the middle of the night!?" I snarled and the fury boiled inside me. "This dickhead—"

I started to rail, but Darren hit my arm and pointed down the small hallway, "Hey."

I met Natalie halfway and pulled her into me. I could feel her body tremble under my hold and it made the storm of anger I felt inside rage. I knew I had to put it away and focus on her.

"Shhhh..." I soothed. "It's okay. You're okay."

"I'm sorry, Finn," her words were muffled in my chest.

I leaned closer to whisper in her ear, "You have nothing to apologize for...as long as you're okay, that's all that matters."

My and Darren's radios crackled to life simultaneously, and Natalie jumped. I held her tighter.

'Bus twenty-one-niner what's your location?'

We heard Marc's voice, "Twenty-one-niner...dispatch, we're a non-medical assist."

'Twenty-one-niner, ten-one as soon as possible.'

"Roger."

I shot a look at Darren. It wasn't common for us to receive a *call your house by telephone* code. Darren put his hand up, "Stay here, let me find out what's going on."

Natalie squeezed my waist before pushing away to sit on the sofa. I sat next to her and neither of us spoke for several seconds, but I watched her. It was in this reserved stillness that a few more of her edges were softened.

"Thank you, Finn. I know I probably should have called the police but, honestly, the only thing I could think was how much I wished you were here." She paused and gave the room a derisive chortle, "That sounds so stupid."

I took her hand, "Not at all. I'm just sorry I got a call."

Pausing, I held a breath in my mouth as I contemplated a question. "Natalie, why is he doing this? Do you have any idea?" I asked.

Her jaw tightened, "When we were together, when we would fight...one of his favorite things to say was that I would be his forever. He would never be without me. It's possession...he really thinks that I *belong* to him."

Before I could respond, Darren knocked on the door and it swung open, "Hey, Rafferty...you're needed at the station. Now."

I looked between him and Natalie and while I'd like to believe I had a choice, I really didn't. Whatever was going on back at the station, I was still on duty for another two hours, so I would have to handle it.

"It's okay," she forced a smile, "I'm awake...I might as well go in."

"I can hang out until she's ready to go," Darren added.

"Alright," I conceded defeat and rose from the sofa. Leaning down, I kissed Natalie on the forehead, "Call me when you get to the hospital, okay?"

She nodded and within a minute, Marc and I were racing back to the station house.

***

We rolled in to find two police cruisers, full flashing lights, and the remainder of our house gathered in the gated side yard. *Yard* is a loose term. In reality, it's our parking lot but includes a covered patio with a smoker, grill, and a couple of lawn chairs. A basketball hoop is attached to a metal pole at the far corner of the lot.

Marc and I jogged through the building to access the yard from our common area door. Hushed whispers fell over the group of people gathered outside as we walked toward them.

"What's going on?" I started to say, but then I saw it.

My heart sunk into my feet as I stared past the group to where my Bronco was parked. I pushed through to take a closer look but as I did, someone grabbed onto my arm and I felt ill.

"We're still getting pictures, don't touch anything," Maria Eleazar, a sergeant with the Hanford PD, explained. "Maybe even some prints off the bottles."

I walked closer to my truck to see scorch marks on the hood and smelled a familiar scent of grain alcohol. It was clear that my comrades did their best to keep the blaze to a minimum, but the damage had been done. A hand rested on my shoulder.

"We tried to save her, but it happened so fast," Nate's voice was apologetic. "Sorry, man."

All I could do is shake my head. It took me three years and countless hours of overtime pay to make her perfect. She was my dream car; was still my dream car.

I sighed, "I can fix it. I'm glad no one was hurt. What the hell happened?"

Nate shook his head as most of the crowd started to move back inside. "We don't know yet...Link was walking by the security desk and saw her on fire."

"We have it on video? Have the cops pulled it yet?"

"Yeah, they're gonna want you to look at it," he nodded.

We left two of our brothers in blue in the yard still bagging bottles from the makeshift Molotov cocktails thrown at my truck to find Maria and her partner skimming through and making copies of the security video. It was kind of funny to me how many people didn't realize what Big Brother was watching and from where. In our large yard, there was a camera at each corner and another at the door. At time stamp three-thirty-five, we saw a dark-colored Dodge charger roll up to the fence in front of my Bronco. A man stepped out of the car, lit, and tossed three bottles of clear liquid onto the truck's hood. He stood for a moment, watching the flames grow bigger. He then flipped off my truck, returned to his car, and drove away.

I immediately recognized the car and the baseball cap. I wanted to be furious at the damage he caused and the danger he put my entire house and crew in, but in the second that the thought crossed my mind, another formed. I was happy it was me and not Natalie this time and nearly ecstatic in the knowledge that this stupid bastard was finished.

Chapter Twenty

Finn

The one thing that I hated more than anything in this world was seeing someone cry. It wasn't that I'm offended by strong emotions because I'm not. And I've never been afraid of my own. But seeing tears flow, for whatever reason, made me uncomfortable in a way that I had a difficult time explaining because I had an overwhelming need to fix the problem. I watched my mother cry too many tears when I was young, either for my deadbeat father or for me. I'd always thought of her and her pain and I wanted to make it go away.

I wanted Natalie's tears to go away too.

My arms were wrapped around her shoulders and she vibrated in terror, but she insisted she come along to the station with me. She had been in this place before, but the last time she was a beaten, bloody shell. This time though, while her insides trembled, her outside was angry and resolute. She was sick of this goddam worm, and so was I.

After catching a few hours of sleep in the rack at the station house, my truck now a burned-out mess, Darren dropped me at Natalie's after her shift. She knew I was coming over, so she picked up take-out for dinner. I was waiting on her front steps when she turned into her short driveway and pulled into the tiny garage. I took the bags from her hands as she pulled her gear and the food from the seat next to her.

"What are you doing here already?" she looked around bewildered. "Where's your truck?"

I motioned for us to go inside, "Darren gave me a ride. We should probably talk."

Our discussion was brief and by the end of it, I noticed something in her I had never before seen in Natalie Shire: I saw her fury.

At six the next day, we sat in the Hanford Police Department waiting for my friend Seargent Maria and a detective to finish the paperwork for an official complaint against Andrew Michael Bonetti. We knew they had him on arson and vandalism, and we were hoping for stalking as well. I finally saw Maria emerge from an office and she smiled at me; I took it as a good sign.

"Hey, I'm sorry to keep you both so long," she approached, reaching to shake our hands.

Turning to Natalie, I motioned back to the officer, "This is Seargent Maria Eleazar...she was on the scene last night at the station."

"Nice to meet you," Natalie's smile was brilliant and genuine.

Maria walked us down a short hallway and into a small room with a desk and four chairs, two on either side. A man sitting in one of the chairs stood as we entered and we exchanged handshakes with him as well.

"Finn, Natalie, this is Detective Callahan. He is looking into the stalking claims," Maria offered us seats and took one beside the detective.

Callahan wasted no time getting to the point, "I understand you have a history with Bonetti?"

"Yes," Natalie nodded.

"And a restraining order. For how long?" Callahan was scribbling on a small legal pad.

"A little over two years now," she replied.

Callahan nodded sharply once, "Can you tell me the nature of the PO?"

I watched Natalie wring her hands. Reaching over, I took one of them to make her stop, but my gentle squeeze also told her she wasn't alone.

"We were in a relationship for about a year and a half. I was his punching bag. He tried to kill me," her attitude was sharp.

Callahan never looked up, "So, that's the six-month stint in county on his record?"

"Yes."

This guy was pissing me off. I knew what cops did, what a lot of us did when there was too much to get emotionally attached to—we looked away. We didn't want to see the nasty, so we detached. We put on our blinders and made believe that the person on our gurney, or in our interview room wasn't a person, not really.

"Excuse me, Detective?" I interrupted.

His eyes raised to meet mine.

"Could you at least pretend that you give a shit that this asshole is a threat? She's not your computer to verify your facts—" I charged.

"Finn..." Maria cut me off. "That's not what's going on. Bill's just doing his job."

I glowered at her, but it was Detective Callahan who spoke.

"Ms. Shire," he finally looked at her over his wired glasses. "I am sorry that I have to make you go through all of this. I can see it makes you uncomfortable, but I appreciate you doing it. I want to get this guy off the streets, for a long time. Thank you for helping me understand him."

Natalie nodded, "Thank you, Detective."

"Please, call me Bill."

We were at the station for another hour before Natalie dropped me off at my apartment. I had invited her to stay, but responsibility and reason won and before long, she left. It would be a week before we could see each other outside work again and I already missed her smile. When I knew she would be home, I sent her a message.

I was still smiling when sleep overtook me and visions of her filled my dreams. Unfortunately, my dreams were interrupted by the buzzing of my phone. I recognized the six-six-nine area code, but not the number.

"Hello?" I asked sleepily.

I was met with dead air for a moment. Finally, a woman's voice cracked, "Finn?"

Realization washed over me like dirty water out of a mop bucket. I didn't want to do this, especially, I looked at my phone again, at three am. She always had the worst timing.

"I should have known," I groaned, sitting up on the edge of my bed.

Lori huffed, "What's that supposed to mean?"

"Well, life is going pretty good...it's about time for you to screw something up and want my help," I huffed with contempt.

The line was quiet again for a second. I hoped she was reconsidering my involvement in whatever she wanted. In reality, I knew I wouldn't be that lucky.

"Does that mean you won't help me?" she asked.

"Yeah, pretty much, Lori," I snapped.

But...Finn...if you don't, I don't know who will."

It was then that I heard her words slur; she was either drunk or high. But, I didn't care. There was no way I would listen to her woes of car repossession, job loss, or maxed-out credit cards. We signed a stack of paperwork six years ago that absolved me of all emotional and financial connections with her and if I had to, I would remind her of that.

"Lori, not my problem," I yawned. "So, take the bus, get a different job, find a therapist...whatever. But, leave me out of it, I'm not interested."

She spoke through a clenched jaw, "I'm in jail...I need to get out by nine. Finn...you have to help me."

Laughter fell from my chest.

"Oh my God, Lori. That's...that's amazing! How many times is this? Four? Just this year? What is it this time? Dui?" I couldn't control myself. My ex was insane if she thought I was going to bail her out.

"It's not funny, Finn," she snarled. "I need to get home to Danny."

She was trying to pull on my emotions, but it wouldn't work. Lori was too intoxicated to remember that I talked to her brother on a regular basis. I knew he wasn't alone and was safe.

"Oh, you're wrong, Lori. It's hilarious. Pro tip...call a bail bondsman. It's their job to get you out, not mine."

I hung up the phone. The audacity of my ex was appalling, but I held hope that the thicker my boundary lines were, the more I said no, Lori would eventually get the hint. I pushed the last ten minutes out of my mind as I rolled over, envisioned my arms around Natalie, and relaxed into sleep.

Chapter Twenty-One

Natalie

The Indian Super Chief rumbled loudly and I covered my ears when Finn revved the engine with a gigantic devilish grin on his face. He shut it off and dismounted. When he called thirty minutes prior asking me to grab a small backpack of only the essentials, I tried to question him but he hung up on me. I was certainly suspicious of the so-called date and raised my eyes at him playfully.

"Where did this beauty come from?" I smirked.

His scheming smile broadened, "Do you have your bag?"

I dropped it at his feet and crossed my arms.

"Did you feed Delilah?" he laughed at my bogus irritation. I tilted my head in a way that made him come undone with delight.

I finally smiled, "Rafferty, what are you doing?"

"It's not what I'm doing," he plucked one of my hands free and pulled me to him. "It's what we're doing for the next couple of days."

He kissed my temple before he glanced back at the bike.

"You're serious?" I chirped. Letting me go, he mounted the bike and turned the engine over.

He bobbed his head back, "I know it's not a Harley, but you wanna go for a ride?"

I did more than ever. Throwing on my backpack, I slid the extra helmet over my head before climbing in behind him. I wrapped my arms around his hard chest and we set off with a roar. Within minutes, the city disappeared in our rearview and we were flying along the highway.

The mid-summer sun was warm on our faces as we cruised through one town after the other. Once we reached Pismo, we made a quick stop for fuel but were back on the one-oh-one in no time. I never asked about our destination, because I was thrilled by the adventure of it. Having the wind in my face and my arms wrapped around Finn with the world soaring by was utter bliss.

It was another hour and a half before we arrived at our stop and my apprehension quickly dissolved when I saw the city limit sign for Santa Barbara pass by. I immediately squeezed Finn's chest with excitement and felt him laugh under my grip. We drove for several more minutes until we glided down a hill and I felt the bike ease to a crawl. Finn rolled into a spot in a parking lot facing the beach.

I could not help myself. Tears welled in my eyes but I didn't want him to see because I'd done enough of that in front of him. I was just overcome with joy for the things this man did for me. I held my embrace around him and pressed further into his back. His hands ran along my jean-covered thighs and I felt every stroke lighting in my core.

"You okay?" he asked.

I nodded, willing my tears to stop, "Absolutely. This is beautiful!"

We dismounted and moved toward the water, our shoes in hand. I curled my toes into the saturated sand and allowed the small laps of waves to wash over the tops of my feet. Closing my eyes, I filled my lungs with salty air and held it. Everything fell away except the sound of the water and the sensation of Finn's hand on my waist. There was no therapy in the world as effective as that moment.

We eventually climbed back on the bike and circled the city, climbing its hills and valleys. As the day waned we rode to a small restaurant on a pier overlooking the ocean. The orange sun reflected off the water and the few clouds dispersed the fading light into shades of purple and pink as we sat close on the outdoor patio and sipped wine.

After dinner, we returned to the bike and I expected us to head back to Hanford, all but forgetting about my bag of essentials. We rode back to the beach and pulled into the Casa Del Mar Inn. It was a beautiful hotel of Spanish tile, wrought iron, and low-lying palms out front. Finn parked and waited for me to climb down.

"What are we doing here?" I asked in awe of the gorgeous building and foliage.

He gave me a sweet grin, "I figured we'd be tired from driving all day. I booked us a room."

I raised my eyebrows. While we had spent several nights together, we were always in separate bedrooms. I knew that sex was an eventuality, as it usually was, but it hadn't been a subject either of us had dared to bring up. Which, in retrospect was completely stupid. We were consenting adults for God's sake. We were both well into our thirties. He was divorced and I had lived with a few boyfriends.

But Finn was slow in that regard. He liked to take his time and get to know a person and didn't seem to like the idea of casual sex. I knew all this because this was exactly what he had shown me; so why were my palms sweating?

"I asked for a double room," he replied in a hurry, clearly quick to explain himself.

A piece of me was a little disappointed as we entered the hotel for our key. When Finn gave the very young front desk attendant his name, her face curled in confusion at her screen. She punched the keys but didn't get the answer she was looking for upon a second and third look.

"Is there a problem?" he asked kindly.

Her face quickly turned apologetic, "I don't think so...maybe? You said you booked a double queen?"

Finn nodded in the affirmative.

"I'm sorry sir, there's been a mix-up of some kind. I'm just not sure which," she said the last part under her breath. "We only have a king room available."

Whether by her mistake or someone else's, I saw the moment the young woman's heart sank into her stomach. She braced for an angry outburst from Finn, but I knew that wouldn't happen. And although the woman at the desk could not see it, I watched as Finn's throat went dry. I decided to step in, sliding the room key into my hand.

"It's completely fine, no worries," I smiled at her before turning to Finn, "We can make it work, right?"

The woman relaxed almost immediately and gave me a huge smile. I widened my eyes, trying to communicate with Finn that it would, indeed be okay. He seemed to get my message before he thanked the attendant and we turned to find our room.

Finn followed me up the tile staircase as I matched our key number to the room. I started to slide the card into the reader when he placed his hand over mine, "I think I'm going to find something else. You stay here...I'll come back early in the morning and we'll get breakfast."

As charming as I found everything about Finn Rafferty, his avoidance was getting out of hand. It wasn't like we couldn't be alone together; and if he wasn't ready, then neither was I. We could discuss it at another time, but eventually, he would have to let me know where we were going.

"No way!" I frowned and he tried to protest.

"Natalie—"

I looked at him in disbelief, "No, Finn. You planned this perfect trip for the both of us...don't bail on me."

I could see in the dim light he was still unsure, but he followed me into the room anyway. We sat our bags on a long table just behind the sofa and took a good look at the accommodations. A king-size bed with a beautiful white comforter hugged the far wall of the room just beyond the sitting area. A bathroom and closet shared space to the right and large windows banked to the left. Finn squeezed the back cushions of the small sofa.

"I guess this will be okay, I can camp here," he gave me a weak grin.

I threw my hand up in resignation and turned from him, "Fine. Do whatever you want."

"Are you mad?" his brow furrowed.

I spun back, "Mad? No, I'm not mad. I'm confused...and completely perplexed by the fact that, apparently, I'm not worthy of sharing a bed with you?"

He took a step in my direction, "Natalie, that's not it at all!"

"Then what is it? Are you not attracted to me? Because that's fine too...otherwise, the only explanation I can come up with is that I've done something wrong!" I bit back angrily, backing away.

"Goddamn it, no!" he growled and his face contorted with pain. "Natalie, please...you don't understand."

At that moment I was mad and I couldn't stop.

Chapter Twenty-Two

Finn

S he said she wasn't mad, but she *definitely* was.

"You wanted to know all my demons, and I let you in. But, seems like there's a double standard here...which, hurts, if I'm being honest. So, no, I'm not mad, Finn...but I am hurt," her words were bitter in my ears.

I stared at her and desperately grasped at whatever would make her understand. She was wrong, so very wrong. I felt things for her that I could genuinely say that I've never felt for anyone, ever. Not even my ex-wife. I wanted so much to feel all of her skin under my fingertips and to have myself buried so deep in her that I got lost and never found a way out. I've wanted all of those things the moment our lips touched. But what I wouldn't do, what I refused to do, is hurt her by setting her up for failure. She stared at me, her deep, golden forest eyes demanding a response. She deserved to know, I owed her that much.

"I can't have children, Natalie," I ground between a clenched jaw. My words were an acrid statement that singed my soul and made it weak and brittle at its edges.

She blinked, "What?"

I looked through the window at the darkened sky as if it would offer me strength, "The kind and amount of chemo and radiation I had as a kid left me sterile. Barring some miracle from the universe...I can't have children."

"Finn, what does that have to do with anything?" sincere confusion settled over her.

"Everything!" I took a step toward her and she didn't back away but allowed me to get within inches of her, "I told you that sleeping with you would mean something to me. But I can't be selfish...I have to think of you too. I can't promise something that I know I won't be able to deliver on."

"Finn, what promises are you making?" Reaching up, she caressed my face with her warm hands.

I rolled my eyes, "A future...a family. I can't have that...and I won't watch your heart break when the answer will always be no."

"How can you know what I want?" her eyes narrowed on me. "You can't. You've been too afraid to ask."

Her bold declaration hit me and the nail on the head. I assumed something because it's ingrained in culture there is a natural progression to relationships which typically culminates in building a family, which is something I physically can't do. I also realized that I *had* been too afraid to ask because I feared the answer: I was afraid of having my heart shattered.

"I'm sorry, Natalie," I apologized. "I shouldn't have presumed to know what you wanted. But, I'd like to."

Her face lightened, "I'm not sure what I want or when or if...but if the person I'm with can't or doesn't want to...then we would talk about that too. But we would do it together...without assumptions."

As if an invisible force took hold, I wrapped her entire body into my arms and crashed into her mouth. I held nothing back and our tongues entwined and danced as our kiss deepened. Lacing my fingers into her long, dark hair I tug gently, exposing her neck to my mouth. A small moan escaped her lips and the erection I'd fought off for weeks struggled against my zipper.

I finally released my hold and took a small step back, "I never meant to make you feel like I wasn't attracted to you...I'm sorry for that."

"I said that out of frustration," Natalie sighed, sitting on the bed.

I knelt in front of her, pulling her hips to my chest. My hands stroked every inch of exposed flesh and our lips found each other again. Delicate fingers raked through my short hair sending gooseflesh from my neck to my boot-covered toes. Every touch from her made my insides tremble. Her head bent toward mine; her breath was hot on my neck. She panted as I scraped my teeth across an earlobe, and arched her back so I felt her tight nipples press into my chest.

"If I go much further, I won't be able to stop," I groaned between her playful bites on my neck.

We locked eyes and her stare bore into me for a few lustful seconds before she whispered, "I don't see anyone telling you no."

With a slick movement, I locked my forearms under her knees and flipped her to her back onto the bed. I hovered over her, my mouth attached to the pillows of her lips and I slowly ground against her. She stripped me out of my shirt which started a frenzy of dispatched clothes and tumbling shoes. In only seconds, her gorgeous, flawless body was under me, and it was all I could do to not stare at her transcendence. She was watching me watch her.

"What?" she asked.

A breath caught in my chest, "You're perfect."

She turned her eyes away, but I wouldn't allow it. I brought her face back to meet mine and lifted her chin with my finger, "Hey...please don't look away. I mean every word."

I brushed my lips against hers and we fell back into place. She allowed my hands to feel her skin and every curve of her body. My fingers moved along the junction of her thighs only to find our sheets already drenched with her excitement. I brought it to my lips and tasted her honey. Her sweetness coated my tongue and I ran it along her collarbone and around the curve of her round breast. I barely grazed her nipples with my fingers when they immediately tightened more to my touch.

Natalie wrapped her arms around my nape and pulled me down on her. Her lips were forceful and demanded attention and I gave it to her. I'd give her everything. My length rubbed against her leg and she moaned every time I got near her entrance. I dipped the head into her for a moment and as I pulled out I grazed the tip against her swollen bud.

She bucked and groaned with pleasure as she begged for more, "Finn, don't stop...please."

She didn't need to beg me because I was desperate to have all of her. I wanted to know what it felt like to sink into her depths and drown in her. I didn't make her wait as I slowly buried my erection into her core. Her muscles stretched around what I gave her, but I had more. My inner voice warned me not to hurt her. But Natalie wrapped her legs around my hips and pushed me inside. I didn't know how long it had been and I was afraid of hurting her.

'It's too much'

She bit my neck, "Why are you holding back? I want all of you."

I pulled out and thrust my cock inside, filling her to her borders. She moaned delightfully and I repeated the move, watching her back arch with each push forward. I set my cadence as I found her clit, enlarged and waiting to be set free. I took it between two fingers and gently rubbed the fleshy bud. I felt her muscles contract around my cock and

I quickened my strokes, my fingers still keeping pace as I drove into her harder.

I had so many thoughts about the positions and places I wanted us to try. I wanted her over me like the Goddess she was, in charge of my body and riding it until she was spent and satisfied. I wanted to take her from behind, her beautiful labia exposed and waiting for me to explore the worlds it holds. I wanted to worship her in every way her divineness deserved. My fantasies of any future encounter turned me on more and my tempo quickened.

I felt Natalie's muscles tighten and I knew she was close to her climax. The sheets beneath us were soaked with her juices as she bellowed my name over and over. As the last of her contracted around my cock, I felt the built energy gather in my sacrum and crash in powerful waves as I bore down and cried her name like a sacred prayer to the Gods.

Chapter Twenty-Three

Natalie

F inn's arms were wrapped around my shoulders and he pulled my back tight into his chest. I thought the air conditioning in the room was on full blast because it was freezing, but it also could have been evaporating sweat. But being next to him, I liked how his warmth balanced me against the chill. His face was buried in my hair, and I could feel his slow and easy breath on my neck. He kissed my ear so I knew he wasn't sleeping. I rubbed his arms with my hands and his tan skin felt soft under my fingers.

"Are you alright?" he whispered in my ear.

I smiled, mostly to myself. It had been a long time since I wanted to be with a man, and even longer since I was. I rolled just under him and he propped himself on an elbow, his hungry ocean blues tracing my face before landing on my lips. I wanted to kiss him again; I wanted to kiss him all night. But, I couldn't forget what he said before our deed: it meant something to him.

"What's wrong?" he asked. "Did I hurt you? I'm sorry if I was rough—"

I shook my head, "No...not at all. But...what did you mean when you said sleeping together would mean something?"

He was quiet for a long moment, I assumed contemplating his answer. I picked and twirled his sandy hair in my fingertips while he thought, lost in my own world. I started to realize he was staring at me again but it was different than a few moments before; he didn't look like he was ready to consume me instead he was peaceful and I saw hope in his eyes.

"If I die tomorrow, I will feel cheated that I didn't get to have any more minutes with you," a small smile pulled on his cheeks and he laid his head on his arm. His eyes never fell from mine, "Being with you brings me peace...I want to hang on to you for as long as you'll have me, Natalie."

My breath stopped in my chest because it was the most romantic thing anyone had ever said to me, but it also brought with it a sense of insecurity. I loved spending time with him and he made me happy, but was this something I wanted? I didn't exactly have the best track record with relationships or picking the right guy. I was so afraid I'd screw this up, but the little voice in my head was screaming to relax and give it a chance. I saw that Finn noticed my apprehension and my palms began to dampen.

His back was rigid as he leaned into me, "Are you okay?"

I closed my eyes and drew in a deep breath that immediately calmed me. When I opened them, Finn's face was full of worry.

"I'm..." I paused. "I'm not very good at any of this anymore, Finn. Give me a minute."

My smile soothed us both and we quietly fell back into each other's arms. We descended into sleep, our nude bodies entwined together with sheets and blankets. I was unsure how long we were like that but the world was still dark outside when I felt a familiar urge crash over me. I wanted more of him.

I nuzzled my face into his bare neck, laying light kisses from his earlobe to his shoulder. His moans were barely audible until my lips worked their way down his chest and I dragged my tongue across one of his nipples. Suddenly, my face was in his hands and our lips were tangled mania.

I reached between his thighs to make him ready, but his cock was hard and waiting. I wasted no time as I climbed over him and slid all of him inside my wet core. His eyes flew open to meet mine.

"Oh God," he growled.

His voice sent gooseflesh down my spine and my muscles squeezed around his cock as I rocked my hips against his. He steadied my gait, grabbing each of my hips with his hands. He was buried inside me and I gave him no relief, no break from the strokes of my pussy as I dug my nails into his chest. His hands tightened on my ass and he forced me to slow my ride. We locked eyes with Every. Deliberate. Stride.

"This is where you belong," he whispered. "On top, in charge."

I blushed but I didn't look away from him, instead, I picked up momentum and watched his eyes roll blissfully in his head. I felt him tighten like a spring for a moment and thought he was ready to release but he pulled it back and pushed his thumb over my clit. I was already so close I nearly came undone but then his finger started to circle me, matching my rhythm. My core dripped over him, my muscles tightened around him, and I felt him buck beneath me.

Finn's hands latched hard onto my thighs as he pushed into me. I felt every throb of his orgasm and he moaned and growled as my name bounced off the room's walls. The sound was glorious music in my ears. I continued to slowly rock on his hips gently until he broke our connection by flipping me on my back between his legs. I laughed wildly as he positioned himself at my glistening junction.

"Your turn," his grin was wicked as he glided his tongue slowly through my valley. I laid back as he went to work and it wasn't long until I saw stars and called his name to the darkness that surrounded us.

Chapter Twenty-Four

Finn

I stared at my wrist and watched the minutes tick down in slow anticipation of my release from the shift. Being short-staffed meant everyone was doing overtime and no one was happy about it. After two weeks of pulling forty-eights with only a twenty-four-hour break between each rotation, it was no wonder why the people in this house were sick of looking at each other.

I hadn't seen Natalie since we got back from Santa Barbara. It was my very next shift when a stomach bug ran through the firehouse and we started dropping like flies. Luckily for me, I had a stomach of iron. The only thing that would ruin my day was if one more person called in and I went from a well-deserved four-day break to moving into the firehouse indefinitely.

Double lucky for me, that didn't happen and the second seven pm hit, I got my gear on my back and the bike started. By seven-twenty, I skated into my parking spot at my apartment and recognized the silver Kia K5 two spaces down from mine.

I sauntered up to the window, cocky grin and all, and leaned inside, "Now, what's a beautiful woman like you doing in a place like this?"

Natalie flashed a smile, "Waiting."

"For?"

"Well, not for you," she laughed, opening the door into my gut. "I forgot my favorite hairbrush in your guest room last month. I need it."

I caged her between myself and the car and as I inclined toward her, her perfume flooded my nostrils.

"Need it?" I purred. "Where are you taking it?"

"I thought I'd move it to the master bedroom," she giggled.

I backed away, smiling, "I think that can be arranged."

"You look tired. How long do you have this time?" First searching my face, her eyes narrowed on mine. This was the first time we laid eyes on each other since the great summer stomach flu event. I knew that of all people, she would be acutely aware of the effects of my exhaustion.

Rubbing the scruff that had accumulated on my face, I sighed, "I've got a full four days. Thankfully, everyone is back and we're working toward some normalcy."

"Good," a smirk rose in the corners of her perfectly plump mouth. Turning, she popped the trunk and pulled out a suitcase and bags of groceries. "That means, we have four days to either sit by your pool or get out of this heat altogether. You're choice. Oh, and we're having pasta for dinner."

Natalie loaded two bags on her arms and sat two more on her wheeled luggage. She turned back to me and by the look on her face, I must've looked dazed because I was missing something.

"What about work?" I asked.

The smile she gave me was kind and graceful, "Okay. First line of business, you...shower and a shave. Then I'll remind you of my vacation...I'm off for a week, remember?"

I didn't, but I did then.

After storing the food away, I obeyed the nurse's orders for a hot shower. When I returned, the apartment smelled of simmering tomatoes and fresh garlic. By nine, the leftovers were stored, the dishwasher was running, and my eyes were heavy. For the life of me, I couldn't remember a time when I felt as tired. It wasn't long after that I was completely content as Natalie's head rose and fell on my chest as we melted into sleep.

The next morning, the pounding on the door sounded distant and out of reach. My groggy eyes refused to open in the vast darkness of the bedroom. The new black-out shades I installed were working quite well at their intended job. More pounding and I finally sat up in the bed.

After stumbling to find a pair of shorts, I staggered into the stark brightness of my living room and peeked through the tiny peephole. I saw the enormous frame of Bill Callahan. I was fully awake.

I swung the door open, "Good morning, Detective."

"Morning?" he looked at his watch.

I realized I actually didn't know what time it was, but I played my ignorance off, "Morning for me. Come in."

I offered the man a seat and something to drink, but both were refused politely. It was then Natalie came out of the bedroom, her hair wrapped in a towel and smelling light of fresh flowers.

"Good afternoon, Detective," her voice pensive.

Bill was quick to get to the point of his visit, "I'm actually glad you're both here. I want to let you know if you haven't been told by the prosecutor's office already, that charges were filed against Bonetti on the vandalism and arson and he's been arrested."

I watched relief wash like a tidal wave over Natalie's face and I thought she might cry out of elation, but she held steady and listened.

"However, we don't think we'll get anywhere with the stalking," he continued grimly.

"How the hell can that be?" I bellowed.

Bill lowered his head, "There isn't enough proof, Finn. The DA doesn't think she can make it stick."

Running a hand through my hair, I sneered, "Proof?! She had a panic attack at the movies when he showed up there...he had someone beat on her door in the middle of the night! That has to be enough."

"I'm sorry, Finn, it's not." He turned to Natalie, "When you saw him at the theater, did he approach you? Talk to you?"

Natalie pursed her lips and shook her head.

"Did the man that came in the middle of the night...did he give you his name? Did you look out and recognize him?" he pressed.

"No."

Bill eyed both of us apologetically, "I'm sorry. Without something that shows a pattern...they won't charge him."

"He showed up at her work...twice. The second time, she had three witnesses...what about that?" I kept pushing, refusing to let it go.

He nodded, "We looked into those incidences. The first time, he was telling the truth...his girlfriend was in the ER that night."

"And the second?" Natalie huffed incredulously. "What was his excuse?"

"He had none...so, that charge will be added later, but I'll be honest, the violation is only a misdemeanor...maybe a class D felony for grabbing your arm. Our best chance at putting him in jail is on the arson."

"Unbelievable," I growled.

"I'll keep you in the loop and I'm sorry this isn't exactly what we were hoping for, but it is something," Bill shook Natalie's hand before letting himself out of the apartment.

"I'm sorry, Natalie," I said softly. Thinking she would be angry about the injustice of having her case overlooked, but, to my surprise, she wasn't.

She wrapped her arms around my waist, "It's okay, Finn. Really. Right now, I don't care how or why he goes to jail, just that he does. And I'm not going to let him or the prosecutor or Detective Callahan ruin my vacation."

Chapter Twenty-Five

Natalie

After lunch, I convinced Finn that our only reprieve from the oppressive July sun was a dip in the complex pool. After some arguments from him about it being overcrowded or loud, I countered with a one-two-punch reminder that it was a weekday and the public pool across the street was far more appealing to rowdy teens. I was right, of course. I should have been a lawyer.

For two hours, we swam laps and played sneaky games of underwater grab-ass all under the not-so-watchful eye of two elderly women who were far more into their Harlequin romance books than us. When the sun became unbearable again and I felt my skin becoming tender, we made our break for conditioned air and filtered light once more. Both of us showered, grabbed a drink, and met back on his sofa.

I snuggled into his hold, laying my head between his neck and shoulder, "Wanna watch a movie?"

"Hmmm...I like that plan," he agreed blissfully. Our selections were slim, but we both giggled when Twister reappeared on the screen.

"It has to be fate at this point," Finn chortled.

We were barely through the opening credits and complaints about map folding when I felt Finn's lips graze my ear. Chills raced down my extremities leaving gooseflesh in their wake. A reaction that didn't go unnoticed by him. More deliberate kisses were placed behind my ear and down my nape. Turning my head, our lips met and fell into a lingering attachment.

His pillowy lips were soft against mine and he pulled me into his tight hold with long, strong arms. He held me in all the right places while running his steady hands through my wet hair. With a gentle, directive tug, he turned me to sit, straddling his lap. I could just make out the fading taste of whiskey on his tongue. My racing heart beat faster as his hands ran underneath my tee-shirt, against my bare skin. More gooseflesh trailed along behind his touch and I felt my body awakening to every movement.

The movie played unattended on the television behind me.

Finn's lips moved down my neck before his tongue traced my collarbone and cleavage, and I moaned softly in his ear. It was then I noticed a growing sensation beneath me and I ground my hips into him.

He immediately flipped me onto the sofa and stripped out of his shirt. Hovering over me, he kissed me with a passion only reserved for the holy and called my name in lascivious whispers.

"I've missed you, Natalie. You're all I've been thinking about for weeks."

Every time he growled my name, delightful sparks rolled through me.

We continued to make out like teenagers before I finally pulled my shirt over my head, exposing my taut, round breasts. Raising on his arm, Finn stared down at me, seemingly memorizing every inch of skin before tracing his finger along my silhouette.

His ocean-blue eyes locked with mine again, "You're my sacred salvation."

I knew my face flushed. His words were far more than just budding romance or a way to get me to have sex with him. In a way, they made me uneasy and embarrassed because no one had ever spoken to me like I was a treasure before. And no one looked at me the way Finn did. The man worshipped me, body, mind, and soul, and meant it.

"Hey," he lifted my chin with his finger, shaking his head, "Please...don't look away."

Our mouths met again and a wave of ecstasy crashed over me as his path of kisses found new places to land on my topless body. Working his way further south, Finn slowly released the tie on my cotton shorts, sliding them and my panties away from my hips.

My thighs throbbed with excitement.

Never moving his eyes from mine, he tossed the rest of his clothes to the floor and covered me with his body. I felt his hard cock against my hip as I became fully aware of my own arousal. I didn't care if he was in love with me or not, I just wanted him inside me. Every move he made was electrifying and I couldn't get enough of his skin on mine.

Finn kissed me slowly as his shaft slid easily into my succulent core.

"Oh, God," his eyes rolled to the back of his head.

He pushed slowly, taking his time with each thrust to fill me, our eyes locked on one another. He wanted me to see his desire and I needed him to see mine. We were lock and key, fitting only each other.

"More," my teeth playfully bit his neck.

His rhythmic thrusting intensified until he was nearly sitting on his knees as he drove ever deeper into my folds harder and faster. My muscles locked onto his long shaft and he groaned in pleasure. He placed his thumb firmly over my swollen clit, rolling it in his fingers.

The wave of orgasm was already building and I felt its electricity pulse as his vibration intensified. He knew I was close to my climax and he worked his fingers in perfect pulse and pattern with each drive of his cock. The louder I moaned and purred, the harder he drove into me until my waves of contraction held him in a vice. I watched every muscle in his body seize as I came and I felt his cock pulsing inside me.

"Oh my God!" he bellowed, thrusting hard.

We bucked and thrashed until we collapsed in sweat-soaked tremors in each other's arms on the soft sofa.

After a long moment of gasping for air, I got out, "That...was...intense."

"Do I owe you an apology?" his words were short as he caught his breath.

I couldn't help but laugh, "No. Why would you say that?"

"Intense is bad, right? I don't want to scare you off," he offered softly.

I had to lean back to get a clear look at his face, "No, intense isn't bad. Intense is good...I like your intense."

Finn smiled and we laid nuzzled into each other's slowly cooling bodies. The television droned until we heard Helen Hunt's voice say, "Cow" and we both erupted in laughter.

Chapter Twenty-Six

Finn

"Hey man, how was your time?" Darren raised his chin in my direction.

Dropping my gear near the foot of the bank of lockers, I sat on the bench and kicked off my tennis shoes, "It was good. Never left my house and had a beautiful woman by my side."

"How's that going? Any more trouble with the asshole?" he shut his locker door and took the other end of the bench.

I shrugged, "In jail for the arson...not much on the stalking. Which, pisses me off, but Natalie's good since he's off the street for now."

"That's good," he finished tying his boot as we heard a knock on the door.

"Rafferty? You in there?" a woman's voice called.

"Yeah, Nieves, come in...we're decent," I replied.

"I'm not!" Darren laughed.

Inez Nievez palmed the door open, "You never are Sanchez. Rafferty, you've got a visitor."

Darren raised his brow at me, "Oh, yeah? That's cute Rafferty. Nieves, is it a beautiful brunette with legs that could kill?"

She looked at us confused, "No, short blonde...but, yeah, I'd call her beautiful."

I looked from Darren to Inez before shoving the rest of my stuff into my locker and sliding out of the open door. I walked through the station and into the open garage from the side door. A petite woman stood with her back turned, hugging her body. Her hair was cut into a short pixie style and her skin was heavily sun-kissed; both much more than I remembered.

"Lori?" I asked, my voice tinged with a little disbelief. She turned and smiled. "What are you doing here?"

Wrapping her arms around my neck she pulled me to her, "Hey Finn! It's good to see you!"

"Yeah," I eyed her. Lori wasn't someone that I trusted entirely. By the end of our relationship, she had cheated, three times that I knew about, lied ad nauseam, and accused me of doing the same things she was doing.

For the record, I wasn't.

We met in high school, two kids from broken homes; one had a giant attitude in a tiny body while the other had a serious case of big man syndrome. Both had a mutual dislike for anyone in authority. Punk kids we were, but we were also completely and madly in lust with each other. I think we eventually found some semblance of love, but we were never really *in* love and it didn't last forever despite what we carved into desks and tree trunks.

I put Lori at arm's length, "Again, what are you doing here?"

"I really wanted to see you. That's okay, right?" her round eyes were like pale marbles.

I chortled a short laugh and shook my head before picking up a rag to polish a light on the ambulance next to us, "You drove down from San Jose just to say hi? What do you want, Lori?"

"Nothing!" she replied a little too quickly for my liking.

"Right." I focused on the chrome.

"I just needed to see my husband—"

"Oh no!" my words cut sharp across hers, "Ex-husband. Ex. That was made very clear by the divorce papers we both signed and I still have several copies of...in case you ever forget."

Her head drooped, "No, I haven't forgotten."

She looked...defeated. It was something I'd never seen in her, but I wouldn't let it deter me. I knew there had to be a reason she was standing here. Lori never did anything without an ulterior motive.

"Get to it, Lori. Why are you here?" I began polishing the same piece of metal again.

"I need help, Finn," her tone uncharacteristically soft.

I smiled to myself in satisfaction, "There it is. What kind of trouble this time? Rent or lawyer?"

"Neither," she replied.

I scoffed, throwing the rag on the table and crossing my arms over my chest, "Well, then you've gotten your car repoed, again. At any rate, you're going to have to grow up sometime, Lori. Bailing you out stopped being my job the second you screwed the bartender at Mickey's Pub."

Lori stayed silent and unmoving. Something that was also wholly against her personality.

What the hell was going on?

I was starting to feel bad that I had come after her so hard. But, honestly, who could blame me? I've known this woman since we were teens and could predict with pinpoint accuracy every move her giant manipulative brain could conceive. But, something had changed. She was sullen and quiet, not the balls-to-the-walls spitfire I knew.

"What's going on?" I asked.

She smiled meekly, "I shouldn't have come. I'm sorry that I bothered you. I'll go."

She turned to leave but my guilt got the better of me.

"Wait."

She turned back.

"Why are you here, Lori?" I asked again, but this time without the accusatory tone. "Really."

She moved closer so that there were only centimeters between us. "I need help, Finn."

I nodded, "What kind of help?"

"I'm sick, Finn. Really sick. I don't have anyone to help me...and no one I can trust with Danny... except you." She didn't cry, but her words shook.

It took me a minute to absorb what she was saying. She was sick? How sick? With what? And Danny...it had been a couple of weeks since I'd spoken to her younger brother.

"What do you mean sick? What's going on?" I pushed.

She swallowed hard, "Cancer. In my ovaries. Stage four."

"Stage four? You're..."

"Dying, Finn. I'm dying. I'll have some treatments to see if that helps lengthen my time, but," she shrugged.

"What happens to Danny?" I asked, concerned about where he would go if anything happened to her.

Danny was the best thing about Lori. He was only two years younger and had been born with a form of congenital mixed triplegia cerebral palsy that affected the motor movement in both legs and his left arm along with his speech. Danny was always a big part of our lives, even when we were on the outs. I loved that guy like my own sister and Lori knew that. I'd never let anything happen to Danny.

She shook her head, "A ward of the state, I guess. But, that's not what I want...or what he wants. We don't have family, Finn."

It was true. Both of their parents were long gone and no extended family to speak of, at least, not in California.

My mind reeled. What exactly was she asking me to do? I stared at her, obviously confused.

"It's a big ask...but, we need you in San Jose. I'm only going to get sicker and Danny needs someone he trusts."

I shook my head, "Lori, I'm sorry, but I can't. I have a life here."

"You've only been here what? Four months? You've barely un-packed, Finn," she countered.

"Yeah, and a lot has happened. I just can't leave, Lori. I'm sorry."

Images of Natalie flashed in my mind and Lori read them like a book.

Her eyebrows raised in understanding, "Oh...you've met someone. I see." Her voice trembled, "I'll a...I'll just call his case worker and get the paperwork drawn up. I just thought having family would make this easier for him."

I put my hand up and stepped in her path before she could turn away, "Lori...wait. Just..." I sighed. "Just give me some time to think, okay? This isn't something I can give you an answer to tonight. When do you go back?"

"Thursday. I start treatments on Friday." She smiled, "I knew I could count on you. Thanks, Finn."

She turned to leave and this time, I let her go. She made it halfway between her rental and where I stood before turning back, "What happened to your Bronco?"

"Vandalism...long story," I replied in the space between us.

"That yours?" she pointed to the motorcycle.

I nodded.

"It suits you," she winked, got into her car, and drove away.

Chapter Twenty-Seven

Natalie

I lay on my sofa, my eyes heavy and drifting in and out to the soft mumble of my television. With Finn back at work, I decided I would spend the next several nights in my own bed if for nothing else, to remember what my pillows felt like. My vacation would be over by Thursday and I would go back to meals of Cheez-Its and thick coffee out of a machine from 1990. Delilah decided that I was no longer Undesirable Number One, and lay curled at my feet purring softly.

The sun set and rose again and I awoke, still on my sofa, to Delilah's mewing for breakfast. I checked my watch: eight am. I checked my phone realizing I hadn't heard a peep out of Finn all night. It was strange, but I figured he had a crazy night.

Stretching out my muscles, I padded into the kitchen, dumped a small cup of kibble in the princess's bowl, and headed for the shower. I just rounded the corner to the bathroom doorway when a light knocking sounded at my door. I turned back more curious with every step who would be here so early. Checking the peephole, I saw Finn.

My heart leaped a bit. It had taken me a while to realize it, but I was really starting to miss him when he wasn't around. I wondered if he felt the same way. He said he was crazy about me, but part of me, the part I knew was probably still a little broken, contemplated that he may be inflating the truth. I also considered things he said while we were naked and sweaty. Was he serious when he called me his salvation? I was still wrapping my head, and the broken part of me, around that as well.

"Good morning!" I chirped, opening the door. His body was rigid, his eyes worn, and his entire demeanor was off somehow. "What's wrong? Bad night?"

His lips were pursed, "Natalie, can I come in...I need to talk."

"Of course," I moved back to allow him to pass. I stood on tiptoe and kissed his cheek but instead of even the slightest smile, he looked like he might cry. I motioned for him to sit on the sofa and took a spot next to him. "What's happened, Finn?"

I could tell his mouth was dry as he struggled to speak.

"I..." he inhaled a deep breath. "There is no easy way to begin...something happened at work yesterday and I need help figuring it out. Figuring everything out."

I gave him a quick shake of my head, "Everything? Like what is everything?"

Another deep breath.

"My whole life," he scoffed.

"Finn, whatever this is, I'll help you. God knows you've done enough for me...time to repay the favor," I smiled at him, hoping it would alleviate even a fraction of the stress he was clearly feeling.

It didn't and his face grew tighter and darker.

"Goddamn it!" he ran his hand through his hair and down his face. "Twenty-four hours ago, it was going exactly where I wanted it to...now? A wrench the size of Texas got thrown into it."

He turned to me, "My ex-wife came by the station house yesterday."

"Lori?" I asked.

"Yeah. I was pretty hard on her...tried to get her to go away because whatever she was into, I wanted no part of it," he nodded. "She's a disaster most days...I thought she needed money for rent or bail like the old days."

"What did she want?" I searched his eyes for a hint of where this conversation was going, but those azure globes just looked sad.

"Not money...God, I wish it were money," he mumbled. "Lori's sick. Stage four cancer."

"Oh, God...Finn, I'm sorry—"

He held up his hand, "That's not all. She has a brother, Danny, who she has sole guardianship of...and no other family to help her. Except..."

His voice trailed off and I raised my brows for him to continue.

"Except...?"

"Me." His shoulders dropped in defeat.

My mind flipped. I tried to put the conversation together and make sense of it but I couldn't. How old was this younger brother, Danny? Did this mean that Finn was considering *adopting* a child?

Seeing the questions on my face, Finn jumped to explain, "Danny is an adult, but he was born with congenital CP. I've known him since he was thirteen...he's the little brother I never had."

The puzzle was coming together, "Lori's ill...very ill and she asked you to take over the guardianship of her brother when something happens to her. And you're considering it? Is that about right?"

"Not exactly. Lori is going to try some treatments starting Friday, just to see if they can at least control the tumor growth. But, she knows they will make her sick, and eventually, she won't be strong enough to care for her brother like he needs." A heavy pause fell between us and he stared at me for a moment before speaking again. "She needs someone to be there to help. They don't have family...except—"

Now I got the whole picture, "For you. She wants you to go back to San Jose, right?"

He nodded, "I don't know how to do this."

I tried to be logical about the situation, not that it helped the crushing reality of what was happening. Cancer was a horrible disease that ravaged its host and destroyed families, but when that family already had a member who needed constant care, its destruction was amplified. If she had no other family, and no other means of physical or emotional support, it made sense to reach out to the person with whom you had a history, right? If I were in her shoes, what would I do?

"You're going to go," I said calmly, keeping the coolness and pain out of my voice.

"What?" his mouth hung agape. "I'm not sure what *to* do. But she needs me to help."

She *needs* him. His simple and kind gesture to her was like a razor-sharp blade passing through me from top to bottom. My heart broke and melted into a pile of nothingness. My insides immediately felt empty and cold and the broken part of my soul that I hoped was healing, went into lockdown. I felt it when my protective barriers materialized out of the ether and hardened again into serrated stone. My stone walls of comfort were familiar like an old friend.

Finn was choosing to go back to his ex-wife.

He paused for a moment and looked a little bewildered, "I mean, I'm willing to do this long distance. We can make it work...I can figure this out."

I shook my head and kept my tears at bay. It seemed like all I could do at the moment. He would figure something out? A long-distance thing? We barely saw each other as it was, adding two hundred miles wouldn't work. Finn's eyes drilled into me, but I kept moving like I'd done my entire life. Keep moving forward. Unless the past pops up like a piece of shit that won't flush, there is no need for reminders and no use in looking back. For a moment, Finn recognized that something was wrong, but just when I thought he sensed my doors closing, I was disappointed again when he didn't seem to notice.

"This isn't something I ever thought would happen. Danny means the world to me," he said softly. "Of course, I also never thought Lori would need anything like this."

There it was again. She needed him.

I nodded and I felt my chin quiver, "Yeah...yeah, you're going to go help. She's going to *need* someone she can trust to be by her side. It will make everything easier in the long run anyway."

I practically jumped from the sofa. I wanted to bolt for the door but realized it was my house so I had nowhere to run. I also remembered a bottle of wine I had in my refrigerator; I would be drinking that later. "I know you've got a lot to do...you've got to talk to your chief, break your lease. And your Bronco isn't ready yet...but I guess you could come back when it is."

I was rushing to get him out of my house so I could cry. My heart was shattered, but she *needed* him.

Finn frowned, "Natalie, I know this is going to be hard...I'm not happy about this either. But, the commute won't be that bad."

I watched the light come on in his head as I stood by the opened door.

"Wait—" He reached out to touch me and I pulled back fiercely. His eyes turned in confusion, staring, but I refused to look at him. I was done and I dared him to say that Lori *needed* him one more time.

"Natalie! Wait a second...Don't! Please don't do this," Finn was still trying to lock eyes. "I didn't mean—"

I took a breath, "Do what, Finn? This is your *family*...there really is no choice, is there? She needs you."

I drew out the words sharply and the bile rose in my throat. I rubbed my eyebrow.

"Natalie, all you have to do is tell me to stay. I'll figure something out," he pleaded.

I steadied myself with a deep breath and set my resolve. When I looked into his eyes, disks of pure gemstone, I gave him my plastered, *everything is fine*, fictitious smile; the exact one I knew he would immediately know was a lie.

"Really, Finn. Take care of your family...they need you now. We're good."

"Natalie! I don't understand," he pleaded. "You just said I should go. If you don't want me to do this, then tell me that."

My impending tears fanned my fury, "I did not say you should go! But you seemed to be concerned about what your ex-wife needs...it's clear that you think you should. Who am I to have a say in what you do with your life?!"

My eyes darted out the opened door and he took my hint. I wanted him to leave so I could crawl into a hole and ignore this bitter feeling that was starting to encompass my soul. He walked slowly out of the threshold before turning to face me. He opened his mouth to speak, but I cut him off.

"I know, Lori needs you. Thanks for a fun summer...I hope you find what you need someday," my voice cracked before I slammed the door in his face.

Chapter Twenty-Eight

Finn

I opened up the throttle of the Indian and barrelled toward my apartment. I was hurt. Furious. Confused.

A *fun* summer?

I thought Natalie felt the same as I did about our relationship. How could she just shut me out? Shut us down? I wanted us to talk about it but more importantly, I needed her advice. I needed her help figuring out what I could do to help Danny and Lori. I didn't want a breakup, but I was pretty sure that's what had happened.

Long-distance wouldn't be without its challenges, but I thought we could make it work. Maybe I pushed her too much. Maybe the last few months had been too intense for her and this was her way of putting on the brakes. I knew after our second date that this relationship would be a minefield of emotions that would need to be carefully navigated. When your ex has tried to kill you, sometimes it takes a while to allow your heart to open up again. But, I thought I'd proven myself to not be like her lunatic ex. I would never treat anyone the way he treated her. Surely she realized that, right? Was I making excuses for her? Maybe she wasn't ready and I was pushing way too hard.

I could commute. I mean, until Lori was at the end. Danny could move here with me and I could help get her into some sort of palliative care. Not that she was ready to give up, because that would be out of my ex-wife's personality. What if I moved both of them to Hanford? It wouldn't be without its own emotional challenges, having both my ex-wife and my girlfriend in the same city. *If* Natalie was still my girlfriend...

I knew everyone came with a small voice in their head; the one that warned of danger or talked you out of a second piece of cake. Mine was screaming obscenities about driving too fast, and about Natalie and Lori and this entire mess.

I made a new life in Hanford. This wasn't fair. Why was the universe doing this to me?

I thought of Danny.

I wouldn't leave him in a world with only strangers. I remember being a scared kid in a hospital and the only people who were around were ones you didn't know. Danny wasn't a child, but, in a way, he was nearly defenseless. I couldn't do that to him and I wouldn't.

I thought about calling Sadie. My sister had always had a good head on her shoulders and always gave great advice. But, I was the protective older brother, and with law school starting and the baby, I didn't want to bring her any more burdens.

I drove faster, weaving through traffic like it was my own video game. I needed Natalie to talk to me. I suddenly remembered the coldness of her eyes and the way she smiled at me. She wasn't just angry, she was shut down. My heart sank.

Without Natalie, I would have to make this decision on my own.

Chapter Twenty-Nine

Finn

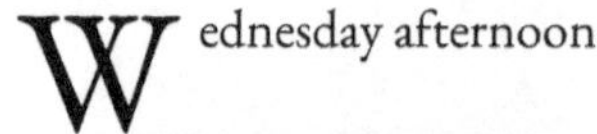

Wednesday afternoon:

> Natalie…please talk to me.

> I DON'T want this to end for us…please. We CAN make this work. I know I probably handled this all wrong. I didn't mean to scare you

Thursday morning:

> Natalie…I know you're angry with me. I just need 5 to explain. Can you give me that?

Thursday evening:

> Natalie…If you want me to stay, just say it. I will stay. I will work something out with Lori. Please, Natalie…just talk to me. I don't want to do this alone.

Friday morning:

Since it's clear you don't want to talk to me, maybe I'm hoping you'll read this. I messed up. I handled this all wrong and now, it's obvious I've lost you. I need you to know that I leave for SJ in the am. I'm sorry I hurt you. I pray at some point you remember how much I care about you. I don't want to give up…so, text back or call whenever…because I'll always answer.

All my love

Seven Months Later...

Chapter Thirty

Natalie

'*Bus Six-two-one enroute, Southwest Haven. Male, thirty-five, GSW, have trauma on stand-by, ETA one minute.*'

"Natalie...where are you right now?" Dr. Carys asked.

I blinked wildly before my eyes focused back on her lightly tapping pencil. I rubbed my brow. Looking over her shoulder, and through the window I watched pigeons perched on a low-hanging line between the two office buildings. I sighed and my eyes shifted back to hers hiding behind dark-rimmed glasses.

"My brain keeps playing the radio over again. I can hear the exact crackles, the pops, the dispatch voice. Every word," I replied.

Dr. Carys wrote something in her notebook then looked over those glasses at me, "It was difficult, losing someone you love like that."

"No," I said flatly.

Her eyebrows arched, "No? It wasn't hard?"

"No," I shook my head. "I don't think that I loved him."

She nodded her head and more scribbling. "So, what do you think your feelings were?"

I thought about my answer. Of course, I'd been thinking about it for a few weeks, ever since I went back to therapy. It was Cece's idea;

she felt that it was a good thing considering the absolute dumpster fire my life had become. I didn't disagree, but it was hard coming back here. I first met Dr. Carys four years prior, after my nightmares and panic attacks became almost debilitating. I learned a lot then, about coping and myself, but it was difficult to admit that while I was perfectly capable of handling any situation when it's someone else's life in shambles, I completely sucked at it with my own.

Trauma was a bitch.

"I cared for him, I know that. But, I don't think I was ever in love," I wrung my hands. "Or...loved him."

Another scribble and, "Do you think, given what happened, that you now feel some guilt?"

"Why should I feel guilty?" I charged, my words a churning pool of anger. "I didn't shoot him. I didn't kill him."

Dr. Carys maintained her zen-like exterior; like she always did, no matter what I said or how angry I got. "Not guilt stemming from responsibility for his death, but maybe you have some strong emotions over how you really felt and that you never got the chance to tell him."

A stinging silence fell between us.

"Do I feel guilt because he died thinking I loved him?" I rephrased and she shrugged.

It was an interesting thought. Was guilt for something I had absolutely zero control over the reason for my new onslaught of ridiculously overwhelming anxiety? I wondered momentarily how long it would take me to digest this new little morsel of information.

Trauma was a bitch.

Before I could open my mouth to speak, the annoyingly cheerful alarm dinged on Dr. Carys' phone, "Looks like our time is up for today. We will continue exploring this next week, okay?"

In the parking garage, I sat in my car for a long time staring at nothing. I felt sick to my stomach and still sad. I looked down at my phone only to realize I would have to be at the hospital in four hours and I still needed to dry my laundry, shower, and feed Delilah. I didn't want to do any of it. I felt numb and dark; like I'd never have any light inside me again. I also felt stupid. He had been killed four weeks ago. And while I was more confident now that I really didn't love him, that didn't mean we weren't friends or I didn't care. But should it be affecting me like this? Now? So many little complications. So many things to consider.

I wondered if death actually did me a favor. It was cruel to think about, but if he were alive right now, we most definitely would be at odds and our friendship would be over. That was an indisputable fact. We both walked into our relationship, if you could call it that, with eyes wide open. We were there to have fun and not be alone; there were no strings. If I thought death was a helpful beast, then it was only there to clean up the mess impulsiveness made.

I turned over the ignition and backed away from where I sat parked.

Trauma was a bitch.

Chapter Thirty-One

Finn

"I didn't mean to lie to you!" Lori's guilt made her voice rise several octaves. It was one of her tells.

I whirled to face her, "Bullshit! You knew exactly how I would react! Your sole purpose was to get me back here and then what? I'd hop right back into your house and bed? Did you really think I wouldn't find out?!"

Her giant crocodile tears spilled over her ruddy cheeks, "I missed you so much, Finn. And so did Danny. We just wanted to be a family again...like we were."

"*We* haven't been a family in a decade, Lori! And don't you dare bring your brother into this...like he was part of this plan. I'm so done with you. This is it. Do not ever...I mean *ever*, call, text, send a smoke signal, or darken my door again. Do you hear me? We are finished!" I bellowed.

"You don't mean that," She swiped at her face angrily.

"Oh, I do. You lying, manipulating, bitch!" I yelled.

Lori's eyes squinted and I watched her overtanned skin flush again, "You listen to me! I am the only person who has ever loved you...and I will be the only person that will ever love you! I didn't do anything wrong! Things were getting back to the way they used to be...you won't leave me again, Finegan Rafferty!"

Spittle flew out of her mouth as she screamed in my face. She stomped her feet like a petulant toddler before reaching for my cereal bowl still sitting with milk from my breakfast that morning. Lifting it over her head her eyes went wild right before she launched the dish at my head.

This was the Lori I remembered.

"That's enough!" I yelled, ducking from the flying stoneware. "You're not coming into my apartment and breaking my shit. Get. Out!"

"I'm not leaving. You're my husband. Mine!" she reached for the spoon, but I knocked it to the floor before she latched on.

I pulled my cell phone out of my back pocket and searched my contacts. Finding the name I needed, I pushed the green button to dial.

"Who are you calling?" she demanded, panting.

"Get out of my house Lori," I warned.

"Get out of my house Lori," she mocked.

"Hey! Yeah," I spoke into the receiver. "I have a situation here that I could use some help with. Yeah, it was exactly what I thought...she's a liar and now she's losing her mind in my house. Can you swing by and get her out of here?"

I listened and she screamed.

"Who are you talking to?!" she reached for the phone, but being that I'm six foot two and she's five feet, it was a futile effort.

I backed away and continued my conversation, "Yep...already threw a bowl at my head. Yeah, thanks, man."

I disconnected the call and Lori seethed at me.

"You love me and you know it. Deep inside, you know it," she said, pointing a sharply manicured nail at me, her panting and fit-throwing seemingly finished.

I knew it wasn't.

A short, derisive laugh fell from my throat, "No, no, I can say with absolute certainty that I don't. You need help, Lori. Professional help. Please, get some...for Danny's sake."

What happened next was so sudden and unexpected, that I couldn't believe it myself. It happened so fast that the motion was like a blur. Lori's nails made contact with my head and raked across my face.

"Ow!" I yelled, grabbing onto my cheek. I felt the moisture forming on my fingers and knew it was blood. I immediately rounded the island and pulled paper towels from the holder to put pressure on the wound.

Her demeanor shifted like warp speed in a sci-fi movie, "Oh, Finn...I'm so sorry. I didn't mean to hurt you. I'm so sorry."

The fake tears started again as a knock hit the door. That was fast.

"Who is that?" her eyes darted from the door to me.

Without another word to her, I opened it, "Hey Elias...please, come in."

I swung the door wide and allowed Elias Palaska, my long-time friend and one of San Jose's finest, inside. Elias joined the force at the same time I was first hired in San Jose, eleven years ago. He was the first person I told about my divorce and the last person I said goodbye to when I moved to Sonoma. His partner, a tall woman in her early thirties, looking like she wouldn't take attitude from the Queen of England, stayed behind in the hallway.

"What's Elias doing here?" Lori's eye twitched.

He ignored her but pointed at my face, "You okay? That from the bowl?"

"Her fingernails," I rolled my eyes.

"Excuse me, why are you ignoring me, Elias?" Lori demanded with her hand on her hip. I knew she was ready to explode again at any second and so did he. Elias knew from experience that my ex-wife was a ticking time bomb.

"My apologies, Lori," he condescended and turned to face her, "Did you throw a bowl at this man?"

She furrowed her brow, "Absolutely not. We were talking and I knocked it off by accident."

Elias looked at me and I pointed into the kitchen where it was still on the floor and the remnants of milk were everywhere.

He nodded.

"Did you scratch this man?" he asked her pointedly.

"I didn't mean to," she growled softly. "He knows that. I don't know why you're here. We were having a private talk...you know, like spouses do?"

Elias pursed his lips, "Except you aren't married and you don't live here. Did the gentleman ask you to leave?"

She didn't answer.

"Lori, are you on anything right now?" he asked.

It was a valid question. My ex-wife was a wild child in our youth and it was she who handed me my first beer. She never used drugs back then but toward the end of our marriage, she became a partier. After our divorce, she was picked up twice for driving while under the influence. She was even caught with two grams of methamphetamine by her probation officer during a check-in for the second DUI.

"I'm being treated for cancer—"

"You don't have cancer!" I interjected, disgusted that she was still playing her little game of Munchausen.

"Lori, if you don't leave this apartment, I will arrest you," Elias warned.

She set her jaw, "Then you need to arrest me because I'm not finished talking to my husband."

Elias shrugged and waved over his partner, "Lori Marcum, you're under arrest for assault and trespassing. Please place your hands behind your back."

I watched her face turn from crimson, then to maroon, before settling on a deep purple, "This is bullshit!"

"Ma'am, please. Do you have anything sharp in your pockets? Needles or a knife?" The female officer started patting her down.

"Fuck you, Elias."

Elias smirked, "This is all on you, Lori. Someday you'll grow up...or you won't. Either way, your actions have consequences."

"I haven't done anything wrong. Oh my God, Finn, you're pathetic." Her laugh was full and on the brink of a little bit crazy. "You pathetic little shit...I should have dropped your ass a long time ago. Blank shooting, motherfucker, Finn! Can't even give a woman what she wants."

Her burning laughter was cruel.

"Thompson, get her out of here," Elias gave his partner a single nod and she walked Lori outside, cuffed, still furious, and spitting obscenities. I took a deep sigh, removing the towel from my face. With as little blood present, I knew it wasn't as bad as it felt.

"You okay, man?" Elias asked.

I rolled my eyes, "I told you. I knew I smelled a rat. I can't believe I fell for it."

"What are you gonna do now?"

"I don't know. But I can't stay here...in Jose. I'll never have a moment's peace." I thumbed over my shoulder, "What's going to happen with her?"

He shrugged, "Well, it's not her first offense. She may have to do some time. What will happen to Danny if she does?"

"He's fine. I convinced her three months ago to let him move into his own place, he's an independent man now," I smiled. "He's got staff that help him and a job to go to. He'll be fine."

"That's great!" he paused. "Look, I'm sorry it turned out this way...but, let me know where you land, okay?"

He patted my shoulder before leaving me alone to clean the mess and my face. I knew I couldn't stay and I didn't want to be in this city if Lori made bail. I wanted to make a clean break once and for all and leave my mistakes in the dust. My first call was to Danny to let him know what happened and he wasn't surprised because he knew his sister. He wished me luck and I promised I would call as soon as I got to where I was going.

I didn't have to think for very long about where I would go. My second call was the most important and long overdue.

Chapter Thirty-Two

Natalie

"*Eight-one twelve en route. Code two-seven GSW... thirty-three-year-old male. Have trauma standing by. ETA two minutes.*"

"Jesus," Cece's groan came from her gut. "Here we go."

She paused, turning to me. I was frozen in place and she watched as terror emerged from somewhere deep inside me. I knew her eyes looked at my hands, and she watched as the tremors violently overtook them and my arms.

She grabbed me with a vice-like grip, "Hey! Nat! It's fine...Carrie and I have this. You stay here and get the chart ready."

My throat was a desert and the act of swallowing felt like sand in the delicate tissue. I squeezed my eyes tight as if trying to dam what was about to happen, but the memories flooded anyway. I took a haggard breath and tried in vain to calm my nerves. Wetness wept from my palms and I was acutely aware of the hospital's seeming lack of air conditioning. My breath, once shallow just seconds before was now heaving with terror. I knew what was about to happen and I willed myself to stop it.

Five, four, three, two, one.

I opened my eyes. Five things I could see. The desk, Cece, the radio, the phone, the paperwork on the desk. Four. Four things I could touch. I laid my sweat-soaked palms on the counter and grasped the stainless steel. I let go and touched my friend's hand. Then the name tag hanging from the bottom of her scrubs; I felt the cracks in the plastic. With my free hand, I pressed it to my chest to feel my heartbeat.

Three. What could I hear? IV alarms, people's voices in the triage room, the whoosh of the glass doors. Two came more easily. I smelled the lavender soap Cece liked and the antiseptic cleaner. By the time I reached one, I was slowly chewing the small piece of mint gum in my mouth. I finally regained my bearings and turned to see Cece's dark eyes smiling encouragingly.

"Better?" she asked.

I nodded.

"You don't have to do this. Let Carrie—" Cece offered.

I shook my head, "No. I'm alright... a little nauseous, but okay. I can do this."

Cece nodded her agreement just as the bay doors slid open and the bedlam erupted. Without a second thought, I jumped into action meeting the medic at the door.

"We're barely holding onto a pulse," Carl, the paramedic nearest me stated with a tinge of urgency. "BP is eighty over fifty."

"Got it. We're taking him to three," I indicated as we pulled the gurney around a corner. As we entered the room, a trauma team met us and jumped in to get their new patient stabilized. After thirty minutes of bloody gauze, intravenous lines, and breathing tubes, I watched two aids and a nurse hurry the man up to the surgery suite via the large staff elevator.

I took a deep breath. It was done. I knew the test was over and I passed with flying colors. Now, whatever may come, the challenge could be met and conquered. Finally feeling good about myself, I made my way back to the nurses' station. To my surprise, Carl was still filling out the normal hand-off paperwork.

"Hey Carl...need to sharpen your pencil or something—" my final words faded in my throat as my stomach filled with stones. Finn Rafferty stood, in uniform next to Carl. Everyone in the immediate area felt the energy shift around them.

Carl looked up, and either was oblivious to the situation or ignored it, "Well, boys in blue followed us in...Rafferty here had to give them a report first." He took a beat. "Oh, sorry...Nat...this is Finn."

"Finn. Nice to see you again," I forced a smile that barely covered the instantaneous pain I felt. My skin crawled with Cece and Carrie's stares and my face blushed with embarrassment.

Trying to ease the awkwardness, Cece interceeded, "Hey Carl...you got a min. Come grab a cup of coffee with me."

Carl agreed and he and Carrie followed her tall frame around a corner. I immediately set to work gathering papers together for a chart. I desperately wanted to look into his eyes, but I also didn't. I knew what we felt for each other months ago was real, but *I* refused to admit it to him.

Was I too ashamed to look at him? Yes, but I still felt his eyes burning into me.

"Natalie..." his voice was soothing like the breeze off the water. Butterflies filled my guts and swarmed up my spine.

I looked at him sharply, "How have...you been?"

I would not cry.

"I've been...good. It's been a long time Natalie," the tenor of his words vibrated in my bones.

I had to play cool. I had to remember that this man chose to go back to an ex-wife that he didn't love and walked away from what he himself described as his *sacred salvation*. I will myself to get mad. I had to be angry with him. That small voice in my head fired back logic and reason softly.

'You didn't stop him.'

Damn it.

My mind reset. There was no way I could have any feelings for this man or any man for that matter; especially if what I suspected was true. There were other priorities now. Other things to consider. I had no time for any of those feelings anymore. The inner voice had no retort and was quiet.

"Yeah, it has been a while," I smiled a little more naturally, placing my hand on my hip. "When did you get back to Hanford?"

"A few days ago," he whispered.

I chuckled, "And you're already working?"

Finn nodded, "Chief was happy to see me. They've been pretty short-staffed."

"Yeah, we all have," we finally locked eyes. The moment hung thick in the air and I began to wonder if he could hear how loudly my heart was beating from where he stood. "I'd better get back to work...full moon, you know."

I brushed past him when I felt his warm and gentle grasp on my arm. Electricity shot through every nerve and every flesh memory I had of him ignited in my cells. I watched every moment we spent together flash before my eyes.

"I'm sorry, Natalie," his voice was low, the words vibrating on my ear drum. "I was wrong. I never should have left...Lori...always shows her true colors."

I looked up into the pained brilliant blueness of his eyes.

Those. Eyes.

He released me, "I'm here for good. Alone."

His hand dropped to his side and I stared again into those globes of sapphire before I took a deep breath and walked away, my words trailing in my wake.

"That's nice. I'm not."

Chapter
Thirty-Three

Natalie

Two days later, I sat on the side of the tub, the tears streamed from my eyes.

There was no denying it. No trick of the mind. No wondering if I was crazy or not. All three told me the same, exact thing. They stared at me like three stark judges, each one reminding me of how stupidly careless I was.

And nauseous. I felt nauseous.

I tried to fight it, but the waves came crashing over me and before I knew it, my head was draped in the toilet, retching. From somewhere beyond the bathroom door, I heard the lock release, an alarm code being punched in, and smelled a familiar scent. It was comforting and welcoming. Then again...

Head back in the toilet.

"Nat!" Cece's voice called out. "Nat! Where are you? Girl, did you oversleep again?"

She pushed the creaking bathroom door with the palm of her hand "Oh my God...Nat! Are you okay?"

"Yeah...I'll be fine. In like nine months," I spat one last time and grabbed a washcloth off the edge of the tub.

"What?"

Reaching for the sink, I pulled the three plastic sticks off its edge and handed them to my friend. As Cece took a moment to allow the information to settle in, I shut the lid of the toilet, flushed, and sat.

"Oh, honey," she muttered. "What are you gonna do?"

I rocked myself gently and closed my eyes. I had choices. I'd thought about every variable of each one for the last week. I didn't have to keep this pregnancy at all or I could give a family that desperately wanted one the child they dreamed of, but neither of those options appealed to me.

I sighed, "I'm going to keep it. I know it's not what Liam would have wanted...he never wanted children. But...I'm sure he didn't want two bullets in his chest either." I choked a sardonic laugh. "I never thought about having a kid before... I accepted that with Liam. I was fine with that decision if we one day got serious. Not that we would have. But he's not here and I am. So...this is what I'm doing."

"Then I'm going to say congratulations, Mom," Cece wrapped her arms around me tight. "I always wanted to be an Auntie!"

"Good! Because this kids' gonna need a family," I laughed through rivers of tears and hugged her back. "Let me wash my face again and I'll be ready to go."

After splashing cold water on my already pale, damp skin, I ran a brush through my hair and swept it into a pony. I grabbed my duffel and the pair of us were out of the door in minutes. Cece pulled from my drive when I noticed a worried expression cross her face.

"What?" I asked, sipping from my water bottle.

She frowned, "Nothing."

I rolled my eyes, "Christ, out with it."

"I just wonder how Finn Rafferty is going to take it, that's all," she lifted a shoulder.

Finn was on my mind from the moment I ran into him a week ago, but thoughts of a potential pregnancy overshadowed everything.

"It doesn't matter," I whispered.

Cece, clearly startled, gave me as much side eye as she could without putting us into jeopardy on the road, "Girl...don't play me. That man is in love with you...always has been. Now, for the life of me, I have no idea why he would leave and go back to his ex. I mean, it was pretty damn clear she was lying, but what he feels for you is as obvious as it is that I'm black and you're white. I mean, I know you said you weren't in love with him but...you don't think he'll have an opinion? You don't think this is going to affect him?"

"Why? Why would it affect him, Cece?" I demanded as her comment tore into my soul. "He left. I can't have a relationship after that? I'm supposed to worry about how it may or may not eventually affect *him*?"

"I'm not trying to upset you—"

"I'm not upset...but...not all of that is entirely true," I murmured more to myself than her.

The ridges in Cece's brow wrinkle upward, "Which part?"

I met her with silence.

"Nat. Which. Part?" she wasn't about to give up or let it go.

"The part about me not being in love with him," I confessed. I couldn't lie anymore and felt a small weight lift when I said it. I did my best to hide my feelings when Finn left seven months ago, even going so far as burying my sorrows in another man. But as deep as I'd like to think I shoved those feelings, in reality, they were always just below the rocky surface.

"I knew it!" she exclaimed. She enjoyed being right. "You aren't as slick as you think you are. I *knew* you were lying...' *It was just a fling, Cece'*. Fling my ass."

We drove in silence for a moment before she dared to ask another question, "Then why on earth did he go back?"

There was the crux of the issue and I didn't want to admit why. I didn't want to tell my best friend that I'd been lying for months about what happened and that Finn wasn't entirely to blame. Part of our breakup was my fault. Calling it a pig-headed overreaction was only the beginning. The nausea churned but I didn't know if it was because of the hormones or shame. I swallowed hard and took a deep breath.

"I never asked him to stay."

Chapter Thirty-Four

Finn

The doors slid wide and the cold, sterile air of the emergency room blasted me in the face. I stepped around the corner of the triage station and determined that someone, anyone would talk to me. It was exactly eight days since our first and only conversation since I moved back. It was bad enough that Natalie was avoiding me at every turn, but now even Becca and Carrie wouldn't make eye contact. I got it and I probably deserved the silent treatment to an extent. I left her but she didn't give me any other options either. One word. One word would have stopped me in my tracks and saved me from the heartache and anger of the better part of a year.

I didn't blame her for any of it. I fully accepted my responsibility for everything that happened. I allowed Lori to manipulate me. She used my willingness to help anyone in need and I was a complete sucker for her lies. Goddamn it! I should have seen it. From the moment she slithered into Hanford, I should have known she was lying. It's all she knows; lies, deceit, and anything that makes life complicated. Life with Natalie wasn't problematic and I missed her every day I was gone.

All of my could haves, and would haves shouldn't have mattered since Natalie had moved on with her life, but I needed to make her understand how sorry I was about leaving. I needed her to know that I'd thought about her every day I was in San Jose and every single minute since I've been back. I knew it wasn't fair to ask for one, but if she would give me a second chance, I'd live my life proving to her how much she meant to me.

I was living a pipe dream because that wasn't going to happen. She said so herself.

I turned another corner and saw the person I was looking for, "Cece."

She huffed a breath, "Rafferty."

"I deserve that," I nodded. "Can we talk? Just five minutes."

She eyed me, her entire body wound like a spring, and for a moment I thought I was done. Cece was a force of nature, I knew that. But to my complete surprise, she pointed for me to follow her to an unused exam room. Setting her bag and keys on the gurney, she crossed her arms, "So talk."

"Yeah, okay." I swallowed hard and rubbed my hands together, "I'm sorry for what happened between Natalie and me. I was and *am* a complete asshole...and I know that."

"Go on," she agreed.

"I just want to talk to her...like, *really* talk to her. I know I can't change what happened and she's with someone...but," I paused. "Damn it! I don't know what to do! She's avoiding me. Even here...she won't even take the report from me. Cece, I didn't mean to hurt her."

"So what? You should've known that girl well enough to know that she hides her feelings...and for good reason." She glowered with a scoff at me, "If you were so in love with her, you would know that much. That isn't rocket science."

I nodded, "You're right. I let myself get played by Lori and it hurt Natalie."

"Speaking of...exactly what story did your ex give you that you thought it was okay to run out on Nat? Because," Cece laughed indignantly, "I can't imagine anything so important."

I shook my head, "It doesn't matter."

"It does to *me*. If you think for one second I'm going to let you get anywhere near that girl without an explanation," she crossed her arms again, unmoving and unwavering. "Then you really have lost your damn mind."

I didn't want to rehash the entire pathetic and albeit infuriating seven months with her. But, Cece's body language told me she wasn't going to hear any further arguments to the contrary or let me out of this room without knowing the whole embarrassing story. And as uncomfortable as it made me to admit that I'd fallen for one of my ex's games again, I would do anything if it meant I would get to talk to Natalie. I drew a deep breath and let it out slowly.

"Lori knows me and all of my soft spots. She got me really good this time," I winced at the painful memory. "Cancer. She told me she had fucking cancer and that she had no one to be with her at the end. She gave me a sob story that no one in the world could understand what it felt like to be close to death...to know that the last breath you took before you went to sleep could very well be your last. And how Danny would be all alone in the world and so confused when she was gone. He needed someone he could trust."

Cece cocked a curious brow in my direction.

"Danny is her brother. He has Cerebral Palsy and she's his sole caregiver," I explained and her expression relaxed in understanding. "She had me, Cece. I know what it's like to look down at death. And Danny? No way I'd ever let him think he had no one...I still love that kid. I struggled over this...I asked Natalie to tell me what she thought. I got the sense she was hiding again. Then when her walls went up...and that was it. You have to know that leaving wasn't the original plan but, the conversation was over. I felt like the choice was made."

I must have looked pathetic or she could see I was ready to fall on my knees begging because I watched her shoulders droop in resignation.

"I know, Finn," she said softly.

I blinked, "What do you know?"

"How she didn't ask you to stay and practically acted like it was no big deal," she paused. "It was, by the way...a very big deal."

My heart pounded in my chest and I wanted to ask so many questions, but I let her continue and didn't interrupt.

She sighed, "She was devastated...we all saw it. She was in love with you. Your leaving crushed her."

My gut was right back then and I ignored it. I hated myself.

"But she pretended she was fine...she's really good at that, you know," she said.

I rolled my eyes because I most certainly knew.

"Look, she's going through some pretty big stuff right now...and that's the reason she's trying to stay out of your way. She doesn't know how to reconcile you being back and this...*situation* she has."

I heard her words but she sounded more worried than I would expect. A flash of Drew with his hand squeezed tight on her wrist came to mind and an old anger churned.

"Situation? Cece, what's going on?" I asked darkly.

She shook her head, "It's not my story to tell. But, you need to talk to her." She raised her brow at me, "Are you hearing me, Rafferty? You *need* to talk to Nat."

She emphasized each word and I was getting her point, "Yeah...yeah, I've got it."

"Good," her head bobbed, and she gathered her stuff off the gurney. "She's home tonight...she doesn't go out much right now."

"I wouldn't want to interrupt if her...guy is over," I swallowed hard. The thought of Natalie with someone else flipped my stomach, even though I knew I had no right to her.

Cece pursed her lips, "There isn't anyone, Finn."

"But, she said she was seeing someone."

The woman shook her head.

"Cece," I braced myself for the answer to my final question, "Is it Drew? Is he bothering her again?"

She huffed a derisive chortle, "The only way that psycho will stop is when he's in a body bag. But for now, the next best thing is that he's still in jail."

I allowed her words to marinate as I followed in her wake. I made a mental note to catch up with Detective Callahan later and then prayed to whoever would listen that Natalie was safe and that he wasn't bothering her from his cell. I slid into the driver's seat of my Bronco and headed for Natalie's.

Chapter Thirty-Five

Natalie

The day was too long and all I could think about was dropping into my bed. My warm, comforting, soft bed. Whether the exhaustion I felt was work or the growing life inside of me, neither mattered, I just had to answer to it.

Delilah curled next to me and purred softly. Deciding to watch one episode of television and then succumb to the power of sleep, my eyes were already heavy when I heard the knock on the door. Checking the clock on the wall, I knew it was too late for Cece or anyone else in our group to pop in. Besides, Cece had a key and a code, so she'd be more likely to just let herself inside anyway. Displacing the cat onto another cushion, an act that elicited a glare of condemnation from her royal highness, I looked through the peephole.

It was Finn.

The butterflies of old reemerged, dancing and flittering their way down my backbone into the bottom of my stomach. I took a heavy breath and opened the door.

"Hey," Finn stared. I took this as a sign that he was unsure what to say.

"Hey," was my response.

"Can we..." he looked around nervously. "I think we need to have a conversation."

I nodded and allowed him to pass by.

"Have a seat...can I get you something to drink? I've got ginger ale," I offered, pointing to my half-full glass.

"I'd rather stand and no thanks," his words were sharp and I wondered if that was their intent. I was certain he wanted to know why I was avoiding him. I could read him like a book and knew he had questions that demanded answers. If I were being honest, I was surprised he hadn't shown up on my doorstep sooner. The more he took me in with those eyes, all the anger or irritation with me that shadowed him was melting away.

"I want to know why you didn't ask me to stay," he blurted boldly.

My throat tightened at his directness. How would I answer that when I don't even know myself? I wanted to scream that I was stupid and scared but that isn't what came out.

"Would it have mattered?" I whispered.

"Yes! Yes Natalie! It would have mattered...it all would have mattered!" Finn's eyes were desperately crazed. "I never would have left you."

"But you did," I saw my words were like hot iron to his flesh, branding and scarring him.

"Because I didn't know how you felt! Jesus Christ, Natalie! How much more obvious did I have to make it for you?" he cried.

"Oh, so you choosing to go back to Lori's bed is my fault?" I shot back angrily.

Finn's hands raised in defense, "No...that's not what I'm saying. I just mean that if I were given all the information, if we could have just talked. If you would have answered one of my texts...I would have made the right choice back then."

He stopped cold and I could see his throat drying. He was *really* nervous.

"I didn't sleep with her."

I glowered, "What?"

"Lori. We didn't...I mean, we never had sex. I had my own place...and it wasn't like that. I know that's what she wanted but..." he swallowed hard. "There's not been anyone...you know...since you."

My brain froze and no words were formed. I was standing, I'm sure quite visibly shocked and the only sound I could make was, "Oh."

"Is that why you're avoiding me?"

"I'm not avoiding you," I lied.

Finn narrowed his eyes, "You are. And I want to know why."

"I'm not—"

"Stop, Natalie. Just stop...I talked to Cece," he raised his hand again, but this time in protest. "You've never lied to me before...except when it was about your feelings. Why are you doing it now?"

"What did she tell you?" my heartbeat flared fiercely and with such strength, I heard the rush of blood in my ears. How much did she tell him? I felt my pulse flutter and a cold sweat break out on my neck; I was starting to panic.

Finn clenched his jaw, "Not much...just that I *had* to talk to you. She was pretty clear on that."

Relief washed over me and it didn't go unnoticed.

"There! You're hiding something," his voice was surgical and he stepped toward me to touch my face softly. "Please, I'm begging you to tell me."

I hung my head in resignation. He would find out eventually and it might as well be from my own mouth and not the gossip mill of Southwest Haven or the Hanford Fire Department. I thought quickly about the words I wanted to say, but nothing sounded right. I finally decided that a direct approach was best, rip the bandaid, so to speak. I drew a breath and held it.

"I'm pregnant."

He looked like I just spoke to him in a foreign language.

"Wh...what?" The shock of my statement broke his words. Another moment of pressurized silence hung between us before he broke it again quietly, "Well...you did say you weren't alone anymore."

All I could read was the heartbreak on his face. While my confession in the hospital wasn't exactly a lie, it was a purposeful misdirection. Technically, I wasn't alone as I had a small human growing inside me, but I knew the inference it made. I also knew it was hitting below the belt and I felt guilt rising.

I shook my head, "Actually...I am. I mean...I'm not with the father. He died...a month ago."

"Natalie, I'm sorry. Cece didn't tell me that," he replied.

"I'm sorry for what it sounded like when we ran into each other. I wasn't exactly sure what to say, but there wasn't and isn't anyone, Finn...I'm alone."

Chapter Thirty-Six

Finn

Natalie's unreleased tears her hazel eyes held glittered like diamonds across the water and I wanted to dive into them. I looked down at her abdomen, imagining it swollen with growing life. Feelings I never imagined I'd have washed over me as I stared at her.

When it was explained to me as a young teen that I would never be a father, I took it as a trade. I gave up my ability to reproduce in exchange for my life. It seemed fair at the time, a deal with a well-meaning devil. But as I grew older and watched friends around me build families, I started to wish life had dealt me a better hand.

I moved toward her slowly, weaving my fingers into hers, and pulled her into me. Her presence was warm against mine and I felt the missing part of my soul lock into place like it did last summer. Our mouths crashed and I kissed her with all the longing of star-crossed lovers. Her body melted into mine; her curves were a perfect match for me. I held her against my chest gently, fearing she would push me away.

Her mouth tasted the same as it always did; soft, strong, and sweet. I touched her back lightly and hoped the same memories flooded her mind. Her tears fell into salty rivers on her cheeks as our lips parted from each other.

"I'm sorry," she wiped the wetness from her face. She turned away from me but not quick enough for me to see her clearly. She looked humiliated. Anger rose in my core and I cursed at myself. I never wanted her to feel anything but happiness.

"Why?" I demanded quietly. "Natalie...you have nothing to be sorry about."

I hated seeing her cry. I swore I could never cause this woman any pain, but I've realized that is exactly what happened when I left. I made a terrible decision seven months ago that wrecked the woman I loved. I turned her to face me and bent, forcing her to look me in the eyes, "Natalie...let me help you. I want to help you."

She continued to swipe at her face with the sleeve of her sweatshirt, "What?"

I knew what I wanted, what I wanted from the second we met, and what I needed to do. My life became immediately clear in that delicate moment. I loved her with every cell of my being and I would not lose her again. I lifted her chin with my finger, "I'm your guy."

"Finn—"

"Natalie...listen to me! You are the only woman I have ever really loved in my life. I made a mistake by not fighting for you harder...making you tell me what I already knew. I pretended that all of the crap you went through didn't matter and that if you did love me, really love me, you would have told me. But I was so wrong...it did matter. Every broken piece of you mattered. I meant everything I said...you are my sacredness. I want to do this with you...please," my excitement rose with every word I spoke.

"I don't need you to save me, Finn. I'm not a damsel in distress," she snapped.

"I don't want to save you! I want to be a part of this... family," I implored. "I want to have this baby with you!"

Natalie shook her head, "Finn, you never wanted children."

"No! I accepted my fate that I *couldn't* have them. There's a differ-ence and I was fine with that...but," I drew a held breath. "If I could, if somehow the universe could give me that ability, I would only want them with you."

"You don't mean that—"

Frustration roiled inside me, "I do! God! Natalie...why are you so opposed to having someone love you? Is it me? Is that it? Just tell me...because this hole inside me that has grown for months is going to swallow me. I knew you were the one from the moment I saw you...I have never lied to you...never then and not now."

Natalie had no way of stopping the rivers that poured from her eyes. I was aware that what I said was the one thing she never knew how to tell people. It was her darkest secret that drilled into her soul and festered like a gangrenous wound. Drew was the trauma that cut deep. I saw her struggle with the memories of old bruises and threats and they clouded her mind as she shut her eyes to shut out the pain.

"You will never understand, Finn. I'm...broken. I'm not even sure if I can be loved...I'm closed off. I have walls...I hate looking in the mirror most days. You will be better off staying as far away from me as possible," she gave up trying to divert the tears.

"Don't say that...none of that is true, Natalie." I grasped her shoul-ders gently, "You're not broken. You are the light in every vision and dream I've ever conceived. You are beautiful. Stop allowing a man who never loved you to get in the way of the one that does. Stop allowing him all that power."

I wrapped my arms around her body as she collapsed to my chest. She was still crying, but she rested her head against me and drowned in the comfort my embrace gave.

"I love you, Natalie," I drew her back, brushing my finger through the loose strands of brunette that haloed her face. I fell to my knees, at her feet, and laid my head on her belly. I resigned to be at peace with whatever choice she made.

She stroked my head and I prayed she knew everything I said was true; she did and had always allowed her past with Drew to get between us. I didn't blame her. I could not imagine the kind of hell he put her through before we knew each other and the hell he still put her through. If I thought about it too long, I knew my own rage would take over which wasn't helpful. I knew she would think of this baby's father just like Lori would always be somewhere for me. But whatever feelings I ever had for Lori were microscopic sand when compared to the hail of stardust I felt for Natalie. That one summer, last summer, was nothing short of sensational, infinite magic. Having her next to me, I felt her raw emotion, and I hoped she felt my devotion to her moving to connect my soul to hers like it did before.

She ran her warm hands over my head, and I heard her whisper, "I love you too."

Chapter Thirty-Seven

Finn

My stunned eyes stared into her face and my gaze never faltered but rose with me as I stood from the floor. Those were the words I waited for what felt like my entire life to hear. I found her delicate lips with mine and we collided in our dance together; our kisses more passionate with every wave of electricity that coursed between us. I was desperate for time to slow down. I wanted to remain in her arms, on her lips like this for an eternity.

I buried my face in her neck and hair and consumed her scent. A gentle mix of honeysuckle and light musk sent another bolt of pleasure to my toes. I laid a light trail of kisses on her neck and took in the sensation of her soft skin. Memories of her nude body on mine drove me to the brink of euphoric delirium and felt my erection growing. I wanted her again like I had never wanted anyone since, but I knew it wasn't the right time. It wasn't befitting of what she deserved. She was vulnerable. I had never taken advantage of any woman, and I certainly wouldn't start. I tilted her head back in my hands and separated from her to stare into her gold-flecked eyes for a long moment.

"What's wrong?" Natalie furrowed her brow.

My sharp breath fell and I shook my head, "I won't do anything to hurt you. This can wait."

"I know I'm kinda a mess—"

"No! No...not that," I pecked her lips. "You're... beautiful. I just want this to be...good. Pure. You know?"

A small scoff fell and a smirk pulled at the corner of Natalie's mouth, "I think that ship has sailed for us, Finn. Two words: Santa. Barbara."

A devilish grin that I knew she thought was wildly sexy spread across my face, and I laughed, "I know, I know. But, Natalie, I would never violate anyone like that... especially you. You mean too much to me. You just let me back in your life five minutes ago...I've got seven months' worth of trust to rebuild with you."

My hands fell to my sides, "I'd better go. I'm sure you're tired."

"No!" she latched my fingers in hers. "Please. Don't. I mean..."

Her voice trailed off and Natalie watched the tiny wrinkles in my forehead peak. I knew she saw my eyes sink into an expression that screamed that I didn't want to leave.

"Unless you *have* to..." she held her breath.

A smile spread on my lips again, "I can stay as long as you want."

An hour passed in complete silence as Natalie leaned, curled into my side on the sofa. Her drowsy, unfocused eyes blinked slowly as I felt her body relax with each minute. Delilah, feeling completely ignored and deciding only twenty minutes ago to accept her suddenly new status as the number two cuddler, lay loafed at my feet.

"I don't think she's jealous," I finally commented softly.

Natalie's eyes batted, "Who?"

"Delilah. She's giving me *the look*," a velvety chortle emanated from my chest.

"Hmmmmm..."

I looked to find her asleep. I slowly retracted my arm, careful not to wake her. I lifted her, cradling her into my chest, and carried her to the bedroom. As I gently pulled the quilt over her, she touched my hand. Her fingertips covered mine and the sensation sent sparks into my arm.

"Are you leaving?" her voice was heavy with fatigue in the darkness.

The street lights created dabbled light in the room but it was just enough that I saw her face clearly and I bent toward her. Brushing a lock of hair from her eyes, I whispered, "Not if you want me to stay."

"Don't go," her fingers held my hand as I caressed her face.

"Okay," I whispered. After kicking my shoes off at the end of the bed, I crawled in next to her and pulled her into my chest. I kissed the soft skin of her cheek. I lay there, my nose in her hair, breathing in her perfume, my protective arms holding my treasure. I waited until her breathing told me she was truly out before I closed my eyes.

"Peaceful dreams, my salvation," my words drifted like an affirmation into the night.

Chapter Thirty-Eight

Natalie

The room was still dark but scattered with light from outside when I jolted awake. It took me several seconds to remember that I wasn't dreaming and that it was Finn's gentle breathing I heard next to me. My back was to him, his arm draped over my waist and his nose buried in my hair. Not wanting to disturb him, I held my breath and rolled to my other side, facing him.

Even in the shadows, his face was gloriously handsome. I noticed his hair was a bit longer than I remembered, but still neatly trimmed. My eyes searched his features in the flecked light of the bedroom and flashes of memory shot through my brain like lightning. Our day on the beach in Morrow Bay and the way his arms felt when he first wrapped them around me. The freedom I felt in the water the day we learned to dive in Pismo. The rush of the world as it flew by me on the back of his motorcycle. The warmth of his nude body as we cuddled in his bed.

That summer seemed endless.

The pain of missing him was the last recollection. I felt the tears grow in my eyes and I squeezed them shut but it didn't stop the drops from falling to my chin. I moved my hand to wipe them away and my fingers accidentally brushed across his stubbled jaw. Finn absently licked his lips in the dark. Those perfect instruments that could curl my toes and make my knees into Jell-O.

A long-familiar quake softly gained traction in my gut and spread to my thighs.

'What in God's name am I thinking?'

He said he didn't want to move too fast, but he was doing it for my sake. Did he want to protect me? From what, exactly? Was he afraid of hurting me or was it me who would hurt him? I knew now how much pain I caused him by ignoring his pleas for contact. We both made mistakes. He said he wanted to regain my trust, but I wondered if I should do the same. I thought maybe the questions rolling in my head would extinguish the fire roaring in my core but they didn't.

Raising my finger I lightly traced the edge of his jaw. I inched closer until I felt his breath on my face and the heat from his face on mine. I desperately wanted to have him in the same way I did months ago. Was he scared? Or was it me?

To my surprise, his eyes slowly opened and he stared at me. I didn't shift or make a sound. We lay in suspended silence for what seemed like an eternity daring the other to move first. In the end, I'm the one that fell over the cliff. I leaned forward slowly and put my lips on his. It was the push he needed because in that instant he consumed me.

Rolling to his back, he lifted me onto his chest and we stared at each other through every motion of our lips. It wasn't until his hand was lost in my hair that my eyes rolled and I broke our gaze. His free hand roved over my body as mine crawled under his tee shirt. I felt his skin pucker and his muscles tremble under my touch. I pulled away from his kiss long enough to slide his shirt over his head and tossed it to the floor. I have never wanted a person as much as I wanted Finn Rafferty at that moment. My soul and my pussy ached for him.

I stripped out of my hoodie and pressed my breasts against his warmth. Our mouths danced again, but this time a little more feverishly as we were like the tides at sea; ebbing and flowing to a passionate rhythm. I found his belt buckle, unlashed it, pulled hard on the button of his pants, and rid him of those too. His wandering hands smoothed over my leggings-covered ass; his fingers just grazing over my valley and my entrance flooded with excitement. His cock was immediately hard.

Flipping to my back, Finn's mouth laid a trail of kisses along my neck and shoulder until he was devouring my nipples. He didn't stay in one spot for long as his tongue ran a path past my navel. Hooking his fingers on either side of my tight pants, Finn pulled them off me and to the floor. He spread my thighs and with the tip of his tongue, massaged my clit gently.

I moaned in delight as I wound my fingers through his sandy hair. He worked my bud until I was ready to give up every molecule of my body to the universe when he stopped. I looked down to find him staring into my eyes; his face begging me to watch him work. I obliged him until the waves of my orgasm crashed over me and my hands clutched onto the sheets as I kept the world from turning upside down. Just as the last sweet sensations of climax rolled over me, Finn drove his cock into my gates. I cried out in relief and waited for the release I needed from him.

But he didn't move, he instead hovered over me propped on his forearms, stroking wisps of hair from my face, his erection buried deep inside me. His gentle timbre cut through the darkness.

"I meant what I said...there's only you. I can't go back."

I kissed him softly, "I know. And there's no one telling you no."

Finn pushed further and my core clung to him. Our bodies rocked in a pulsing rhythm, magnetically drawn to each other. Wrapping my hands around his tight ass, my fingers latched into his muscle and drove him harder. Finn's eyes rolled as his knees dug further into the mattress and grasped onto my shoulders, holding on as if his life depended on it. It occurred to me that this simply wasn't enough. I wanted to be with him, but I wanted him to remember it for the rest of his life. I never wanted him to forget that I was the one that he loved and I knew exactly how to seal that image in his mind.

I moved my body so he would roll me on top, which he did flawlessly. My knees pressed into his hips as I began my rhythmic stride, my muscles stroking his length from base to tip. I flipped my long hair away from my face and to the side so he knew I was watching every movement his body made with mine. I cupped my breasts in my hands making sure to draw his attention as they bounced with each measured stroke. The headboard knocked fiercely against the wall and I felt Finn's abs tighten under my hands as I balanced myself. His eyes rolled and I hooked my finger under his chin.

"Don't look away," I whispered breathlessly.

I picked up my pace, driving him to the edge of the cosmos as Finn came undone.

Chapter Thirty-Nine

Natalie

"Oh God, will this ever stop?"

I wasn't exactly sure to whom I was speaking as I sat, crossed-legged, at the base of my toilet. If there was a God, his sense of humor was as shitty as I felt. The bathroom door swung open behind me and I felt familiar hands gently gather my hair.

"Get out of here, you don't need to see this," I groaned.

Finn didn't move, "Yeah, you've said that the past three weeks. Just shut up and let me hold your hair."

I could hear the smile in his voice and while I'd like to say it annoyed me, it was also comforting. We hadn't officially said it out loud or even told our friends, but we had effectively been living together for almost a month. There were adjustments for both of us, but mostly Finn wasn't exactly comfortable moving into my bedroom initially and insisted on staying in the guest room for the first few days. But, as my morning sickness evolved into an all-day and night vomit fest, he was quickly convinced that the closer he was to me, the better. While I loved having him here, my guilt burned as much as my indigestion because he did everything for me.

Not only did he hold my hair, but he cooked and did the laundry. He catered to anything I needed. We spent our evenings watching TV or talking until late at night and reacquainting with each other. A lot had happened in seven months but we didn't seem to miss a beat and picked up where we left off. I really missed him on the nights he was on duty. I could not stress enough just how much his being here meant to me.

It was during one of our long talks after dinner one night when he asked about Liam. This time, I didn't try to hide or evade anything like I did with Drew. I knew I could be open with him and that he was a safe place for me to be honest and raw. My relationship with Liam was vastly different than with my ex or Finn. While we shared a friendship, everything else was casual. We were never emotionally deep. Liam was never a replacement for Finn, only a placeholder.

"What exactly happened?" Finn asked.

I drew in a long breath, laying my head against the back of the sofa, "Liam was the manager of a restaurant downtown. He was working one night and from all accounts, helping his kitchen staff close up. He told them he would take the last two bags of trash out. Next thing they hear is two shots and a car racing down the street."

Finn took my hand and squeezed.

"I was working the night they brought him in," my eyes were cloudy with tears. "I froze when I saw him. I only remember Cece pulling me out of the room and Carrie running in. I stood outside and watched...they couldn't bring him back."

I let the tears fall but I didn't sob, "Liam was a good man and didn't deserve to be killed. I don't know what I would have done had he lived though. He...was adamant about not having children. I know he would be furious right now."

Finn sighed, "Natalie, you don't know what he would have said or done. There is a very good chance he would have loved this child."

"I don't think so. It was definitely a deal breaker," I laughed tensely. "I guess it doesn't matter now."

"It's hard losing someone you love," he tried to console me.

"I didn't love him, Finn. Like I said, he was convenient and fun to be around...but he was never you."

A heavy silence filled the space and his hand tightened on mine. Besides Dr. Carys, I had never admitted to anyone how I really felt about Liam. In a way, it was cathartic to recognize that while Liam and I had some good times, had he lived, our days as a couple, as loose as it was, would have had an expiration date.

"Natalie," Finn's brow furrowed, "Did they ever find the shooter? Did he have enemies?"

I shook my head, "No. Nothing. From what I understand, the police think it was a drive-by...maybe mistaken identity."

Part of me feared after our talk, that when he knew everything, Finn might decide that this wasn't what he wanted, and that much like Liam, children were a non-starter. But, he did the exact opposite: it made him more determined to be whatever I needed him to be for me and this child. With him, and Cece, I didn't think this baby would ever want for a single thing; and neither would I.

"Damn it! God...I'll do anything," I retched again.

Finn's hand was cool on my face, "Don't make promises you can't keep."

I groaned and finally flushed. He helped me to my feet, handing me a wet cloth to wipe my face. I leaned into him, resting my head on his chest as he held me against him.

"When is this going to end?" I whined.

He looked at me in the mirror, "What is it they call it? The glow? You've got that."

"It's the blood rushing to my head from the handstands in the toilet," I jabbed him hard in the side with my elbow. He threw back his head in deep laughter, but after a moment he was still watching me.

"What?" I asked, grabbing my toothbrush.

His face was serious but pleasant when he said, "You're beautiful."

Chapter Forty

Finn

Late spring turned to summer then turned into fall and I watched with impatient anticipation as the child inside Natalie grew. By mid-September, our lives were fully melded and our routines were yen and yang. I was grateful that she allowed me to hold her while I fell asleep every night and wake up next to her every day.

As immeasurable as our blissful existence had become, there were still lives to be lived and bills to be paid. With a new baby on the way, I wanted to be sure he or she would have everything they needed. Because Natalie's morning sickness ran well into her second trimester, I waited until the worst was over and took all the overtime I could physically handle. It was on one of these extra shifts when someone I never thought would show his face again; because he swore he wouldn't after his retirement, walked in the door early one morning.

"I thought you got a real job, Rafferty," Marc bellowed, his round face shaking in laughter. "How the hell are you kid?"

"Hey old man, I thought you retired?" I laughed as my old partner wrapped me in a bear hug. "I'm good."

I was good. Very good.

"I understand better than good," he smirked.

Crinkling my face in confusion, I chuckled, "What are you talking about?"

"Boy, don't play games with me. I hear that gorgeous woman took your sorry ass back and now you're gonna be a dad in a couple of months," he laughed. "You sure didn't waste any time, huh kid. Congratulations!"

"Oh, yeah!" I lied. "Thanks, old man."

While we tried to keep the rumor mills at bay, Natalie and I neglected to tell people the complete and whole story. In my opinion, it was none of anyone's business what was going on in her life or mine. If they made assumptions, it was fine, but I didn't think either of us anticipated that I being the baby's father would be one of them. I also couldn't blame anyone either, no one other than Natalie and probably Cece knew my story.

"Natalie!" I called out, tossing my bag next to the door that night. "Baby? Where are you?"

A small voice called out, "Back here."

Walking through the house, I found the bathroom door closed but the light shining under its crack. I knocked, "Hey, you okay?"

"Yeah."

Water splashed and I started changing out of my uniform and into a pair of shorts and a tee shirt, "You'll never believe who came by today...Marc! It was good to see him, but...I don't think we did a very good job with gossip control. Even he knows...well, he knows a version that I think is the narrative right—"

"Uhmm...Finn. Can you help me for a second?" her voice behind the door sounded defeated.

"Sure...what's wrong?" I said as I opened the door to find Natalie sitting in the bathtub full of water on all fours. I grabbed a towel and jumped to the edge, "What the hell are you doing!?"

"Trying to crane me and this baby out of the bath. But I can't," her voice shook and for a second I thought she was getting ready to cry, but the sound that came out was rolls of laughter. "Oh my God...Finn...call for a lift assist. I can't get out."

Her uninhibited amusement sent me into full roars. I finally got her pulled upright, between breaks of raucous laughter, and sitting on the edge of the tub with her robe. She had to take several deep breaths to finally stop giggling at herself.

After a moment, and one final deep breath, she looked at me curiously, "What narrative?"

"What?"

"Before. You said Marc came by and we didn't control the story enough. What did you mean?" she grabbed a towel off the hook and wrapped her hair up.

I shrugged, "The little game of telephone has you taking me back and that the baby is mine."

She stared at me for a long moment but it wasn't something I could read. I didn't want her to be angry that I didn't correct my old partner on the spot, but I also didn't think it was my place to tell her business. Neither of us could blame people for what they thought because it did look exactly what Marc described. Only Cece knew Natalie was six weeks pregnant when I showed back up in Hanford, and it was a week later that she told me. So, the assumptions made sense. But at that moment, I was regretting even telling her what Marc said.

"I'm sorry...I'll call him and explain," I offered.

"No," her head shook and she moved closer to me. Wrapping her arms around my neck, her swollen abdomen was pressed against me, "I'm glad that's what he thinks. We don't have to tell anyone anything different...if you're okay with it?"

Her large hazel eyes bore into my soul and my breath caught in my chest. I was more than okay with that option and it was something I wanted more than anything.

"I've been thinking about something else too...but, it's a much bigger ask," she continued and waited for my nod for her to go on. "You can say no, and I won't be upset, okay?"

I nodded again.

She took a deep breath, "I want you to be this baby's father...I mean, you already are, but officially. I want to give it your name."

Now, I couldn't breathe at all. All the wind had been knocked out of my lungs and I didn't know if my brain remembered how to inhale. Elation filled my veins and I felt like I might explode. It was my turn for tears and I found Natalie's lips with mine.

"Are you serious?" I could hardly contain my excitement.

"Yes, I'm serious," she beamed.

Falling to my knees, I open her robe to expose her belly. I placed my hands on either side, kissed her navel, and rested my head.

"I can't wait to meet you, Baby Rafferty."

Chapter Forty-One

Finn

"Did you remember the little pink bag?" Natalie asked suddenly. "The one with the glitter?"

We were up early and set out to make the three-hour drive to Palo Alto. It was Harbor's second birthday and the first time Natalie would meet my sister, her wife, and their daughter and we wanted to make a whole day of it. I would also tell my sister about the surprise I had hinted at for a week.

The traffic on Charleston Road was running as good as could be expected as we cruised along toward Sadie's apartment on Arastradero. We had made good time which made me happy because it meant more fun with my niece.

I smiled at Natalie, who I could tell was nervous, "Baby, relax. I got all the gifts. Why are you so edgy?"

She gave me a look of exasperation that made me chuckle. She tugged at the sleeves of her loose-fitting dress; she was still trying to get used to the changes in her body, but I secretly suspected she felt self-conscious.

"Seriously? I'm meeting your family, Finn. I just hope your sister likes me," she started to wring her hands together. "I mean, how is she going to feel about this...situation? I just wished you would have told her before we came."

I realized this was more than just her being apprehensive, this was full-on anxiety and I may have inadvertently made it worse. I cupped my free hand on hers, "I'm so sorry. It's hard to get Sadie on the phone long enough to have a real conversation with her...she's so busy with school. But, that's no excuse. You're right, I should have told them already. But, Natalie...she's going to love you."

"How can you know that?" she snorted.

"Because I do," I squeezed her hand.

After finding an empty guest spot on the street next to Sadie's complex, Natalie and I unloaded our packages and found our way to her second-floor apartment. Before I could ring the bell, the door swung open and my little sister greeted us with a squeal.

"Finny! I'm so glad you're here!" she threw her arms around my neck and pulled me tight.

I cut my eyes at Natalie and saw her sly smile at the mention of my sister's nickname for me. I gave her a playful look of warning but I knew the name would be used against me at some point. Sadie's hug broke away and I turned toward Natalie.

"Sadie, this is Natalie."

My sister gave her a wide and genuinely happy smile, "It's so nice to meet you! Finny talks about you all the time...I'm so glad you came."

I watched Natalie's entire body relax before my eyes as we followed Sadie inside.

"Brooke will be out in a minute, she's changing Harbor. Can I get you guys some coffee?" she walked into the kitchen of the open-plan room.

"Sure sis, I'll take one," I replied then turned to Natalie who shook her head.

Sadie busied herself with her espresso machine, "What about you, Natalie? Can I get you one?"

"Oh, no thank you," she replied.

"You sure? I guess I've hung around too many law students and paramedics. I thought ER nurses had the same caffeine addictions," my sister laughed, as she packed coffee in the portafilter.

Natalie cut her eyes at me and stared, "Oh, we do for sure. I'm just not drinking a lot of coffee right now."

She gave me a look that told me to open my mouth and explain.

"Hey Sade, can you put all that stuff down for a minute so we can talk?" I asked as Natalie and I took a seat at the barstools. My sister stopped tamping the coffee and turned to face us.

Her eyes narrowed but before I could speak, she looked through us and smiled, "There's my girl!"

We turned as Brooke walked into the living room with my niece clinging to one finger and high-stepping with her chubby legs. My mouth gaped as I watched her walk toward me, her hands held out for me to take her.

"Hi, Princess!" I cooed. "How is Uncle Finn's girl?"

Harbor babbled like we were having a very intense conversation.

"I know!" I answered her. "You're two now. And we brought you all kinds of presents. But, no pony yet...mommy said no."

"Oh, that's not fair Finn," Brooke laughed. She extended her hand out to Natalie, "Hi! I'm Brooke, Sadie's wife."

"It's so nice to meet you."

Brooke eyed Natalie and then looked suspiciously at me, "Uhh...Finn. Question...when were you going to tell us?"

Sadie and I said in unison, "Tell you, us what?"

"Sade, you don't see it?" Brooke smirked. "She's glowing."

"What?!" my sister raced around the island to stand by her wife. The pair stared at Natalie.

"Cover her ears," Sadie ordered and I cupped my hands over Harbor's head. "You're an asshole Finny!"

I released my niece's ears, "What? Why?"

My sister poked a finger in my chest, "Why didn't you tell us you're girlfriend is pregnant?"

My jaw dropped and the pair laughed wildly.

"Did you think we wouldn't see it?" Brooke giggled.

"I can't believe you made me look like an ass by offering her coffee," my sister scolded and returned to the kitchen. She opened a cabinet and pulled a box of herbal tea from the shelf before flipping a switch on an electric kettle. "Natalie, why don't you sit down. My brother will bring you tea when it's ready."

The look on her face told the whole story; Natalie was beside herself in amusement. She giggled softly and shrugged as she walked by me on her way to the sofa.

"I...I was getting ready to tell you," I muttered under my breath.

My sister rolled her eyes and whispered, "You're an idiot."

Brooke sat beside Natalie on the sofa as Harbor wiggled out of my arms. I put her down and she toddled to a small basket of toys, still chattering.

"How many weeks?" my sister-in-law smiled.

Sadie handed me a steaming cup and pointed to Natalie as if I didn't know who it was for or what I was supposed to do with it. She smirked at me and I rolled my eyes before walking the beverage to the sofa. Sadie again busied herself with the espresso machine.

Natalie took the cup from me before answering, "Almost twenty-five weeks."

I felt two pairs of eyes turn on me, "Finegan Dean Rafferty! I can't believe you kept this from us. Wow...anything else you want to tell us?"

Their voices overlapped as both of them scolded me in unison. I looked to my girlfriend for a lifeline, but there was none. Natalie sat sipping her tea looking quite pleased with my situation.

"How are you feeling?" Brooke turned to her.

Natalie nodded, "Pretty good now. The morning sickness comes and goes still."

"Oh, God," Sadie groaned. "That is something I don't miss."

They all burst into chatter and I sat back and watched, my heart filling with pride. Both Sadie and Brooke understood my quiet wish for a family; they had similar desires of their own. While my sister and I always had our mom and each other, life wasn't always easy for us. There were nights when our mother worked late at her second and, sometimes, third job, leaving Sadie and me to feed ourselves and go to bed on our own. A lot of responsibility was put on our mom that should have been shared with a partner and sometimes, my sister and I didn't make life any easier.

Early in the afternoon the apartment filled with friends and their families. The rooms were buzzing with the giggles of toddlers and the conversations among their parents. My niece was a beautiful angel even when stripped to her diaper and covered in pink frosting. After cake, punch, and so many presents that Harbor's room would look like a toy store, most everyone said their goodbyes and left to put little ones down for naps.

We stayed through my niece's nap and into dinner. While Brooke and Natalie played with Harbor on the living room floor, I rinsed dishes as Sadie loaded the washer.

"You look happy, Finny," she smiled, waiting for me to pass her another plate.

I nodded, "I am. More than I've ever been."

"I'm glad. I know you really missed her," she said. "You know, I've got to ask..."

I glanced at my sister and the concern in her eyes. I knew what she wanted to know and if it were anyone else, I'd tell them to mind their damn business. But, I wouldn't say that to her.

"My goal in Jose was always to get back to Natalie. I hurt her when I left...she needed to forget the pain," I explained softly. "It wasn't intentional."

Sadie was quiet for a moment and I knew she was mulling her next question. She was becoming a very good lawyer.

"What about the father?" she asked. "Finny, I know you've always wanted your own family...but, you know this is complicated."

I shook my head, "It's actually not, Sade."

"Finn—"

My sister started to protest with a raised voice and I shot her a look of warning.

"He died, Sade. He was shot and killed before she knew. But, from what she says, he wouldn't be around anyway," I whispered, looking to see my niece blowing kisses at Natalie.

"That's awful. So, what now?" she took the final bowl from my hand, placing it in the rack of the machine.

I dried my hands on a towel, "That baby will be a Rafferty."

"Uh," my sister's snicker fell from her mouth. "That's pretty bold, Finny. Even if the father was an asshole...he died. She may want to name the child in his memory."

My head shook emphatically, "This is what she wants. *She* asked *me*."

Sadie's jaw dropped and a broad smile spread across my face.

"You mean—"

"That's *my* son...or daughter," I laughed. "We don't know and we want it to be a surprise."

Elation filled my sister's eyes, "I'm going to be an Auntie!"

Chapter Forty-Two

Finn

The trip from Palo Alto was long and when we arrived home around one am, Natalie wanted nothing more than our bed. I watched her curl onto her side and drift to sleep. She didn't feel the bed move when I lay next to her after my shower ten minutes later nor did she feel my arm when I laid it over her waist and my broad hand cradled her belly as I spooned against her back.

But, she heard the squalling of the house alarm when it activated two hours later.

She flailed wildly as she covered her ears to the wailing but I was already out of bed as she felt for me in the darkness.

"Stay here!" I barked from the direction of the door before racing down the hallway to the threshold of the living room. I stopped immediately as my eyes were wide awake and perfectly adjusted to the lack of light. The siren of the alarm screamed but I carefully took in each room from my vantage point before making my way to the panel by the door.

But nothing moved. Taking a deep breath, I reached the glowing numbers on the keypad and punched in my code; even the sharp silence was deafening. Within seconds, the speaker buzzed and a woman drawled, "Atticus security. Do you need assistance?"

I checked the locks on the door and my eyes were still scanning every shape in the darkness, "Hold, please. I need to check the back door."

"It looks like the alarm originated in the front right window. Do you want me to dispatch an officer?" the woman's voice asked as I jogged to the door leading to the backyard and jiggled the handle. I hurried back to the living room, moved the loveseat across the wood floor, and checked the window. I couldn't see anything out of place.

"No. Everything is secure. False alarm," I shook my head as if she could see me.

"No problem, sir. I'll just need your code word," she replied.

"Carribean."

The woman in the box thanked me and disconnected. I stood for another long moment in the dark before flipping on the porch light. The house seemed tight as a drum and my once-racing heart slowed its pace. Making my way back toward the bedroom, I called to Natalie.

"Baby, everything is fine. I checked the doors and—"

The bed was empty and took me a second to make out the crouching shape in the darkness. Carefully, I pulled the switch on my bedside lamp and a soft glow illuminated the room. Natalie was wedged between the tall chest of drawers and the edge of the wall, a small knife in her right hand. Her eyes were wide and unblinking.

"Natalie?" I walked slowly toward her. "Hey...it's okay. Everything's fine."

She didn't move or bat an eye. When I was within a few feet of her, but out of arm's reach of the knife, I held my hands up, crouching to meet her eyes.

"Hey...Natalie...can you look at me?" I asked softly and the immensity of her gaze drifted to my face. I forced a smile, "That's it, baby. Hey...you're okay. Can you hand me the knife?"

I watched her chest rise and fall quickly as her breathing became heavier, the tears welling in her eyes. Slowly, her shaking hand extended and she dropped the blade in my hand. I threw it behind me and pulled her from the tiny space in one fluid motion. As her head hit my chest she sobbed.

"Shhh," I soothed calmly. "It's okay. It was a false alarm."

I held her there until her tears dried and her breath was steady again. I took her to the edge of the bed and we sat. Picking up the knife again, I handed it back to her.

"Where did that come from?" I asked.

Natalie shrugged, "It was my dad's. I found it in a box when I moved into this house and I've always kept it here."

She pointed to a space between the mattress and the bed frame.

"I'm sorry, Finn." A small derisive laugh fell from her lips. "I just freaked out a little bit."

Taking the leather sheath from its hiding place, I placed the knife back inside and tucked it back into the frame of the bed. If it made her feel safer having it beside her, so be it; it could live there forever.

I shook my head at her, "There is no apology for that. Ever. It's hard to remember in the middle of the night that he's locked away. But, everything is fine now."

I brushed my hand across her cheek and kissed her temple, "How about we try to get some sleep?

Chapter Forty-Three

Natalie

"So, what time did Cece say to meet her?" I called from the side of the bed. I was trying on dresses for twenty minutes and hated every one of them. Everything felt confining and strangely alien because nothing fit quite right.

"We've got plenty of time."

Finn shut the water off at the sink, poked his head around the corner, and after seeing my scowl asked, "What's wrong?"

I sighed, plopping on the corner of the mattress; my white tank stretched over my ever-growing belly.

"Nothing fits," I complained. "I'm hungry. And..."

I blushed. I didn't want to admit what I really wanted. Physically, I knew that my body was getting overloaded with large amounts of hormones and I knew those hormones affected women in different ways. One of those common afflictions was a heightened sex drive.

Mine was currently in overdrive.

"And?" Finn knelt in front of me.

"Never mind."

"Baby, what is it? If you need a snack, I just got another giant bag of apples...want me to cut you one?" His beautiful ocean eyes sparkled.

Damn it. This was so hard. Why did he have to be so damn hot? And now, he's feeding my cravings too. I imagined him in a toga as he fed slices of apples to me with one hand, a fan in another.

I shook the fantasy from my head.

His brow furrowed, "Okay...let's go shopping. Nothing fits? Let's find something that does."

I sighed again. He was too perfect.

"Alright Natalie, what is it? It's not food...a new outfit isn't the key. I'm running out of ideas from my pregnant girlfriend handbook," he laughed.

Jesus! This man was killing me. My junction throbbed when he called me his girlfriend.

"Wait a minute...how could I forget?" a wicked smile spread across his lips. He leaned into me, cupping one hand around my face as his lips brushed my ear. "You want something more *hands-on*, don't you?"

He ran the tip of his tongue over the curve of my lobe and fire exploded in my nerves.

"Yes," my breath shuttered and I felt my underwear soak.

Finn stood over me and stripped out of his shirt, "I have to say, this is one of my favorite parts of this pregnancy so far."

"Shut up and put that cock to work," I demanded as I yanked him on top of me.

***

An hour later and fully satiated, for now, we were on our way to meet Cece and her new mystery man for dinner. I had no idea she was even seeing anyone but was excited for the invite because Casa Azul was only a ten-minute drive from my house and my favorite. Believe me, when you're pregnant, proximity is an important detail. We pulled in a few minutes after six to a packed parking lot.

"I hope they got a table okay," I eyed the large amount of vehicles.

Finn shrugged, "Probably some kind of happy hour deal. Hey! We're in luck."

We were. I saw the single open space near the door right as he did. I was secretly ecstatic because my feet were already beginning to hurt a bit in the shoes I chose. Finn helped me out of the truck and we headed for the door.

Once inside, we stood at the hostess stand for a few moments before a young girl, somewhere in her late teens approached. Without asking our names, or getting us menus, she smiled at us, "Your party is ready."

Following her down the short hallway we turned into a room full of familiar faces.

"Surprise!" they called in unison.

The entire restaurant was decorated with streamers, poms, and ribbons of all pastel colors. Over the oak bar at the far end of the room, balloons spelled out 'WELCOME LITTLE ONE' and I was immediately in tears. Cece was the first person I laid eyes on and she rushed to my side with tissues.

"I knew you'd be a bawling mess," she laughed through the rivers barreling down her face.

I dabbed at the corners of my eyes, "Did you do this?"

Finn squeezed my hand as Cece winked at him, "I had some help...Becca and Carrie too."

"Thank you!" I wrapped my arms around her neck and squeezed tight.

"We can't wait for this kid to get here. So, there's plenty of food...Casa set a spectacular buffet. And I think just about everyone from Southwest Haven and Hanford Fire is here. Oh! And there are presents...but, we'll get to those later, maybe at your house. And we're taking bets on if there's a boy or a girl in here...since I can't convince you to find out." She kissed my cheek, "Just have fun tonight."

And we did. An entire restaurant filled with all of our friends and family; even Sadie and Brooke made the trip with little Harbor. It had been a month since her birthday and Finn's face lit like the sun when she reached for him and squeezed his neck tight with her tiny arms.

I stuffed my belly with chips, salsa, tamales, tacos, and tres leches cake but my heart was brimming with love from all the well wishes and desperately needed parenting advice. It was well past the Casa Azul's closing when the last of our guests finally said their goodbyes and Cece, Finn, and I loaded the last of the gifts into the truck.

"I'll come by this weekend and take notes so you can write thank you cards," she offered before shutting the door of her car. Finn and I waved as she turned right from the lot and her taillights turned to specks in the dark.

I walked around to the passenger side and Finn followed. Getting in and out of almost any vehicle was becoming a chore, but his truck was a huge challenge; I wasn't good at climbing up or down. I opened the door, but Finn closed it. I turned around to face him as he caged me between himself and the vehicle.

"What are you doing?" I giggled, my heart pounding in my throat.

He lowered himself closer to my face, his breath making light puffs in the cool air, "Wondering."

I raised my eyebrow in a question. Did he want to mess around here? In this parking lot? In October? I couldn't lie, the thought of it excited me and my body was definitely responding.

Those hormones were legit.

"I'm all ears," I cooed.

He pulled back a bit, staring at me, "You little fiend. Here? Now?"

"Me? You're the one that..."

Lightbulb moment. Sex was not what he was *wondering* about.

Finn burst into laughter, "I was just going to ask how I got so lucky to fall in love with someone like you. Now, I—"

An engine roared. Screeching tires. Metal crashing and a resounding boom.

Chapter Forty-Four

Finn

"Hang on!" I commanded. Throwing the truck into drive, I laid on the gas and flew from the parking lot. A mere half mile down the road, it was Natalie who saw the car first.

"Stop!" she yelled. "There...oh, God. Cece!"

The brakes squelched and Natalie's door was open before I reached for the handle of mine. The little red Mazda sat nose first in the small embankment, its engine still running. Reaching around my seat, I grabbed my gear and called after her.

"Natalie! Be careful."

When I reached her just seconds later, it was as if a different person stood before me. I expected her to be upset or emotional since the victim was someone she loved, but she wasn't. She held her cell phone to her ear and spoke with a defined coolness that I had witnessed no less than a hundred times in the emergency room.

"We're on Parkland Road, one half mile west of Casa Azul. Victim is a thirty-three-year-old female, named Cece Pullis."

She paused to listen as I entered the car on the passenger side, rolled down the driver's side window, and shut off the engine.

"Off-duty paramedic and nurse currently on scene. Yes, she's breathing...okay, thank you." She disconnected the call and turned to me, "Bus is on the way."

I checked Cece's pulse and noticed a large bump forming over her right eye. Not wanting to move her until a crew arrived, I checked her legs and arms for more injuries but found none. With the wails of sirens crying on the cold air in the distance, I applied a pressure pack to the bleeding on her forehead, and her face puckered in pain.

"Son of bitch! That hurts," she complained thickly.

"Hey...glad you're awake," I said.

Reaching through the window, Natalie picked up Cece's wrist and placed her fingers over the pulse point while simultaneously counting the seconds ticking by on her watch, "Ce...how you doing?"

She moved her head to look in Natalie's direction, "Nat? What are you doing here? What happened?"

"Penlight, please," Natalie held her hand out to me. I pulled one out of a side pocket of my bag and gave it to her.

"Ce...look at me, honey," she commanded gently and Cece obeyed. Natalie made quick motions with the light back and forth in her eyes. When she was satisfied, she handed the light back to me. "Normal and reactive."

"Cece, can you tell us what happened?" I asked as I dabbed the swab on her eye.

After a few seconds, her head bobbed, "Yeah...yeah, some asshole ran me off the road. He flew up behind me then got in the inner lane to pass...but he cut in too soon."

Flashes of red and blue enveloped the area as the ambulance and a police cruiser parked. Natalie squeezed Cece's hand, "Okay...the calvary's here. They're going to help you out then we're going to South to have you checked out."

Cece shook her head, "I'm fine...I think just this knock to my eye."

Natalie looked at me and I shook my head. I worried that the *knock* could have been more than just the giant lump over her eye. And there were other things to consider as well; automobile accidents almost always came with some form of soft tissue damage. I'd rather be safe, than sorry.

"I tell you what, let these guys check you out and I'll meet you at the hospital. Dr. Harris is working tonight...she can look you over and if she clears you, Finn and I will take you home," Natalie was firm but gentle as she spoke.

We gave over care to Darren and Inez before we had a chat with the officer on the scene. It wasn't long until Sanchez had opened the driver's side door and helped Cece to her feet, obviously refusing the backboard. She steadied herself against him as he helped her back to the bus. After giving the police a description of the vehicle, a dark, blue or black, late-model Ford truck, Cece sat on a gurney in the back of the ambulance with Darren as Inez drove them away.

We waited until the tow truck arrived and gave them instructions on what shop to deliver the Mazda to before we climbed back in the Bronco and turned toward the hospital. I glanced cautiously at Natalie.

"You okay?"

Her head bobbed, "Yeah, I'm good."

Once we arrived at the hospital, it didn't take Cece long to convince the attending physician on duty, Dr. Harris, that she was fine and that the ER was crowded with other people with *"real problems"*. Then, after promptly coaching her co-workers on getting her paperwork processed in a more timely manner, we had her back home around one a.m.

Luckily for us, we were both off the next day. However, when a heavy fist knocked on the door at nine o'clock in the morning, it was not a welcome sound. Throwing on a shirt, I stomped to the door, determined to give whoever was doing the pounding a piece of my mind if they woke my very pregnant and *sleeping* girlfriend. I shut off the alarm, turned the deadbolt and, without looking through the peephole, yanked on the door.

"Can I help you?" I growled then hesitated. Sargeant Eleazar stood on the porch with a uniformed officer I didn't know. "Oh, Maria...hi."

"Hey," her voice apologetic. "I'm sorry to bother you, I know it's kinda early."

I waved her off. "No worries. Just..." I looked over my shoulder and then stepped out on the porch with them, shutting the door behind me. "It was a late night...Natalie's sleeping."

"Got it. Unfortunately, Finn, she needs to be a part of this conversation too," she replied.

My eyes bounced from Maria to the uniform with her. It occurred to me that there was only one reason that any Hanford police officer would want to speak with both of us. An old anger surged in my nerves and I knew this had something to do with Drew.

"Is he out?" I narrowed my eyes on them both.

"Finn, can we go inside..."

I shook my head, "No. Maria, she's barely in her third trimester...you're not going to add any stress."

"Finn, she needs to know. If she wants the PO reinstated, she needs to do it today," she insisted. "I know you want to protect her—"

"She's carrying my child! Of course, I want to protect her, Maria." I hissed. Something about Maria's tone and demeanor caused me to pause. My mind was still clearing and I thought about what she said.

"Wait. He's already out, isn't he?"

The thought that the ball had been dropped and this notification was being done in retrospect made me furious. If that was the case, I would insist that whoever failed to inform me or Natalie was at the very least given an official reprimand. Maria's expression fell and I had my answer before she spoke another word.

"Goddamn it!" I snarled through clenched teeth. "How long?"

Maria shook her head, "Not long, Finn. A week...out early on good behavior. They gave the assignment to a rookie. Callahan and I just found out this morning. When we realized you didn't know, I made a line right over."

I took a deep breath and gave myself a moment to think.

"Let me tell her when she wakes up. Neither of us is on duty today...I'll make sure we get down to the station by noon. It was a late night...her friend was run off the road last night after the party," I offered.

"I heard about that from someone this morning. She okay?" she asked.

"Yeah...bump on the head." I raised my eyebrows, "Are we good? You'll let me handle this?"

Maria was reluctant but finally agreed to let me tell Natalie about Drew's release. After watching the pair return to their cruiser, I walked back inside to find Natalie standing in the living room, a look of interest on her face.

"What was that about?"

Chapter Forty-Five

Natalie

"A week? He's been out a week and no one told us?" I paced my living room. "Good behavior, my ass! He was sentenced to two years! Two years! And he only serves seven months? What kind of justice is that?"

Drew Bonetti, the ex who tried to kill me, the man who had me completely terrified of anything that moved, the wingnut who set Finn's truck on fire was out of jail for a week and someone failed in their responsibility to inform me. I was pissed, to say the least.

"Baby...you gotta stay calm," Finn soothed. "You're at the finish line...stress isn't good for either of you."

I glowered at him and he put his hands up, palms out in an act of surrender. I rolled my eyes and turned away. I really didn't want to hear logic, I wanted to be angry.

"I'm not telling you how to feel...I'm pissed off too. But, right now, we just need to handle it. I'll make some breakfast, we'll get dressed, and we'll file the restraining order," he wrapped his arms around my shoulders and hugged me to his chest. A tiny bit of my anger melted away. "We're not going to let him run our life, okay?"

"I know. It's just," I faced him. "You weren't there when he was sentenced. You didn't see the look in his eyes. Finn, I've seen it before, he doesn't forgive or forget."

"I get that, Natalie. We just have to work within the..." He took a step back and stared. "When he was sentenced? You were there?!"

"Yes."

Finn let go of me, "Natalie! What the hell were you thinking?! Why? Why would you do that?"

It was his turn to pace, but I had to admit I was a little surprised by his reaction. Just because he didn't care or wasn't curious enough to be there didn't mean I felt the same. To that point, Drew took up most of my space and my mind; at least the parts that weren't still missing Finn. To see him finally defeated, even a little bit, gave me hope that he wouldn't be a part of my life forever.

"Because I had to see it for myself! I wanted him to know that he didn't break me...that no matter how many people he intimidated because of me...or how many times he tried to knock me down, I would always get back up. I wasn't going to be afraid of him anymore," I thundered because I was finished crying over anything Drew Bonetti touched.

Finn stared at me, unblinking for a long moment. "You're the bravest woman I've ever met."

"I think I've been told once I've got guts," I huffed.

"I don't think. I know." He wrapped his hands around my hips again, "I owe you an apology. I should have been there...Callahan called and gave me the details. But with work and everything with...*her*...I couldn't make it. I wish I would have."

I didn't know how to respond to that. I honestly don't know how I would have reacted had he shown up that day. Knowing myself, I would have cried, eaten a tub of ice cream, and told everyone I was fine. I would have been so far from fine.

It didn't take us long to eat and make ourselves ready. By eleven o'clock, we were cruising toward Hanford Police headquarters. From the car, Finn called Maria to let her know we were on our way and I checked in with Cece. She gave me the same line as earlier that morning; she was fine, makeup would cover the worst of it, and she thanked us again.

We entered the squat brick building on Lewis Street ten minutes later. The desk sergeant handed me a clipboard with a very familiar application attached to it by its metal clasp. Finn plucked a pen from the cup and we chose two seats in the corner of the small waiting area. Once I was halfway through the information, Maria came out to greet us.

"I'm glad you could make it so quickly," she stared at my growing belly. "Wow! You look like you're ready any day now."

I gave her a small smile, "About ten weeks and counting."

She led us through narrow hallways and into a room I recognized all too well. Maria leaned against a small bookshelf as we sat at the conference table.

"Are you finished with the application?" she asked.

I looked down at the board, "Almost."

I wondered what the hurry was all about, but I didn't have time to express my question before Finn did it for me.

"Maria, what's the hurry? I thought restraining orders were put on hold until the person was out."

She crossed her arms over her chest, sighing, "That's true. But, the time left runs out today. If we don't get this on record now, you'll have to start over."

My face contorted in a noticeable look of shock. I couldn't believe that I had forgotten about this. The past few years had been nothing but thinking about where he would turn up. But with Liam's death, Finn returning, and a baby, it was something I completely overlooked.

"Damn it!" I grumbled, irritated with myself.

Maria shifted her position, "Don't worry about it. You're here taking care of it...that's what matters."

I hurriedly finished the form and handed it to her. She promised she would call later that day once a judge had the information and it was signed. She also let me know that there would be a hearing most likely in the next couple of weeks to make the time frame official. We said our goodbyes and left.

As we drove back home, I wondered if this would set all the drama back in motion again, part of me hoped that Drew had forgotten all about me. I was living a simple, quiet life now; one where Finn, our baby, and I would be happy and content. We could be a family; better than Finn had and more than I ever expected.

I settled into our bed that night as exhaustion from the last twenty-four hours abraded every nerve ending but sleep would not come for me. I found myself reliving every second of every moment I had ever spent with Drew. Deciding it was ridiculous to continue to toss in bed, I went to the kitchen for some milk. I would settle for a while on the sofa, snuggle with Delilah, and find something on a streaming service to relax my brain.

Shutting off the kitchen light, with my glass, I walked into the darkened living room and reached to turn on a lamp. I saw the shadow move but I wasn't fast enough and large hands reached out, wrapping me tight around my bulging belly and mouth.

"Hello, gorgeous," Drew's breath was hot in my ear.

I tried to scream, but his hand pulled tighter and pressed my lips against my teeth. I wanted to bite him, but the pressure was too much.

"You stupid whore. It bothers me when you don't listen. That was always your problem, Nat. If you had ever done what I told you, I never would have hit you like that. But, you deserved it, didn't you?" he growled. Moving his hand from my waist, he drove it into my hair and yanked hard. My head and neck were bent back and I gazed into his dark eyes.

"Say it, Nat. Say that you deserved it. If you weren't fucking all those guys behind my back...you know, I'm the only one that loves you," he nestled his nose close to my ear. "Say it!"

His grip was like a vice and I could barely shake my head. I felt his nails digging into my flesh, and it was a sensation I was familiar with. I could feel his lips move against my ear when he spoke.

"Say it you lying slut. You made me do those things to you...I love you, Nat. But, you can't treat the people that love you like garbage. Sneaking around and bending over for every man that comes sniffing," he pulled my hair even tighter and I felt pieces beginning to tear from my scalp. He uncovered my mouth. "Say. It."

"No!" I screamed in his face as I kicked back with my bare heel. His grip loosened and I flung myself away...

"Natalie! Natalie!!" Finn's voice came sharply in the dark and I felt his broad hands shaking my shoulder and hip.

I blinked several times only to realize sweat poured from my face. I sat up, grounding my bare feet onto the floor. I felt the heat radiating from Finn behind me and he stroked my damp hair and face.

"Are you okay?" his words laced with shock.

I couldn't blame him. It had been a very long time since I had a nightmare and I had never had one since he moved in with me. I was completely alert and thoughts raced around the track in my mind. I took a deep breath and exhaled slowly. Without saying a word, I walked to the bathroom to splash cold water on my face.

When I returned, Finn had turned on a light and was sitting on the edge of the bed. "Natalie?"

I looked him in the eye.

"What the hell was that?" his forehead creased with concern.

"I'm sorry," I apologized.

"No, Natalie, stop. Stop doing that," Finn's head shook. "I want to know what happened."

I took another breath, "It was just a nightmare."

"Oh, baby, I get that. I want to know what he did," Finn's tone was hard like steel. It was a sound I hadn't heard from him before. He was angry, but not with me. It was as if he thought Drew was actually in our house; and, in a way, he was.

"I don't want to talk about all this—"

"Natalie, this time, that's not good enough," he cut me off.

My eyes narrowed on him, "Well, it's going to have to be. I don't want to think about him, I don't want to dream about him and I certainly don't want to talk about him! I'm so goddamn *tired* of talking about him! Of him being any part of our lives!"

Finn stared at me and his eyes never left mine, "Natalie, I want you to talk to me. Let me help carry this!"

"Why?" I cried.

"Because it's my job! And I love you and it's what being together means!" he charged.

I was silent because I wasn't sure what to say so, I remained quiet and considered his words. My tongue felt like cotton and my lips were dry. It was hard enough telling Dr. Carys all the darkness and I've spoken even less about it to Cece. I understood what Finn wanted, what he needed, never realizing that it was what I needed too.

I told him everything. Every dirty, sadistic detail was laid out for him. I described every busted lip, every bruise, and every scar; including the one in my eyebrow. What he didn't know, was that it went beyond the physical sufferings. I exposed every verbal thrashing Drew threw at me; whore, slut, cunt, bitch; Finn heard them all. Then I described his control and obsession. How I was allowed to fix my hair, nails, makeup, and clothes. What was demanded of my behavior in public, all so I could fit the mold of his perfect mate, and when I finally broke free, how he told me it wasn't over; that he refused to ever let me go.

By the end, Finn was in tears; but it wasn't sadness or sympathy or pity reflected on his face.

It was rage.

Chapter Forty-Six

Finn

While I'd like to think the week following the new restraining order was slow and quiet, it would only be a half-truth. The leaves on the trees, once brilliant with oranges, yellows, and reds, now drying and falling to the ground, meant the days were turning to night more quickly. We were quiet in that week. I worried about Natalie's stress and her nightmares and raking the leaves while she struggled some nights to sleep.

I had to think about the leaves. It kept me from finding Drew Bonetti and doing to him all the things he did to Natalie.

I knew she didn't want me to worry, but we didn't hide from each other. And I was thankful that her current nightly torments paled in comparison to that first one. I did everything to get her mind off Drew's release, but I knew what haunted her; why she was so afraid. How his shadow oozed its way back into her mind like an oily film, and why she sometimes cried in the night. The piece of shit didn't even have to set foot anywhere near her to inflict his torture. It made me hate him more if that were even possible, and added to my constant concern.

Natalie was primarily on desk duty from now until she delivered, which, eased some of my anxiety while she was working. The ER, while not the constant eruption of chaos that one sees on television, can still be the Wild West. I worried constantly about the next addict or psych patient that came through losing it and hurting her and the baby.

They were never far from my mind. My heart lightened when I thought about how crazy lucky I was and that Natalie was allowing me to be this baby's father. I would never be able to put into words how incredibly happy it made me and how grateful I felt. But in my mind, a soft voice that clawed at me for a long time was screaming and demanded my attention. Something was still missing and it was the one thing that would wrap everything in a neat bow.

I wanted to marry her.

It was something I was thinking about for months; ever since we moved in together. I knew that more than anything, I would spend the rest of my life with her, and while I was confident she felt the same, neither of us ever hinted at the topic. I wasn't afraid to get married again and on some level, I knew from the beginning, Natalie was *the* one. But there never seemed to be the right time to talk about it.

I decided to stop being a spineless ass. And while nothing about our relationship was exactly traditional, I wanted this to be done right. I arranged for Natalie to get a New Mommy massage one bright November afternoon then, I asked Cece to meet me at the Pig and Fly for coffee under the guise of discussing Natalie's birthday a month later.

"Hey, that eye looks pretty good!" I said as Cece slid into the booth in front of me.

She touched it absently, "I think so. Thanks again for everything."

I waived my hand dismissively.

"Get your car back yet?" I asked.

"Tomorrow...about damn time too. I hate rentals. And now...I'm seeing that stupid truck everywhere. It's like everyone is driving it," she said as our waitress strolled up to our table. I ordered an iced tea for myself while Cece ordered a diet Coke. "How did you get rid of Nat?"

I smirked, "An hour-long massage at Lotus Spa. Manicure, pedicure, facial."

Cece's eyes widened in approval, "Good job, Rafferty."

She paused, "How are the nightmares?"

"Getting better, I think," I knew she watched the concern shadow my face, but she nodded anyway.

"I wanted to talk to you about something," my throat was becoming a desert, and I looked impatiently for our waitress to bring our drinks.

"Yeah, Nat's birthday. What are you thinking? Another surprise party?" she grinned conspiratorially. "If so, let's do a brunch. I'm thinking super posh...rose gold and ivory."

"Actually," I began as our drinks arrived and I took a long pull from my glass. "I need to talk to you about something else."

Cece frowned, "Okay."

A small pause fell and I heard the blood rushing in my head. I placed my hand in my pocket and pulled out a grey box, holding it under the table. I drew a deep breath, "I need something from you."

"From me?" she chortled. "Alright...what?"

Opening the box, I placed it on the table in front of her, "Permission. Cece, you're the closest thing to family Natalie has....it wouldn't be right if I didn't run it by you first."

Her eyes grew and flitted between my face and the ring, "May I?"

I nodded and she picked up the box, twirling it in the light. After she was finished, Cece brushed a quick tear from her cheek before she sat back against the faux leather with crossed arms.

"Well, it's about time, Rafferty," her smile spread quickly and I know she saw my relief. "I mean, she is having your kid and all."

She gave me a quick wink.

"Do you think she'll like it?" I asked, closing the box and placing it back in the pocket of my jeans.

Cece snorted, "Well, if she doesn't let me know...I'll take it."

"Thank you, Cece," I replied and took another long drink from my glass.

I paid our check, we said our goodbyes and it wasn't long until I was on the road. After making a couple of short stops for takeout and other things to make the night perfect, I was back home in plenty of time to dim the lights and wait for Natalie.

I watched her headlights float across the candlelit room. I checked off my list quickly in my head: flowers, candles, and the ring were all accounted for along with a light dinner from her favorite Chinese restaurant and dessert. My heart raced uncontrollably and I anxiously waited for her to come inside.

Other than setting the scene and the actual ring, I had no real plan. I was winging it. All I knew was that I wanted to propose and I needed to hear her answer. When she finally opened the door, my mind went blank for a moment and I struggled to find my words.

"Oh my God!" her face glowed in the flickering light. "What's going on?"

Her voice was like ice water on my brain, startling me back to reality. I noticed she was staring at the obscene amount of flowers covering every flat surface of the living room.

"Did you buy the florist out of hydrangeas?" she giggled.

"They're your favorite," I replied softly. The smile she gave me in return was nothing short of unmitigated beauty.

She laid her jacket over the arm of the sofa and tossed her keys on a table before leaning over a bouquet to pull in a long, deep breath.

"They're beautiful." Natalie tucked a loose strand of hair behind her ear, "What's with all the candles?"

Licking my lips, I took a step in her direction, weaving her fingers into mine. "Natalie, I hope you know that you are the one true love of my life. There is nothing in this world that means more to me than you and our baby. So, I have a question."

I released her hands and slipped the box out of my pocket. Lifting the lid, I showed her the ring.

"Will you marry me?"

Chapter Forty-Seven

Natalie

I mean it when I say that the world glitched for a second and everything around me was still.

I stared unblinking at the most dazzling piece of jewelry I ever laid eyes on. Shock and disbelief could not come close to describing how I felt at that moment. Finn and I had never, not even once, discussed marriage. I don't know why we hadn't, but it never came up in conversation. From the placement of the candles and flowers to the gorgeous ring, it was fast becoming clear that this had been on his mind for a while. I mean...that ring; even Cece would approve.

I realized he was staring at me and expecting an answer. I opened my mouth to speak, but what came out wasn't from the English language.

"Oof!" my hands went to my thick belly and I frowned downward.

The ring box snapped shut and Finn's hands were immediately on mine, "What's wrong?"

"Nothing." I looked into his eyes, "He just kicked me...hard.

Finn smirked, "He?"

"Well, I mean, it's bad luck to call him anything else until we know for sure, right?" I smiled, looking down at the box. Finn caught my eyes drifting and he held it up once more.

"I know it's never come up before. I was just hoping that we could talk about it."

"No talking," I shook my head and paused."Yes."

Finn's face contorted in disbelief, "Did you say, yes?"

My head bobbed as laughter erupted from my throat. Getting married wasn't what I expected, but neither was anything else that happened in the past year. I saw my future and the entire universe in those ocean-blue eyes and I wasn't about to live another moment without him. I held my shaking hand out for him to slip the ring on my finger and it fit perfectly.

"You said yes!" Finn exclaimed through whoops of laughter as he picked me up and twirled me. "You said yes!"

I giggled as he put me down, "Yes, Finn Rafferty, I will marry you."

After a long moment of kissing that made every fiber in my body quake, we spent the rest of our night loafing on our sofa. We were surrounded by Chinese take-out boxes filled with vegetable lo mein, chicken fried rice, and a prowling feline that seemed to be too interested in my fortune cookies. We lay content in each other's arms as he watched me twirl my new gift on my finger.

It was several days later before I had to be back at the hospital for a shift. After word spread about my recent engagement, I was congratulated by nearly every coworker who crossed my path. But, it was my core girls that were the most excited. Becca, who had transferred out of the ER three months prior, came down from pediatrics to have lunch with me, Cece, and Carrie.

"Holy. Shit," Becca's eyes gleamed as she pulled my hand closer to her face. "Okay, maybe I was wrong about only dating doctors."

"I knew that boy had good taste," Cece cocked an eyebrow and sipped her coffee. "I told him if you didn't want it, I'd take it for you."

I roared with laughter. Of course, she knew about the proposal; there was no way he would ask before running it by her first.

"So, have you picked a date? Where are you thinking? Do you want something big?" Carrie's excitement grew with each question.

But, I didn't have answers. We discussed a lot of options the past few days, but neither of us could come up with anything that seemed to fit. Did we want to get married before the baby came, or after? I really didn't care about a huge production and honestly, didn't want to pay for one either. There were just too many options and Finn just wanted me to be happy.

"We're thinking small...just close friends and Finn's sister. We really don't have a date or anything else yet...and with the baby coming soon, this may not be the best time to plan," I replied, pushing the fruit on my plate around with my fork.

"Hey!" Cece's gentle command forced me to look up. "If you don't want big, don't do big. If you want to get married in your backyard, we'll make it happen. Don't use my niece as an excuse to put it off."

I rolled my eyes, "Still sure it's a girl, huh?"

"She's got a hundred dollars on it," Becca chortled.

"Two hundred, actually," Cece took another pull from her cup. "And when I win my cut of the pot," she eyed her friends carefully, "Little Miss and Auntie are going shopping."

Carrie and Becca snorted their laughter. I knew I would have my hands full reeling Cece and her shopping habit in when this baby came; the reveal of her little scheme just proved my point. But, I was thrilled that this kid would be smothered in love and well cared for, no matter what.

I rested my chin in my palm, "So, you think we should get married before the baby comes?"

"It's up to you. I'm just saying that intimate is on trend right now. And you know, your girls do like planning a party," Cece snatched a grape off my plate and laughed.

Carrie and Becca agreed in unison, "Absolutely! We can make this happen. No problem!"

I smiled, "I mean, I'll see what Finn thinks. Maybe...next weekend?"

After that, our watches told us that lunch was over and it was back to patient care. Spending the rest of my shift doing paperwork, I had plenty of time to daydream. Just when I didn't think I would be able to crawl out of the hole I dug for myself, my deepest wish happened and Finn walked back into my life. I still felt a tiny twinge of guilt that Liam died not really knowing how I felt; that other than friendship and a roll in the sheets, I wasn't in love with him. Or, maybe he did know, maybe we both did. While we dated each other exclusively, there was no pretense of commitment and no talk of long-term plans. We were there to have fun and hide from our real feelings, if even for a night. I think my only regret for him is that he never found the kindred spirit he was destined to be with.

Like I did in Finn.

Chapter Forty-Eight

Finn

"We're not late, Ce," I steadied my tone because my best man and I were indeed late. Her sharp voice filled my truck as Elias smirked in the passenger seat.

"Rafferty, I'm not playing with you. We have planned this day to the minute...Darren got here on time. Don't make me reconsider my very high opinion of you," she warned. "Natalie is ready to go."

I rolled my eyes, "That's not fair. Darren drove you...we wouldn't be having this conversation if I drove Natalie."

"Uh-huh. No way," she pitched higher. "It's bad luck to see your bride the day of."

Elias laughed, "You're not gonna win, man. She's got you."

"Elias, you're a smart man. I like you," the smile resounded in Cece's voice.

"Fine," I relented and pushed the gas peddle harder. "Ten minutes, I promise."

I disconnected the call.

Exactly nine minutes later, I rolled the Bronco into the sparsely occupied parking lot and easily found a spot. The bright sun shone overhead and looked like diamonds on the water. I noticed Darren's black Yukon parked several spaces to my right and an archway dec-orated with blushed roses and white hydrangeas on a grassy plot a hundred yards from me. Around twenty white folding chairs were set up in pairs on either side of the arch, creating an aisle.

"This look different than your first wedding?" Elias grinned.

I chuckled, "I didn't have a wedding the first time."

It was then Cece exited the black truck and walked toward mine. Elias rolled down the window as she approached.

"Everyone is here," she motioned to the few cars around us. "You, Elias, and Darren need to go to the arch. Once everyone is seated and the violinist plays, Becca, Carrie, and I will head down the aisle. Then, showtime!"

I nodded and all the moisture left my mouth; it wasn't nerves, it was excitement. I had to be honest, I didn't think Cece would be able to pull off a wedding in seven days. But there I stood. And, before the end of the night, Natalie and I would sleep in the same bed as husband and wife.

Elias and I did as we were directed and met the minister, a short, older woman with gray hair and eyes locked in smile mode. Darren followed closely and she greeted us all with grandmotherly hugs. I wondered for a split second where Cece found her, but she was quick to explain, as our small crowd was seated, that she was Cece's god-mother.

The breeze off the ocean was cool, but luckily the sun was bright overhead and it was warm in Santa Barbara for mid-November. The violinist took her seat and drew her bow across the strings. It was the last thing I heard as I spotted Natalie on the sidewalk and my heartbeat filled my ears. She was the absolute, most beautiful person I ever laid eyes on; she was ethereal and divine and I could not pry my eyes from her.

The white lace of Natalie's dress flitted in the breeze as Cece adjusted the circle of baby's breath woven into her hair. After being handed a small bouquet by Carrie, the volume of the violin's song grew and everyone stood as Becca first, then Carrie, and finally Cece led Natalie down the small grassy aisle. Only then did the world come back into focus for me.

The minister spoke joyfully of soul mates and finding the one person to spend the rest of your life with. How sometimes, life throws curves your way and it is in those moments when our true fortitude is tested. I barely remember any of the actual words she spoke because I was too mesmerized by the woman in front of me. The woman who said yes a week ago and the one who just said "I do."

It was well after midnight before we coasted back into our driveway. After the ceremony, we and all of our guests enjoyed a champagne and cake reception at the beach. Afterward, our small wedding party watched the sunset over the water as we ate fish tacos and seared steak at Anchor Rose. Natalie was exhausted and I noticed her eyes drifting as we came through San Luis Obispo a little after nine.

She didn't move when I opened her door. Brushing her cheek with my fingers, I whispered, "Natalie...hey, we're home."

"What? Already?" her eyes fluttered.

I helped her down out of the truck and she leaned on me as we made our way onto the porch. Before I could unlock and open the door, I looked down to see a neatly wrapped box shoved against the corner. I bent to pick it up only to realize the package was incredibly heavy. Natalie took the bags and I carried the gift inside.

"Looks like a wedding present," I commented as I reset the alarm. I walked the gift to the kitchen to get a better look.

Natalie's nose wrinkled, "Kinda weird paper to wrap a wedding gift in."

I couldn't disagree. The bright yellow paper and obnoxiously neon pink bow looked more like something that could be found at a birthday party.

"Who's it from?" Natalie asked.

I looked for a tag, "No idea. I can't find a card. Should we open it now?"

"Might as well," she shrugged.

We both tore off the paper and found a plain cardboard box. After cutting through the tape running along the top, we folded the flaps down and slid out the protective styrofoam packing. I peeked inside.

"Oh, this is nice," I whistled then slid the hefty knife set and wood block from the box.

Natalie's heavy eyes widened, "It really is. I wonder why they didn't leave a card."

I shrugged, "Maybe it blew away. Who knows how long this was out there."

I didn't bother putting anything out of her bags or the knife set away since it could wait until morning. As she made her way to the bedroom, I reset the alarm and fed a very perturbed, very cranky Delilah before shuffling off my shirt and slacks and jumping in for a quick shower. When I finally got to the bedroom, I expected to find Natalie fast asleep, but she wasn't.

"You should be asleep," I grinned down at her as I toweled my hair.

Natalie yawned, "I'm okay. I thought maybe...I mean, are we supposed to consummate our marriage?"

While I realized no one would believe me, the thought hadn't crossed my mind. It had been a long day; I mean, I was tired and I wasn't the one nearly eight months pregnant. But the mere thought of her body on mine made me harden a little.

I sat next to her, chuckling, "We *could*...but, honestly, when have we ever done anything unless it was on our own time?"

She yawned again.

"I tell you what," I leaned into her. "Let's put that part on hold until tomorrow...until we both have a little bit more to give."

I kissed her as she softly protested but eventually gave in, "Alright...have it your way."

Another yawn before she snuggled into her pillow and drifted off to sleep.

Chapter Forty-Nine

Finn

I threw the polishing rag back into the box just as the buzzer rang with a call. Our radios came alive as dispatch crackled over the air.

'Code four Alpha, 1833 Pepper Drive, Clearwater Condos, number twelve ...Hanford PD also en route, request EMS assist'

"We're up, kid," Carl grunted as the garage door lifted for our bus.

I jumped in and shut the door as Carl rolled us out onto the street. Clearwater Condiminimums was a new development located on the northeast edge of our station's territory. The gated community offered three pools, a tennis court, a community room, and a security team, all of it for a price well outside the average for the area.

After the gate guard moved us through without question, we found three police cruisers parked along the sidewalk of the third building on our left. Carl eased into the empty drive and we donned gloves and grabbed our bags from the back of the unit.

A woman of around sixty stood near the front door talking to Officer Jackson, "I am telling you, sir, she did not fall down those stairs. Do not believe her...that boyfriend of hers hit her again. I've heard them...they go at it all the time. He's just terrible."

I raised my eyes at Jackson and he nodded for us to go inside.

The entryway and living room of the spacious home were immaculate. Decorated in shades of white and beige, the condo looked like it was straight out of the pages of Architectural Digest and it was no wonder why the price tag was so high. As we looked around, neither Carl nor I noticed a lamp or a seat cushion out of place. The only thing that indicated that there was even a problem was the brunette woman sitting on the carpeted floor at the bottom of the lengthy staircase. The underside of her eyes was just beginning to turn a sickly purple and she held a towel under her nose.

Another officer standing near her raised his chin at us and met us a couple of feet from where she lay on her back.

"Hey Charlie," Carl said, "What's going on?"

Charlie Huang scratched his chin, whispering, "She says she just polished the wood floor at the top of the stairs, slipped at the edge, and took a tumble."

"You believe her?" I asked softly.

Charlie's face contorted and he made a quick shake of his head, "But that's her story."

"Anyone else here?"

"Not when we arrived. Reed's wandered the whole place," he replied. "Her name's Gia."

Carl and I thanked him before I squatted next to her, "Hey, my name is Finn...I'm with the Hanford Fire Department. Can I take a look at that?"

The woman's quickly swelling eyes struggled to open and look in the direction of my voice. She nodded and slowly removed the blood-soaked towel from her nose. I saw the bridge was also swollen, but the bleeding had mostly subsided. Carl and I worked together giving her some basic first aid as she rested her head on a riser.

There was something oddly familiar about her. I knew we had never met, but familiarity permeated my head but I couldn't put my finger on it. It was then I started to take in the rest of her injuries. A cut lip, a scratch on her neck, and three older bruises around her wrist.

"Gia?" I said gently as I touched the corner of her mouth with a bandage. Her dark eyes, just barely slits, looked in my direction. "We're going to get you to Southwest Haven to get this nose looked at, okay?"

She nodded.

"It might be a good idea if you talk to someone while you're there," I continued.

Her eyes narrowed and looked closed, "Why?"

"Honey, we can see that the stairs aren't the only thing that might be hurting you around here," Carl offered.

Gia shook her head, "I just slipped on the floor...I just cleaned it."

She tried to smile, but her face was too painful to move and she winced.

"Okay. But, you might be there a while...if you feel like—"

My sentence was cut short by a commotion outside. The woman, who turned out to be a neighbor, was yelling at the top of her lungs. Charlie was at the door in seconds, helping the other two officers diffuse the situation when another voice bellowed over them all.

"This is my girlfriend's house! I want to see her!" the voice yelled.

An alarm went off in the back of my head and the hair on my arms rose. I shot a look at Carl, "Stay here."

"You're the reason she's hurt! I can't believe you would come back here after what you did!" the neighbor screamed.

"Hey! Hey! That's enough!" I heard Charlie, Jackson, and Reed bark.

"Look, you nosy bitch, I don't know what you've done, but stay out of our business!" the voice snarled as I walked up.

My eyes locked with Drew Bonetti.

I watched his face darken, "What the hell are you doing here?"

"Did you do this, Bonetti?" I growled and my blood boiled. This is what Natalie's life was before she escaped. Before he tried to kill her.

"Do you know each other?" Charlie's eyes bounced from mine to Drew's.

I nodded, "Yeah, this is the guy that burned my truck last year at the station."

Charlie's eyes rose, "I see. Mr. Bonetti, are you on parole right now?"

Rage filled Drew's eyes but he was smart enough to keep his voice steady, "I am."

"Charlie, he's the reason she's in this condition," I snapped. He turned toward me, but I never took my eyes off Drew.

"You're probably right...but unless she reports it, we can't do anything. You *know* that. Get your gurney and get her out of here. I'll stall him," he whispered in low tones. I nodded as Jackson and Reed moved Drew and the neighbor so I could walk through.

I opened the door only to notice a fifth vehicle parked just to the side of our rig: A black Ford F150. It took a moment to register the significance but when I did, my adrenaline rose. I couldn't believe what I was seeing. Questions and rage ran through my mind but I put them in my back pocket. I made a mental note to call Bob Callahan when we were back at the station. I returned a few moments later and as I moved to push the wheels of the gurney closer to the door, Drew looked at me, smirking.

"Tell Nat I said hi when you get home tonight."

Without thinking, I let go of the bed and had Drew's collar wrapped in my fists. I shoved him against the brick facade of the condo twice, fury spilling from my soul as he laughed.

"You son of a bitch!" I screamed, my face contorting with madness. "Stay away from my wife!"

His laughter stopped abruptly and his eyes went dark. I watched them flicker to my hand where Natalie placed a gold band not ten days prior.

"Hey! Hey...it's okay, Finn. C'mon, Finn. Don't do this," Charlie and Carl were pulling me away. I dropped my hands but the look in Drew's eyes as they followed me into the house was concerning. As if a lightbulb turned on over my head, I knew what it was about Gia that was so familiar. The perfume. She was wearing the exact perfume that Natalie wore.

My stomach turned and I realized her hair color was nearly the same as my wife's as well.

I had to put the thoughts away and refocus my attention. I peered in the open door and I again saw Gia's broken nose and blackened eyes. I walked through the threshold and knelt, taking her hand gently, "C'mon, Gia...let's get you out of here."

Chapter Fifty

Finn

For better or worse, I kept Natalie in the dark about the incident at Clearwater. Cece, who heard the entire story from who I assumed was Darren, called me a few days later to agree that it was better that she not know, at least for now.

"It's a good call. There's no need to get her stressed out when everything is fine now," she said over her speakerphone.

I hated keeping anything from Natalie, but Cece was right, "I know. There's something else though...something you need to know."

"Okay?"

"Bonetti's driving a brand new black truck," I waited for her response, but the air was dead for a moment like she had me on mute.

"That little piece of rat shit!" she snapped suddenly. "I'm going to rip his lungs out."

"Ce, don't go looking for trouble. I'm only telling you because I want you to keep an eye out...Darren too," at this point, I almost grinned. Darren and Cece thought they were discreet with their new relationship, but it was hard to miss.

"I don't know what you're talking about, Rafferty." she denied playfully.

"Uh-huh," I mused. "Ce...can I ask you something? About Bonetti?"

"Sure."

"Do you remember the incident last summer? When he showed up at the hospital?" I prodded her memory. I had a suspicious itch that needed scratching. If it was only the hair, I could dismiss the intrusive thought, but the whiff of that perfume at Gia's had me spinning.

Her sigh was heavy, "Yeah, sure do. What about it?"

"Natalie told me that night he had been there before. He had a girlfriend in the ER and she ran into him in the parking lot," I explained, hoping she would remember the incident. I had an idea of the depth of his obsession with my wife and that idea terrified me.

"I actually do! I'm telling you, Rafferty, had I recognized him that night; I would have slapped the cuffs on myself," she snapped. "What about it?"

"Did you see the girlfriend?" I asked. "Do you know what she looked like?"

She was quiet for a long moment, "No, she wasn't one of mine or Natalie's. Why do you ask?"

"Nothing...just curious, I guess." I was disappointed but, I didn't want her to know why. I switched gears, "Just so you know, Sanchez is a louse and a terrible cook. I hope you can turn him around, but that chili he makes needs an exorcist."

Bellows of familiar laughter poured through my handset before Darren said, "You're a dick, Finn."

I chortled, "I figured you were nearby."

"Okay you two," I could hear Cece's eye roll. "Rafferty, you better keep this under wraps."

"Does that include Natalie?" I chuckled.

"Yeah, right. She's known from the beginning," Cece snickered.

"Hey, Finn. I'll keep an eye out for that truck...and another on this one. You do the same, man," Darren said before we said goodbye and disconnected.

Dinner was nearly finished when Natalie walked through the door that night. Delilah made an immediate line for her legs, purring fiercely for attention. Natalie walked into the kitchen and I kissed her then her belly as she sat a small clutch of lillies on the table.

"How was your day?" I asked as I stirred garlic cream sauce in a pan.

Natalie sighed, "Four falls from roofs, because, you know 'tis the season. Three strokes, two overdoses—"

"And a partridge in a pear tree?"

"Close. One Mr. Bob," she laughed, popping a piece of raw carrot in her mouth. "Looks like the neighbors got a new car and the light is out on the porch."

"Oh yeah?" I poured the sauce into a bowl of linguine. "Hey, what's with the flowers? Should I be jealous?"

"Hilarious, Mr. Rafferty," she smacked my ass with a towel. "Thank you though. After today, I needed them."

I began to toss the pasta and sauce with forks, "Well, I'm glad they made you happy...but you should probably thank Cece because I didn't do it."

Pulling salad out of the refrigerator and plates from the cabinet, I looked back at my wife. Natalie's face wasn't one of amusement. Turning, I grabbed our silverware and began setting our places at the small round table in our eat-in kitchen.

"What's wrong?" I asked.

She shook her head, "Cece most definitely did not give me these flowers. Just admit it...why would you give someone else credit for something so sweet?"

"I'm not. Baby, I'm telling you, I didn't send you flowers today," I contested firmly.

"Well, I know you didn't send them...but leaving them on the car was nice."

I pulled the chair out for her, "Again...not me. Cece. Unless you've got someone else that knows how amazing you are."

"Finn, stop!" she seemed to be getting angry. I took my seat next to her and stared. "There is no way these came from her...she hates lilies. Despises them in fact...even the smell. So, if you didn't leave them and she didn't—"

"Who did?" I interjected and a chill ran down my spine.

Damn it. My mind debated confessing about the altercation with Drew, but as soon as the thought crossed my mind, another formed. Natalie was weeks from having the baby, and anything outside of normal, everyday stress could be dangerous. I wouldn't risk her or the baby's health. I smiled at her, "Well, I think you may have been the accidental recipient of someone else's gift. Too bad for whoever was supposed to get them...they're very pretty."

Any apprehension she held melted immediately, "Oh...I never thought of that. Now, that makes me feel bad they didn't get to the right person."

I watched her fill her plate before I did the same. In reality, I was stalling before I asked my next question.

"What car did the neighbor buy?" I put a fork full of pasta in my mouth and chewed.

Natalie wiped sauce from her lips, "It's too dark to see the color, but it's a big truck."

It took every ounce of control I had to macerate and swallow the mouth full of food. I wanted to fly from my chair and charge through the door, but I couldn't. Instead, I thought of any excuse to look out the window. Wiping my mouth, I went to the door and opened it wide.

"What are you doing?" Natalie giggled.

There was nothing there. Drew was gone.

While I was relieved at the moment, I was furious that he likely left those flowers on her car before following her home. I worried how far his fixation with her would go and if it would ever be over.

When I returned to the kitchen, I was smiling, "Well, you said they got a new car. I wanted to see it. Looks like they left though."

"I'm sure you'll get a better look in the light of day anyway," she stabbed at a clump salad.

I smiled at her as one thought ran through my mind.

'I'm counting on it.'

Chapter Fifty-One

Natalie

I guided my Kia into the small driveway, shut the engine off, and released the trunk. I sat for a moment admiring the twinkling Christmas lights hanging from nearly every house but ours. We would have lights and a tree soon, but holidays were just different when you had the careers Finn and I did. Thanksgiving came and went as we both spent the day on shift and with our work families. That's not to say we didn't celebrate together; it was just postponed until the following Sunday and involved a few friends, nachos, and football.

Twilight was settling over the neighborhood and the late autumn air was crisp in my nose when I finally exited the car. After retrieving my backpack from the back seat, I loaded the groceries from the trunk in my empty arm and set off for the front door. I walked up the stairs and onto the porch, bumping into two flower pots on the way.

"Thank you, Finn," I mumbled realizing the light on the porch was fixed.

I fumbled with my keys hanging off my wrist and with a lot of effort, unlocked the door. Not wanting Delilah to escape through my legs, I swiped back with my foot, and the heavy door shut with a loud thud. My breath was heavy as I huffed and struggled with my bags. I knew

I should have made more than one trip, but I just wanted to get into the house.

In the dim lighting of the house, I made my way through the living room and into the small kitchen, dropping my bags on the table with a loud thud. I let out a long and calming sigh as the blood rushed back into my arms.

"Delilah!" I called to the house. I didn't hear the tiny bell attached to her collar or any scratching from distant rooms. It wouldn't be the first time my tiny terroristic princess had holed up under a bed or sofa, completely ignoring my presence. "Where did that little brat run off to?"

My phone vibrated in my pocket.

"Hello?" I answered without looking at the screen, walking to the living room to turn on the lamps.

"Hey, baby! Did you make it home okay?" Finn's voice was like a quilt on a cold day.

I smiled, "Yeah, now, I'm ready to shower and go to bed."

"You need to eat," he replied.

I let out a playful whine, "Nooo...shower first. Then I'll order a pizza. Promise."

Finn laughed.

"I'm going to get off here...I need to find Delilah. Oh! and Finn?"

"Yes?" he said using his sexiest voice.

"Thanks for fixing the light. You're the best...I love you."

I disconnected the phone and dropped it into the pocket of my scrubs. I moved to the kitchen looking under the table but didn't see my cat. I started to the laundry room when Drew's large mass stepped around the corner filling the doorway between my kitchen and my destination.

"Oh my God! What the hell are you doing in my house?" panic shooting through me like lightning. "Get out!"

I thought of the alarm. Why didn't it go off?

His eyes stared at my belly, "Nat...wow. You've gotten...big."

As if instinct took over, my hands immediately ran protectively over my stomach. He stepped closer, reaching his hand out to touch me. My blood ran cold like ice.

"Don't touch me," I ordered and I felt my eyebrow twitch.

Drew moved closer, caging me between himself and the table. He leaned in, whispering into my ear and weaving his fingers in my hair, "I'm not going to hurt you, Nat. But, you need to sit down and listen."

His fingers tightened on my head. Fear spread through my muscles and my body convulsed to the invasion. I felt the tiny droplets forming on my nape and palms as I followed his eyes with mine. His pupils were deep caverns of darkness that threatened to swallow me and my child. Drew tugged on my hair, forcing me to follow. At the edge of the small table, he withdrew a chair and let go of my head. I stood, still never taking my eyes off him as he took a step back.

"Sit down!" he screamed.

I sat as he ordered and dread made my body tremor uncontrollably. I knew, better than anyone, what Drew was capable of but I had to control my emotions. If he knew how afraid I was, it would cause him to escalate. After so many years of therapy, I knew how much he liked fear. I had to play his game until I could come up with an exit.

He pulled out another chair and sat across from me, "I just want to talk."

My body shook and I swallowed hard, "Okay."

He was nodding his agreement but his eyes wandered all over my kitchen before they fell back on me. He took me in for a long time in an unnerving and uncomfortable silence. Without moving my eyes from his, I searched my house in my mind for anything that would make a good weapon when I had a chance to run from the table.

When or if.

He pointed to the new knife set, "I see you got my gift."

I swallowed hard.

'His gift?

"I thought since yours got taken by the police, I'd replace it," he grinned. "It's the least I could do...an early birthday present."

I was frozen as I played my wedding night over in my mind. I saw the tacky yellow paper and the pink bow. It disgusted me that something from him had been sitting on my counter for weeks.

"Tell me, Nat...who'd you decide to spread your legs and get knocked up with?" he asked with a deadly calm.

Bile rose in my throat, "My husband."

An oily smirk spread across his lips which only made my stomach churn more. I couldn't read his face. I used to be able to. Back in the old days, I would know by now if I was going to have to call out of work the next day or not just by reading his mannerisms. But it seemed as much as I had grown in the last few years, he did as well, just not for the better. He slammed his left hand on my table causing the salt and pepper shakers and me to jump.

"You're still a liar. A filthy, whore liar," he growled. "That little bastard isn't your *husbands*."

My voice caught in my throat. How did he know that?

"I can't believe you would do this to me, Nat. After everything I've done...I mean, I'm really trying here. I buy you flowers...thoughtful gifts."

He paused.

"But, I can forgive you. I can. You know... you're supposed to be with me...I get to have you. But you need to tell me the truth!" his voice bounced off every surface of the small room.

No one outside Cece and I knew that Finn couldn't have children, and she only learned of his condition a few months ago. Finn never discussed it with anyone he worked with, except maybe Elias, who was one of his best friends. But Elias was in San Jose and Drew and he certainly didn't know each other. My heart was racing.

"Tell me again, Nat...who's the little bastard's father? Was it that bartender you were banging a few months back?" Drew's eyes narrowed on mine.

"Liam is dead," I choked out.

His eyebrows rose, "Oh, I know. I kinda got tired of him fucking my girl every night."

At that moment, my world imploded.

Chapter Fifty-Two

Finn

"Who's turn is it?" Carl called out.

Inez let out a laugh, "God, if I have to eat chili one more night..."

"I vote pizza," I called out from behind my rig. I just finished the inventory and was running through the end of my checklist. I was already two hours into my shift and ahead of the game for the night.

"Pizza's good," Darren agreed. "I'll go out back and find out what everybody wants."

It promised to be a decent night. The air felt calm and for the first time in a month, the house was fully staffed. I finished my task and sat at the table with Carl, Inez, Darren, and our rookie, Quade. Flipping cards like a Vegas dealer, Carl gave Darren and Inez a quick wink.

"Should we take all the newbie's money tonight?"

"More likely I'll take all of yours," I straddled my chair as everyone at the table laughed.

Carl waived me off, "Well, I can't in good conscience deal you in, Rafferty. I'd hate to spend your kid's college fund before he gets here."

"*She* gets here," Darren corrected.

"Oh, my mistake," my partner chortled.

I shook my head in resignation, "Oh Jesus, not you too."

Darren shrugged. Carl dealt our hand and we settled into a friendly game of poker. We were just finishing up our third hand when several of the guys who had been either cleaning around the station or working on paperwork came carrying in armloads of pizza boxes. Nate Yeung, bringing up the rear, made a direct path for me.

"Hey, there's a woman here to see you. And it's not Natalie," he said, dropping two pizza boxes on the granite countertop.

My eyes shot at Darren. The last time a woman who wasn't my wife visited, I ended up wasting seven months of my life being lied to by my ex. As I stood, I peeked around the doorway to see a petite woman with beautiful dark eyes staring back at me.

Carl leaned into my shoulder, "Isn't that the woman from Clearwater a few days ago?"

"I think so," I agreed. "Eat your dinner, old man."

I motioned for Darren to come with me. As we drew closer, I saw the cut on her lip was just about gone, and the dark bruises under her eyes had faded to pale yellow and green. But she looked nervous like scared prey looking for an opportunity to bolt.

"Gia?" I asked, reaching out my hand.

"Yeah," she replied hoarsely.

I smiled, "This is my friend, Darren Sanchez."

He shook the woman's hand, "Nice to meet you."

She nodded, looking behind us, "I'm sorry to interrupt your meal time. I thought...well, I have to talk to you. It's important."

"Okay," I grabbed some folding chairs from a cabinet and offered her a seat. After we were settled, I continued, "What can I do for you?"

Gia picked at her fingers and I saw her nails had been bitten to the quick. When she wasn't pulling at the frayed skin, she wrung her hands tightly. The nervous tick saddened me as I pictured Natalie sitting in the Hanford PD conference room last year. But, it wasn't the only thing about Gia that reminded me of my wife.

"I think...uhmm," Gia's eyes filled with tears. "Drew's been really angry since I... *fell.*"

I raised my eyebrows but didn't speak.

"He's been going out for months at night and not coming home until morning. I thought he was working nights, but he wasn't. Last week, he took off for a couple of days and didn't come home. But when he did, he was really quiet. Then, tonight, I asked him where he was going...I asked if there was someone else," she continued hesitantly.

I was getting a disturbing feeling in my gut; a confirmation of everything. The puzzle pieces were coming together.

"What did he say, Gia?" I prodded.

Tears welled in her eyes, "He slammed me into a cabinet and said I didn't matter. I was only his *'backup'* and not even a good one. *I* was a dumb whore who was only good for one thing. Then said he was going to take the real love of his life back and it didn't matter that she was married now."

My heart dropped and I jumped from my seat, "Natalie."

"Wait!" Darren snatched my arm before I ran out of the door.

"I'm so sorry," Gia cried. "I heard the fight you had with Drew outside my house that day. I knew he had to be talking about you. I didn't want what happened to me to happen to her."

"Nievez!" Darren whistled sharply and Inez jogged over to where we stood.

"What's up?" she looked down at Gia, concerned.

"This is Gia. Can you get her something to drink and someplace to wash her face? After that, make sure she gets home, okay?" he ordered.

Inez put her arm around the woman, "Sure thing. Hey, hon...let's get you cleaned up."

My body shook with anger as the potential possibilities ran circles in my brain. I yanked my phone out of my pocket and dialed Natalie's number. Her voicemail answered. Was she still in the shower? My heart pounded in my ears and panic set in my bones. Was Drew already in my house?

I heard Natalie's voice in my head.

'Thanks for fixing the light. You're the best...I love you.'

I bolted for the door, but Darren hung on, "Finn! What are you going to do? Remember, you told Cece not to go looking for trouble."

"He knows where I live! Natalie's not answering the phone...he's got her, Darren," I growled. "He fixed the light!"

"Finn, breathe. You just talked to her not twenty minutes ago," he reasoned. "What light?"

"I didn't have time...I was going to do it when I got home."

Terror shot through me like a bolt and I was frantic.

"Darren, listen to me. Didn't you notice anything familiar about Gia? She looks really similar to Natalie...she even wears the same perfume. I called Detective Callahan. He finally got back to me yesterday. I asked him about the woman Bonetti was dating last year. He texted me a picture of her." I pulled the message up on my phone and showed my friend.

"She and Natalie could have been sisters!" I yelled.

"Okay, Okay...he's a sick bastard. *Really* sick. But man, do you think he got into your house?" Darren questioned carefully, but I saw the same panic I felt falling over his face. He knew it was more than probable.

"Call HPD. Tell them to send someone over to my house. Tell them to find Detective Callahan and Sergeant Eleazar."

I turned and did the only thing I could.

I ran.

Chapter Fifty-Three

Natalie

I felt the vibration of my phone against my leg. I wanted to reach for it, but I knew he would never allow me to answer. I wanted to scream to whoever was calling that there was a murderer in my house and I was probably his next target.

'No. You're not. You will protect this child.'

The little voice in my head was doing its best to keep me on task and so far it was working. I took a deep breath and glared at Drew.

"You killed Liam," I whispered as more of a statement than a question.

His shoulders moved in a shrug, "I didn't see what kind of things you and he were doing at night, but I was obviously right."

He glanced at my belly but my eyes narrowed into even smaller slits.

"Sorry to disappoint you. But this baby is Finn's."

"Lying fucking bitch!" he screamed, throwing himself out of the chair. "Why are you doing this to me, Nat? Can't you see that I'm the only one that will ever love you? You are making it so hard...I do everything for you. I even fixed that light! Some appreciation would be nice and you need to stop lying to me!"

Drew was centimeters from my face and his spit hit my cheek when he spoke, "I took a little trip to San Jose, Nat. Want to know what I found out?"

He leaned into my ear, "Your husband has an affinity for whores too...just like me. I found his little skank in a bar and she was awfully chatty when I told her about you. But you know what she said to me? Imagine my surprise when she said that ole Finn shoots blanks." He rose to stand over me, but my eyes never waivered. "Tell me another lie, slut."

I jumped from my chair and Drew took a step back, startled. I ground my teeth to fight off the urge to vomit because the fear was overwhelming. I had no idea where any of this was going but I had to put distance between him and myself. I needed to make a run for the door. Without any warning, I shoved Drew as hard as I could.

"You asshole! How dare you come into my house and threaten me! You're a piece of absolute shit, Drew. Oh, big powerful man threatening a pregnant woman! You're a bully! That's all you'll ever be—"

The backhand across the face sent me backward, but it also put the table between us once more. Before Drew could charge at me, I flipped the table over and ran for the living room. I latched onto the keypad of my security system and hit the number nine four times. I heard Drew shoving the heavy wood table out of the way as I grabbed onto the knob of the door. But, before I could pull it open, Drew's fingers snatched my hair and flung me into the entertainment center. My side and back hit hard but, I remained standing.

"You've got a big mouth, Nat. Especially for a stupid little skank," he pulled my head back and I felt blood trickle down my mouth. His body was pressed against mine when I felt my phone vibrate again. "Hubby must be calling. Pick it up."

"No," I snarled defiantly through clenched teeth.

Drew grabbed my cheeks with his hand and squeezed, "I said pick it up or you're going to find out that I'm not shooting blanks."

Feeling down my scrub pants, I found my thigh pocket and drew the phone out. Drew latched onto my hair tighter.

"Tell him everything is fine, understand?"

I nodded but when I pushed the green button, the vibrating stopped. Drew pulled my head back and shoved me against the large cabinet once more. I felt a run of blood slide down my face where the bridge of my nose connected with the wood shelf, but it wasn't the only thing running out of my body.

A fiery shot of pain exploded in my back and I looked down at the floor to see water spreading along both of my pant legs and dripping on the floor. Drew jumped back as the amniotic fluid splashed on his shoes.

"Did you just piss your pants?" he screamed and raised his hand to hit me again. Another wave of searing pain raced through me and my knees buckled.

"No, no, no!" I cried. "My water broke, shithead! You've got to call an ambulance."

Drew stood frozen in shock and shook his head. His eyes darted from me to the floor and back again.

"Listen I know you hate me...but this baby didn't do anything wrong. You have to call nine-one-one! It's too early," my voice strained as another torrent of pain swept over me. This time, my knees gave way and I collapsed to the floor. Drew stood over me and looked at me blankly. It was then we heard sirens getting closer. Drew finally curled his lip in anger and ran back into the kitchen. I heard someone yell as the backdoor slammed against the house as he left.

"Oh God," the tears I had been fighting finally fell from my eyes as I rolled onto my hands and knees and tried to crawl to the front door.

I wasn't going to make it. The surges of pain contracted like swells of electricity and encompassed my entire midsection. A large ball of white darted from under the sofa and leaped onto its cushion. Delilah's large eyes gazed at me as if she knew I was in pain, but her sudden presence gave me something to focus on.

"There you are, pretty girl," I cooed between the now-settling contraction. "Where have you been?"

The front door flew open and the cat bolted for the safety of the underside of the sofa as Finn slid to me, runner-on-third style.

"Oh my God, Natalie! What's wrong?" he eyed the damp floor. "Jesus...it's okay. I'm gonna get someone here."

He grabbed the radio off his shoulder, "Dispatch, code two-four, delta-three at eight six one Rosewood Ave. Paramedic on site, send a bus." Finn ran his hands over my face. "I'm so sorry Natalie...I should have been here."

Within seconds of his call, the room exploded with flashes of red and blue, and the room was filled with police officers. It was a flurry of activity that I had a difficult time getting a handle on through the increasing waves of pain.

I watched Darren and Carl enter the house with gear in hand, and Finn's face contorted in confusion, "How the hell did everyone get here so fast? I just called it in."

I latched onto Finn's hand, "Silent alarm. I used the keypad."

"It calls nine-one-one. Everyone shows up," he kissed my hand. "Good job, baby."

My back lurched as another contraction pulled at my insides, this time, it was the pain and not fear that made me want to vomit.

"Breathe," Finn said calmly.

"It's too early...it's too soon," I ground my teeth and tears filled my eyes.

Darren pulled the velcro on his blood pressure cuff, "Nat...we need to get you in the bus. Someone needs to check if you've dilated."

I, like Cece, refused the backboard. But, with Finn's help, the guys got me upright and onto the porch where the gurney was waiting. The contractions, which had weakened for a few minutes were ramping up again and I groaned in pain.

Darren and Finn were just ready to shut the doors of the ambulance when Eleazar grabbed the handle. Finn's face turned three shades of red but Darren spoke before he could utter a word.

"Sergeant, we've got no time," he ordered.

"I just need to know where Bonetti is going," she replied quickly. "Callahan is in pursuit."

I shook my head, "No...no idea."

"Sorry Maria, that's all you get right now," Darren shut the door on her and banged on the window, "Move out."

Chapter Fifty-Four

Finn

Jaisen Hope Rafferty, my beautiful, perfect daughter, was born shortly after midnight and weighed five pounds, ten ounces, looking like the spitting image of her mother. As a precaution, she would spend the next few days in the Southwest Haven Neo-Natal Intensive Care Unit, NICU, for observation, but, her prognosis was very good.

I spent the night in a fold-out recliner next to my exhausted wife. After delivering, she was finally able to get her cuts and bruises treated and luckily, there were no other serious injuries. Natalie fell asleep around three a.m. but I was still completely wired. I knew our daughter was safe with the nursing staff in the NICU, and I couldn't imagine being anywhere but next to Natalie. I watched her chest rise and fall easily with each slow, delicate breath and I thanked the universe that she was still with me. While the sun rose behind me outside, I contemplated calling Maria or Detective Callahan and getting an update on whether Bonetti had been found but decided it could wait until later that day.

Natalie's eyes fluttered open around nine and even though she only had a few hours of sleep, she looked well-rested. I was still sitting bedside when her head lolled in my direction.

"Good morning," I whispered, picking up her hand. I held her fingers close to my mouth, kissing them lightly.

She drew a deep breath, "Good morning. How is Jaisen?"

"Beautiful and brave, like her mother," I smiled. I watched my wife's face flush with a rosy hue. "Are you hungry? I can run down and get you something."

She shook her head, "No, not right now. Have you heard...anything?"

Her face turned dark when she spoke. I knew her hope as well as I could feel my own and she of all people deserved to finally have some peace.

"No, but I'm sure as soon as they find him, we'll know," I rubbed her hand between mine, but I still felt the tremble start.

I hated Drew Bonetti more than I have despised anyone in my life. Not only for what he did to Natalie years ago, but what he did to her last night. And to Gia. And to my daughter. But all the anger and outrage I held for him was quelled at that moment while I held Natalie's hand. I had everything I ever wanted and it was all located within two rooms of this hospital.

Within the hour, I helped Natalie with a well-deserved shower and change out of her hospital gown. Ready to make the short trip down the hall to visit Jaisen, we were interrupted by a soft knock on the door as three NICU nurses entered with our daughter in her acrylic incubator. As two of the women plugged in the unit and arraigned supplies in the room, the third explained that since she was doing so well, and Natalie was already staying in what was called a nesting room, a post-partum room for parents with NICU babies that are close to discharge, the decision was made to allow the baby to stay with us until we could go home. So, after a few lessons on how and when she could be taken out of her warming crib, we were left to enjoy our daughter together.

It was late afternoon and Natalie was giving Jaisen her third bottle when Cece and Darren arrived. At my request, Cece got permission to enter our house, which was still a crime scene, to pick up more clothes for Natalie and some things for the baby. What the pair arrived with looked more like dorm room move-in day.

"Jesus, Ce," I chortled. "We aren't going to be here that long."

She waived a hand dismissively, "Look, Rafferty...you've got your job, and I've got mine. Now, give that child to Auntie Cece."

Several department store bags slid down her arms and onto the floor near the sofa. She turned to Natalie, who was laughing at the shopping-addicted friend, and wiggled her fingers.

"Give me my new BFF," she grinned wide, scooping Jaisen and her wrappings into her arms.

Natalie's brows arched as she looked at me, "Looks like I've been replaced."

I nodded.

"We had to pick up a few more things before we came over," Darren indicated the piles of bags. "The old-new stuff wasn't good enough."

Natalie and I rolled with laughter.

"Don't you listen to any of them," Cece cooed and swayed gently as she finished giving Jaisen her bottle. "You're a queen. And you need to dress like one...Auntie Cece will teach you all you need to know."

Chapter Fifty-Five

Natalie

Finn's hands rarely left mine in that hospital room. I love those hands. The length of his digits, the shape of his fingers, and the vein structure told a story. He was a nail-biter, but not a nervous one. The rounded areas of his tips were stripped and clean and his beds were markedly shortened by years of abuse. But those hands were also strong and skillful tools that led to muscular and protective arms. It didn't go unnoticed by me that the only time he wasn't touching me was when he was holding our daughter.

Our daughter. Drew's hateful voice and words still echoed softly in my mind.

'That little bastard isn't your husbands.'

I deconstructed and picked that sentence apart over and over in my mind until I heard the lie and remembered the truth. My daughter, our daughter wasn't and would never be a bastard; Finn made sure of that. Jaisen was as much part of his soul as she was mine, that I was sure of. He told me the night he found out I was pregnant that his deepest wish, the most hidden and private of all his prayers, was to be a father and have a family. But, they weren't just words, in the months that followed, Finn showed me with every moment that what he confessed to me was the truth. I was in love with him then, but it paled in comparison to the devotion, passion, and respect I had for him now.

Cece and Darren stayed for a little more than an hour that first day and Carrie and Becca each visited after their shifts. It wasn't until day two that I became tiresome of our surroundings and I really wanted to go home. But, it would be three more days before Jaisen and I were released, both with clean bills of health.

To my surprise, our house was no longer a crime scene and had been completely cleaned, thanks to our Hanford Fire family. They even went so far as to erect and decorate a Christmas tree in our living room and hang lights along the porch outside.

It was just after noon when Finn unlocked the front door carrying our tiny bundle of joy securely in her car seat and I followed close behind. Any hint of what happened almost a week prior was gone and while I would be eternally grateful for their hard work, I was a little apprehensive. I didn't want to remember what happened in those rooms, because part of me still felt unsafe. But it wouldn't last long because that feeling disappeared later that night.

I just sat on the sofa to feed Jaisen when a firm knock rattled the door. I started to get up to answer it when Finn came from the kitchen, potholder in hand, and motioned for me to stay where I was. He looked through the peephole and then looked at me.

"It's Sergeant Eleazar," he told me as he turned the knob. He pulled the door wide, "Maria, come in."

"Hey Finn," she stepped inside, her eyes bouncing from him to me. "Is this a bad time?"

I smiled, shaking my head, "Not at all. I'm just getting ready to give her another bottle."

"Oh my! She's so tiny," Maria's voice pitched higher in tone as she peeked at the baby. "Is she eating well?"

Finn and I laughed.

"Like crazy," he said. The sergeant grinned as she took one last look before her demeanor morphed into stark professionalism.

"I'm sorry to just come over like this, but we wanted you to know... we found Drew Bonetti," she said with an inflection of regret.

I thought my heart would beat out of my chest and I was instantly on alert. Thoughts of filing reports at the station and hours sitting in courtrooms flooded my mind. But they had him and that is what really mattered.

"You've got him in custody?" Finn blurted.

Maria shook her head curtly, "No. Mr. Bonetti is dead. Detective Callahan and several HPD and CHP cornered him just on the edge of town. He raised a gun at Callahan and he returned fire. We believe it was suicide by cop."

I gasped, "He's...Drew's dead?"

Her lips pursed as her head bobbed in the affirmative, "Callahan wanted to tell you himself, but he couldn't get away."

Raw emotion overtook my entire body and I drew several deep breaths but they weren't enough to keep the tears at bay. All my years of fear and looking over my shoulder were over. It was as if the weight of the planet was lifted by some invisible force from my chest. I looked down at my little girl and finally felt the real freedom I was missing for so long.

"There's more," she continued. "Callahan put a rush on the ballistics from the gun Bonetti had in his truck. We've matched it to the same weapon that killed Liam Monahan earlier this year. You knew Mr. Monahan?"

She was looking at me.

My eyes glanced quickly to Finn but rested back on Maria's, "I did. We dated briefly, but that's it. I was actually working the night he was killed."

"That answers our next question which was why Bonetti would target Monahan," she sighed. "I want you to know, Natalie that you were braver than you realize that night. From the note that was found in his truck...it looks like his original plan may have included killing you as well. So, whatever you did, it saved you...and her."

I was speechless. Part of me wanted to remember what I did that changed his mind. But, as I looked down at Jaisen, I knew it was her. *She* saved my life. It wasn't long and Maria said her goodbyes and left.

A palpable lightness spread, seeping into every room of our home, and a sense of satisfied relief washed over me. Anyone who abuses another is a coward and Drew proved, beyond a reasonable doubt, the depth of his cowardness when he forced another person to kill him. I felt no guilt for his death because, from the moment he entered my house, I knew deep inside what he was planning; I knew what I did, that night in our apartment all those years ago: it was him or me.

Finn took Jaisen, who was finally asleep, out of my arms and placed her in the bassinet. When he turned back to me, he knelt beside where I sat. We laced our fingers together right before he pulled my face to his and rested his lips on mine. We stayed that way for a long moment before he drew back.

"I love you, Natalie," he said softly. I fell into his large gemstone eyes and lost myself for a minute in their sparkle.

I smirked, "Why is that?"

"A lot of reasons, too many to name," he chuckled, tucking a lock of hair behind my ear.

I wondered about those reasons and if they were the same as I had for him. I knew I could spend hours thinking and reciting every one of them, and I'd never come close to being finished. He called me his sacred salvation, but he was mine. Warmth spread through all of my limbs. Here he was; this man I fell in love with that summer— in all his juxtaposed, wholesome beauty. He won my heart in the warm ocean air as we stood on a beach and now, he owned it. I knew there would be no going back to the darkness. The world could end around us and I would still be his.

Finn spent what felt like an eternity searching my face. "You are the bravest woman I've ever met."

My face flushed, "I've been told I've got guts."

Finn's beautiful laughter filled the room and he held me close, "You sure do, Mrs. Rafferty. You sure do."

Epilogue

Chapter Fifty-Six

Finn

"Daddy! Where's Mommy?" Jaisen asked me excitedly. "When's everybody coming?"

I lifted my daughter high in the air and she squealed. I held her on my hip, "She's on her way, sweetheart. Why don't you find Uncle Darren and tell him you want to slide down the pole."

She wriggled out of my arms, and took off out of the side door yelling, "Uncle Darren!"

I laughed to myself as I watched her run. The last five years have flown by and I can't believe how much my daughter has grown. She's smart and kind and beautiful. She's still an identical copy of Natalie; from her long brunette hair, which is usually in pigtails, to the golden flecks in her hazel eyes.

The front door creaked open and before long, I watched Danny roll his motorized wheelchair over the threshold.

Having him in Hanford was a long time coming. After Lori found out from Drew that Natalie and I were married and starting a family, she spiraled even more out of control. She was convicted of her third DUI a year after Jaisen was born and was let off with a two-year probation. Just six months in though, she was arrested again but this time the prosecutor threw the book at her and she was charged with a felony.

After she was sentenced to four years in Santa Clara County Jail, Lori's guardianship of Danny was pulled. The conversation, if it could even be called that, between Natalie and me about Danny's conservatorship was nearly as short as my marriage proposal. Neither of us batted an eye or had any reservations. Danny was family and we loved him.

After our application was granted, we took short leaves from work to get him settled in his new town. But it was Natalie who really deserved the most credit. Through the hospital, Natalie found a case worker who put us in contact with a local organization that provided long-term staffing for people like Danny, much like he had in San Jose. She worked tirelessly to find him an accessible, ground-level apartment and placement on a job crew with others in his situation. Everyone at the station got in on the action and built ramps for our house so Danny could visit whenever he liked. Danny found his tribe and it thrilled me to see him thriving.

"Danny!" I bellowed as he maneuvered around one of the trucks.

"Wh....where's my JaiJai?" he asked, after giving me a high five.

I nodded at his helper, a college kid named Justin who we had also adopted into our ever-growing flock, "She's out back. She's trying to talk Darren into a ride down the pole."

Danny's laughter echoed off the walls, "Oh, N...Nat's not gonna like that."

"Well, don't tell her then," I chuckled before turning to Justin. "The guys got burgers and hotdogs on the grill out back. There's soda on the bar there, help yourself."

I pointed him toward the open kitchen.

He nodded, "Awesome. Hey, Dan...let's go find JaiJai."

The door swung open again as Natalie and Cece appeared with armloads of bags and boxes. I jogged over to help them unload.

"Hi, beautiful," I said, relieving Natalie of three gift bags, a cake box, and candles. "Is this everything?"

Her smile was weary, "From our house? Yes. But, *she* had to stop for one more thing."

My wife rolled her eyes teasingly and asked, "Did Sadie and Brooke make it?"

"They're all out back," I nodded.

"Hey, I'm not telling my niece she can't have everything she asked for on her birthday list," Cece pursed her lips in defiance. "Besides, she's only going to be five once."

Natalie sat the enormous sheet cake with purple frosting on the dining table in the middle of the room, "You know, after her first four birthdays, I don't think that excuse is allowed anymore."

"Huh," Cece chuckled, "Try and stop me."

Darren came through the door leading from the courtyard, "Hey ladies, just in time! The food is ready."

He stopped to kiss Cece, "Hello, love of my life."

"Darren," Natalie warned playfully, "Tell your wife that she's going to get a taste of her own medicine when that baby comes."

We all burst into laughter.

I called the crew and our guests in from every corner of the station for dinner. When planning Jaisen's big day, we couldn't think of a more perfect place for her to celebrate with her entire, extended family. This firehouse was her second home.

It was well after eleven o'clock when we finally made it back to our house and I carried a sleeping Jaisen to her room, gently lying her in bed. After Natalie and I kissed her forehead, I pulled the covers over her, turned on her nightlight, and quietly shut her door. I walked to the end of the hall, but I saw Natalie sitting quietly on the corner of our bed before I made it to the bathroom for a quick shower.

"Hey," I called from the doorway. "You okay?"

She nodded but, I knew my wife; there was some thought weighing on her mind. Making my way to her, I crouched on my knees to eye level.

"You wanna try again?" I asked. "What's wrong?"

I saw the unshed tears glistening in her eyes.

"She's five, Finn! Our baby girl is five," the salty rivers fell over her cheeks. "She'll go to school in the fall...then, before we know it, it will be her Prom. Then graduation...college...she'll get married—"

"Whoa! Slow down," a grin pulled at my mouth. "Baby, she's *five*. Yeah, all those things are going to happen, but there's so much more in between. Why don't we take a breath and enjoy each day, okay? Remember...we're living in the moment. And I promise she's not moving out tomorrow."

Natalie laughed, wiping her face. "Yeah, okay...you're right. I'm being ridiculous."

"No, you're just a great mom," I kissed her temple.

She smiled at me and I lost myself in the golden green of her eyes. It wasn't the first time today that it had happened, and it wouldn't be the last. I was still grateful every minute that this incredible woman put up with me.

"I thought you were headed to the shower," she mused.

"I was. But..." Reaching over, I closed our door before pulling my shirt over my head and squaring up to her. I took her face in my hands and leaned into her ear, "I got distracted by a beautiful woman."

Natalie shivered and I watched gooseflesh rise on her neck.

"Want to join me?" I whispered before our lips crashed together and we dissolved into the night.

About the Author

January Kelly is a longtime writer and holds a BS in Sociology with an interest in Religious Studies. She is an avid reader of fantasy and science fiction and a lover of all genres of music. January is based in the wilds of the Missouri Midwest where she loves to embroider bad words on bookmarks, have cocktails and queso with her friends, and go on long walks with her husband, Jarritt.

www.januarykelly.com

Follow on Facebook:

https://www.facebook.com/profile.php?id=100067850730415

Instagram:

https://www.instagram.com/januarykelly.author/?next=%2F